Wednesday's Girl

Cheryl Bateman

Copyright © 2024 by Cheryl Bateman

ISBN 979-8-9858903-1-0 (paperback)
ISBN 979-8-9858903-0-3 (e-book)

For the love of my life

Thanks for always being there and for loving me through the years. I want you to know you made this so much easier for me and that you brought me happiness.

I Love You

Special thanks to "P" for finding another way to get it done. You rock my go to girl. I love you.

Shortly after moving to New Orleans, Chelsea's husband John mysteriously withdraws from their happy marriage. She tries everything to bring him back to her. When she is unable to do that, but not willing to leave him, she looks for companionship and pleasure elsewhere.

Then a friend introduces her to Adam Irons, a ruggedly handsome, wealthy, southern gentleman. When on their second date he introduces her to bondage, he unleashes something in her she did not know existed. Together they indulge in an erotic relationship that has no limits and no boundaries.

Present Day

As I board the plane to New Orleans, my heart flutters with excitement. It has been years since I have been there. I am happy to be going to the city that I love, the city I called home so many years ago. My excitement escalates as I think of my time there ...

I begin to think back and remember.

Part One

Chapter 1

I am sitting in the living room when I hear my husband John burst in the front door.

"Chelsea, Chelsea, where are you?" he calls out.

"I'm in the living room."

He rushes in out of breath and visually excited. He leans over, gives me a quick kiss on the cheek and announces.

"We're moving to New Orleans!"

My heart sank as panic and fear come over me. I knew right then that New Orleans would be the end of our marriage. John and I have not been married long; we met at a resort in my hometown in upstate New York. I had been working there since graduating high school. He had come up from the south for a beverage manager position and I was working in the dining room as a server. We were dating for six months when John decided to move on. He asked me to go with him and I happily agreed.

We married shortly after we left New York, bounced around to a couple of states never staying too long. It was a little hard not knowing anyone, but I did not mind much since we were together.

John is seven years older than I and had moved around quite a bit before we met. So, whenever he decided it was time to move,

3

I happily followed his lead. Not minding that he never asked me. This time should not have been any different, but it was.

"I got a job at a hotel in the French Quarter; you can get a waitress job in one of the many restaurants in the city."

So that was it; I was packing again but this time with a heavy heart. We had only lived in small towns, and I was nervous about living in a big city. Worried that it would change us and our life together. As we drive towards New Orleans on the I-10 we get our first glimpse of the skyline.

"Look, sweetie, isn't it beautiful?" John said. "Don't worry you're going to like it here," he said sensing my nervousness.

"Yes, it is beautiful," I said looking out the window with a sense of dread.

We check into the hotel and go out to get our first look of the infamous French Quarter or as it is also known, the Vieux Carre. There are bars, restaurants, strip clubs and T-shirt shops. The buildings are all assorted bright colors with hurricane shutters and cast-iron balconies.

As people are hosing down the streets, opening shutters and doors, we walk to the river and watch the boats going up and down the Mississippi. Then we head to Jackson Square and watch the artists, set up their easels, as the French Quarter comes alive for the days business.

As we walk through the streets people are courteous to us and greet us with "Hello" giving us a taste of Louisiana's southern hospitality. We walk by a shop that has a sign overhead, "Johnny's Po-Boys."

"I wonder what that is?" I spoke.

"I guess we'll find out," John said as he holds the door open for me and we walked up to the counter and read the menu on the wall.

"I would like a shrimp po-boy please," I said to the woman behind the counter.

"Would you like it dressed?" she asked.

"Dressed?"

"With lettuce, tomato, and mayo?"

"Yes please," I said with a giggle as she turned to John.

"I will have an oyster po-boy dressed," he said sounding like a local.

The sandwiches come on paper plates with the seafood piled on fresh warm French bread. I close my eyes as I take my first bite of New Orleans.

"Yum!" I exclaim as the flavors fill my mouth.

"See, you already found something you like here." John said with a laugh.

Next on the list is to find a place to live. John's boss told him we should look uptown. We find a great shotgun house on Second Street. The rooms are in a straight line in a shotgun style house so you must walk through one room to get to the next. They say that a bullet shot from the front door would pass through the house and not hit anything but go through the back door. When the doors align it helps the air circulate in the summer. The house has lofty ceilings, beautiful hardwood floors and ceiling to floor windows.

Our landlords Roger and Linda are a nice couple a few years older than us. They live in the other side of the house; they tell us all about the neighborhood.

"If you are looking for a job, Chelsea, we know an excellent restaurant uptown on Carrolton Avenue called the Riverbend. It is a casual place with tasty food, and a pleasant atmosphere," Linda said.

"Thanks, I will check it out."

I had tried to find a job in the French Quarter. Everywhere I applied they told me that I had to live in New Orleans for five years before I could work there. Which made me even more apprehensive about New Orleans.

The next day as I get ready to go to the Riverbend to apply for a job, I choose a green blouse and black skirt with black pumps. I look at myself in the full-length mirror as my five-foot-four petite body fills the frame. The just above the knee skirt and pumps enhance my shapely legs.

I read somewhere that if you have great legs, you will see three diamond shaped gaps going down your legs. I pull up my skirt and look at my three diamonds. As I comb my short wavy light brown hair, I notice the color of the blouse brings out the green flecks of my hazel eyes. I apply a little mascara and a light blush since I do not wear very much makeup; I decide that is enough. After a quick head to toe check I decide I am ready to go.

"Hello, I am looking for a job. Can I get an application, please?" I said to the hostess as I enter the restaurant.

"Sure," she said as she reaches for an application.

"Thank you, Sara," I said noting her name tag.

I quickly scan the place and see it is a decent size and it has a pleasant atmosphere. There are rattan chairs, glass top tables, brass railings divide the sections and booths lining the wall. I grab a menu to lean on and sit on the bench next to the register to fill out the application. I hand Sara my completed application and she takes it to the back of the restaurant.

"Someone will be right with you," Sara said when she returns. "Thank you."

Minutes later a tall handsome man with a nice physique, healthy tan, blonde hair, and blue eyes approaches me as he extends his hand.

"Hi, I'm Eric the night manager."

"Hello, I'm Chelsea," I said as I stand and shake his hand.

"Follow me," he said as he turns and walks to the back of the restaurant. We enter the bar area and take a seat at a table.

"I read your application; looks like you have plenty of experience Chelsea. Are you looking for days, nights, full or part time?"

"Full time nights," I reply.

"Can you work weekends?"

"Yes."

"Great. Would you be interested in being a hostess one night and a waitress four nights?"

"Sounds good to me."

"When can you start?"

"Is Thursday, ok?"

"That's great. Let me get you some shirts and an apron," he said as he stands and leaves the bar. He returns in a few minutes and hands me a couple of green shirts and an apron. "Wear this with black pants; see you Thursday at four."

"Ok great, thanks, see you Thursday," I said as I reach for the shirts and apron.

I walk out the bar door happy that I had found a job, I could not wait to tell John. My news would have to wait until he gets home tonight. We have plans to go out for drinks.

I shower, dress, and am waiting for John when he gets home. He quickly showers, dresses, and joins me in the living room.

"Wow, you look great!" I said as he enters the room dressed in a tight black T-shirt with black jeans and boots. It looks good on his tall thin frame. I reach up and run my fingers through his short light brown hair and his big brown eyes light up as he smiles.

"Where are we going?"

"To the French Quarter," he said with a smile.

"Oh really," I said less than thrilled.

"Come on it's going to be fun; it's nothing like what we saw when we first got here."

He was right; Bourbon Street is quite different at night. People are out in front of their businesses offering menus, telling drink specials, T-shirt sales, and girls sparsely dressed are outside of strip clubs.

"Let's get a drink to-go at Old Absinthe House before we hit the street," John said as he holds the door open for me. "What would you like to drink?" John asks as we approach the bar.

"I'll try a Planters Punch," I said as I see a sign advertising the cocktail on the wall. I look at the wall that is adorned with business cards randomly stuck in with push pins as John orders the drinks.

"Look, Chelsea, I wonder what this is," John said as he points to a tall green marble fountain sitting on top of the bar.

"The fountain was used to drip water into a glass of Absinthe," the bartender said as he delivers our drinks in plastic cups.

"Wow, that's interesting," John said as he gives the bartender money and collects our drinks.

We walk out of the bar and see an old-fashioned cancan cabaret show advertised at the Royal Sonesta hotel and I think that would be fun to see one day.

"Welcome to the Big Easy. We got the finest girls in New Orleans," a man say as he stands outside a nearby strip club.

I look up to where he is pointing and see two girls in silk bras and panties dancing in the window. As we continue to walk, we pass a group of people standing in line outside the Chris Owens Club. Next, I see Big Daddy's strip club and a pair of stocking clad mannequin legs swinging in and out of an open window. Next door is Unisex Love Acts and I wonder, "Are people having sex on stage?"

The street is full of people walking up and down with drinks in their hands. There are people standing on the balconies offering beads to women in the street if they show their breasts and women are lifting their shirts in exchange for the beads.

The lights from the neon signs light up the bar windows as jazz, blues, rock, punk, and new wave music fills the street. There are groups of people watching people performing in the street. We see a man sitting on a stool playing the drums on the bottom of a five-gallon pickle bucket. Next, we see a group of children tap dancing on the sidewalk. A crowd watches while they do a dance routine as they keep time with the music. As I look, I realize they are wearing sneakers; then I see bottle caps on the bottom of their shoes when they kick their legs. How clever I think as I walk up and put money in the hat they have set out for tips.

As we walk, I see two New Orleans police officers on horseback just outside Maison Bourbon and we decide to go in.

"Good evening, officers," I said.

"Good evening," they reply with a smile.

We are lucky two people are just getting up, so we get seats at the bar.

"What can I get you?" the bartender said.

"I'll have a Corona," John said.

"I'll have a Planter's Punch please."

"Is it always this crowded and crazy?" I ask the bartender.

"This is nothing, just a typical night, wait until Mardi Gras that's when it gets crazy," she said with a smile.

We sip our drinks while listening to live jazz music. When we finish our drinks, we decide to walk a bit more. As we walk, I notice the beautiful gas lanterns that are outside the shops, restaurants, and bars along the street. We pop into Fritzel's Jazz Pub, a great little bar with live jazz music. We have another drink and enjoy the jazz music before heading back down Bourbon Street. As we walk back, we pass Ripley's Believe It or Not.

"Do you want to go in?" John said.

"No, not tonight, let's go home," I said as we continue to take in the sights as we head back on Bourbon Street.

"I have a surprise for you tomorrow," John said as we climb into bed.

"Oh?"

"I am taking you to Commanders Palace for lunch to celebrate your new job. It's a famous New Orleans restaurant."

"That sounds great," I said as I put my head on his shoulder and drift off to sleep.

I wake up the next morning excited about going out to lunch. We slept in since we had a late night; we skip breakfast and just have coffee. As I get ready for lunch, I choose a silk blouse and long flowing skirt that has buttons from my waist to my feet and a pair of sandals. I style my bangs down over my forehead and spike a couple of pieces of hair with spray. As I walk into the living room, I see John wearing a crisp white shirt with a blue sports coat and khaki pants. He walks across the room and takes my hand in his, brings it to his lips and kisses it.

"You look lovely."

"Thank you handsome," I said as I put my arm in his.

"Are you ready to go, sweetie?" John said in his sexy southern accent.

"Yes," I said with a smile.

We head out to the Garden District and as we pull up to the big corner restaurant with blue and white awnings, I notice that there is a cemetery across the street.

"Hello, I am John Stevens, we have a reservation."

"Oh yes," the maître d' replies as he consults his reservation book.

"We requested the garden room if possible."

"Yes, I see. Follow me please."

We follow him upstairs and through a couple of rooms until we reach the garden room. A room with large windows and a big beautiful, graceful old oak tree with cascading branches is standing outside the window. The tables are set in crisp white linen, sparkling glasses, and gleaming silver. When we get to the table, the maître d' pulls out a brass backed chair for me and as I sit, he places a napkin in my lap.

"Peter will be with you in a moment, enjoy your meal," he said as he places the menus on the table. A busser comes to the table and pours water in our glasses and in a moment Peter arrives.

"Hello, I am Peter. I will be your server today. Can I get you a drink?"

"I will have a mimosa," I said. Although it is not Sunday it is for us, and John orders one as well. Peter returns with our drinks and recites the specials. He gives us a moment to decide and as he walks away John raises his glass.

"To us."

"To us," I said as we ring our glasses.

"We will both have the turtle soup, Caesar salads, and red snapper topped with crawfish," John said when Peter returns.

"Excellent choices," Peter said as he takes our menus.

"I want to have sex with you in the cemetery across the street," John said the moment Peter leaves the table.

"Very funny," I said with a laugh.

"I'm serious, I'm going to be on you like white on rice."

I cannot believe it as we have never done anything like this. This is not like him at all. We have a good sex life, but I am the aggressor, the one who initiates sex. This is out of character for him but as I look at him, I realize he is serious.

"Ok, I'm game," I said as Peter brings our soup.

"Let's skip dessert and go over right after we eat."

"Sounds good to me." I said smiling as I taste my turtle soup.

As we enjoy the rest of our delicious meal, I begin to get excited as I think about us having sex in the cemetery.

We enter the cemetery through two iron columns with an iron sign overhead reading, Lafayette Cemetery No 1. There are groups of people milling about as a tour is about to start. We pass them as we walk into the cemetery through the rows of tombs.

"Let's hurry to the back," John said as he takes my hand, and we move swiftly towards the back of the cemetery. When we get to the far end of the cemetery, we find a mausoleum with a short marble wall around it with a marble pillar in each corner. It is out in the open which makes it more exciting.

"Take off your panties, I'm going to sit you on top of this

pillar," John said as I slide my panties off, he picks me up and sits me on top of the pillar.

I look around to see if anyone is nearby, I unbutton my skirt and it flows over my thighs and cascades over the pillar. I feel the coolness of the marble through my thin skirt. John unzips his pants, spreads my legs apart and pulls me closer, I like this aggressive John. He kisses me as he cups my breasts in his hands. He kisses my neck and I throw my head back as my hands grip the back of the pillar and I look up at the clear blue sky. I get excited as I hear people off in the distance. His hands slide down my stomach to each side of my hips pulling me closer to him as he thrusts himself inside me.

"Ah," I moan with pleasure, and I kiss him passionately as he moves himself in and out of me. I wrap my legs around him and move my behind up and down to meet his thrusts. "Ah," I moan again as I wrap my arms around his back clutching his shirt in my hands. As he moves himself in and out of me faster, I keep with his rhythm and meet his thrusts.

I am trying hard not to moan aloud but it is hard because he feels so good inside me. He puts his arms under each of my legs and holds them up as he pushes himself in and out of me harder and deeper. He thrusts his cock in and out of me faster and faster and I cannot hold back anymore. "Oooh," I moan aloud with pleasure as he puts his hand over my mouth as he comes inside me. I giggle and push his hand away and we are both laughing now as he pulls himself out of me and zips up his pants. He lifts me off the pillar and I put my panties on, button my skirt, and adjust my shirt and hair.

"Do I look ok?"

"You look beautiful," he said as he grabs me and kisses me, then he takes my hand, and we slowly walk towards the gate.

As we walk, we stop to look at some of the old graves. We hear the tour guide telling the tourist that the city of New Orleans is under sea level. Which is why the graves are all above ground; if buried under ground the water would push them up. As I listen to the guide I wonder if anyone saw us as we leave the cemetery.

I am still giggling the next morning as John, and I have breakfast before he goes to work.

"I had a wonderful day yesterday," I said as I kiss him goodbye.

"So did I. Good luck on your first day at work," he said with a kiss.

"I will see you tonight, my love," I said as I shut the door and start to get ready for my first day.

"Hi, I'm Chelsea. I'm a new waitress starting today. Is Eric here?" I said to the hostess Claire just as Eric walks up.

"Hey, Chelsea, good to see you. I have some papers for you to fill out," he said as he reaches for the papers and hands them to me.

"Thank you," I said taking the papers.

"Follow me," he said, as he walks towards the server station.

"Ok."

"Hey, Anna, this is Chelsea. Can you please train her tonight?" Eric said as we enter the server station.

"Sure," Anna calls out.

"Thank you, Eric," I said.

"You're welcome," he said as he walks away.

I walk over to Anna as she is getting ketchup bottles off a shelf. When she stands, I see she is about five-foot-six with long dirty blonde hair, brown eyes, and a shapely figure.

"Hi, Anna, nice to meet you."

"Nice to meet you, Chelsea. Follow me, I'll show you around," she said. She shows me the seating chart, stations, and menu. In the server area she shows me the set up and the side work list of opening and closing jobs for the servers. In the kitchen she shows me the hot line, salad, coffee, and dessert stations.

The restaurant begins to fill up and the night goes smoothly, and I catch on fast. The dining room turns over a couple of times. The food looks nice, and the price is moderate, so the check average is good and so are the tips. I already see this will be a great place to work and I can make decent money here. After work we head over to Madigan's, a bar across the street. We grab seats at the bar and order two beers.

"So, like the other girls at work you are going to college; are you dating anyone?" I ask.

"I've been dating Mike since high school, and we plan to get married someday."

Anna is easy-going and I get a feeling we are going to be good friends. I can already see living in New Orleans will be much different than all the other places we have lived. There is more to do here and the girls at work are friends and hang out together. All the other places we lived in were rural and my coworkers were older than me and we all went home after work. Things may be looking up for me. The other girls have joined us by now; we all have a couple of drinks and unwind before heading home.

I get home to find John asleep. I am surprised since it is not that late. I shower and slip into bed and try to wake him with no success. I put my arm over him and drift off to sleep.

The next morning, I am sitting in the living room drinking coffee when I hear John come out of the bathroom.

"Good morning," I call out as I hear him walk into the kitchen.

"Good morning," he grunts as he strides into the room, walks by me, and goes to the desk where I see him write something.

"What's wrong?" I ask as he joins me on the couch.

"I'm getting old. I feel like I am going to die before I reach forty."

"What?" I said half laughing thinking this must be a joke.

"I am not interested in much of anything anymore. I do not want to go to anymore concerts, I only want to go to a movie if it is a comedy, I still enjoy going out to eat but that's about it."

"What are you talking about; what is wrong? You are barely twenty-seven, what makes you think you are going to die by forty?" I said not believing what I am hearing.

"It's just how I feel," he said as he gets up and walks out of the room.

I start to cry as I walk over to the desk to see what he wrote earlier. He had put a big red X on today's date on the calendar and I think he is crossing off the day before it even starts. I see now he has been doing this for weeks. I know he seemed a little off lately; he turned me down the last two times I tried to have sex which is not like him. I just thought he was tired. Then we had that hot sex in the cemetery, so I did not give it another thought.

"Maybe you should see a doctor?" I spoke.

"There is nothing wrong with me," he replies sternly.

I call his parents for help; I do not give them all the details but let them know he is depressed, hoping they can talk to him. He assures them he is fine so that does not help me. I try to get him interested in different things with no success. I try to get him to go for walks, play cards, go to movies, give him a massage, give him a bath, anything to get him engaged. I am heartbroken, I do not know what to do and I cannot think of anything else. Funny thing, John seems like nothing is wrong. Then I think what if it is me, what if he has someone else.

I decide to follow him one night after work, so I get off early and go to his job. As I wait for him to come out, I park where he cannot see me. I watch him go out of the parking garage and turn onto the street. I wait a moment for a couple of cars to get behind him and then I follow him. He went right home. I follow him a couple of times and he always goes right home.

Sometimes after work we meet for a drink but mostly, we just go home and watch tv. He barely even speaks to me. This went on for weeks; then weeks turns into months. I am so sad and lonely, and I have a brief affair with a bartender, Luke, that I met while out one night. He wanted more, wanted me to leave John. I could not so I ended it. I try to keep myself occupied with work and the girls there. I hostess on Monday nights and Eric's wife Gina is the cashier.

The rest of the week she is a server at a restaurant in the French Quarter. Gina is tall, and very fit from her daily workout. She is extremely attractive with long dark hair and big, beautiful chestnut eyes that sparkle when she smiles. Over the last few months, we have gotten to know each other and have become friends.

"Hey, Gina, do you want to have lunch on Wednesday?" I spoke.

"I can't; I'm meeting Josh on Wednesday."

"Who's Josh?"

"Josh is my lover."

"Are you kidding me?" I said with a laugh.

"No," she said with a smile.

17

"So, you and Eric have an open marriage?"

"No, we do not have an open marriage, there are rules. I don't just pick up any guy."

"Oh, is Eric seeing anyone?"

"No, it does not really work out when he sees someone; he gets to attached. He was seeing someone, but she just wanted him for herself so that had to end."

"How does anyone have sex with someone on a regular basis and not get attached? Are you attached to Josh?"

"No, we just have sex once a week," she said with a smile.

So, they do not have an open marriage, she just gets to have sex with someone else once a week I thought to myself. Well, who am I to judge what they do in their marriage?

"I wish I had someone to have sex with once a week!" I spoke. Not realizing I said that aloud until I hear Gina laugh and I laugh myself, just as a customer approaches the register to pay and we get back to work. At the end of the shift, Eric walks over to the hostess station as Gina is cashing out and I am wiping down the menus.

"Hey, Chelsea Gina and I are having friends over for drinks on Wednesday evening. Would you like to join us?"

"Sure, sounds like fun."

"Great, seven o'clock," he said as he scribbles their address on a piece of paper and hands it to me.

I get excited as I think about what to wear to the party on Wednesday morning as John and I have breakfast before he goes to work.

"Have fun tonight I love you," he said as he kisses my cheek and heads out the door.

"Thanks, I love you too," I said as I watch him leave.

I spend the rest of the day doing laundry and cleaning until it is time to get ready, and at five o'clock I jump in the shower. I choose a black skirt and sleeveless beige blouse with a pair of heels. I apply my usual light makeup with a touch of lip stick. I style my bangs across my forehead and touch up my nails with pink polish.

I arrive shortly after seven and Gina answers the door. We greet each other with a kiss as I walk in, and I see there is already quite a few people there. She calls out to Eric who is working on something in the kitchen. He runs over to us and bends down to kiss me on the cheek.

"Hello welcome, so glad you came. Would you like a drink? We have a full bar: wine, champagne, beer, or a cocktail?"

"Hello, thanks for having me. Champagne would be great."

"Ok, wait right here," he said as he rushes off.

"Your dress is beautiful," I said to Gina.

"Thank you. So is your blouse," she said as Eric returns with a glass of champagne and hands it to me.

"Thank you," I said as I take the glass.

"Gina, can you please finish fixing that tray of shrimp while I introduce Chelsea to everyone?"

"Sure, I'll see you later," she said as she walks away.

"Ok, see you later."

Eric takes me by the arm as we walk around the room. He introduces me to several people, mostly couples. Everyone is enjoying the hors d'oeuvres as they sip their drinks. He moves us around the room quickly, not staying long with anyone before he pulls me on to the next few people. As we approach the couch, I see Gina sitting there with a man and he stands when we are in front of him.

"Chelsea this is Adam Irons; Adam this is Chelsea Stevens," Eric said.

"Hello, nice to meet you," Adam said as he extends his hand as I reach my hand out and he takes it into his.

"Nice to meet you too," I said as our eyes lock and a warmth comes over me. Eric's voice brings my attention back to him and I gently pull my hand away and turn towards Eric.

"You two have fun," he said as he and Gina walk away.

"See you later," Gina said with a smile.

"Ok," I said as something told me they had accomplished their mission and I turn towards Adam and see he is smiling at me. As I look at him again, I see that he is ruggedly handsome with dark hair, a mustache and piercing deep blue eyes. He is about six feet tall with a medium build and a nice tan. He is wearing a crisp white shirt with khaki shorts and loafers. He is obviously older than me as he looks to be in his mid-thirties. He takes my hand again and the electricity shoots up my arm as he steers me towards the couch to sit down.

"How do you know Eric and Gina?" I ask as we sit on the couch.

"I used to live in this complex before I bought my house, and you?"

"I work with Eric at the restaurant," I said although I am sure he already knows that.

After a moment Adam pulls a joint out of his shirt pocket. He lights it, takes a hit, and passes it to me, I take a hit and pass it back.

"I'm going to give you a shotgun," he said as he moves closer to me.

"Ok," I said excited about being closer to him. We are facing each other, and I bring my face closer to his as he puts the lit end of the joint into his mouth. I cross my legs at my feet as I rest my arm on the back of the couch.

As I lean in and put my lips near the end of the joint, he put his hand on my bare shoulder. He let it linger there for a moment as he blows the smoke from his mouth, and I suck it into mine. His hand slowly slips down my arm and I nervously move my leg. As I do my ankle ends up on top of his ankle. I do not realize for a moment that I am moving it up and down caressing his calf with mine. I enjoy the feeling of his skin on mine, as the moment is very intoxicating.

I pull my mouth away and hold the smoke in for a moment before I turn my head and blow it out. He moves his hand from my arm and takes the joint from his mouth. As I slide my leg from his, I turn my head and look at him and our eyes meet as I lick my lips and catch my breath.

"Ok, smile," Eric said while holding a Polaroid camera to his face as I turn and smile.

When the picture shoots out of the camera, he pulls it out and put it and the rest of the pictures in his hand on the table in front of us. "I'm going to get a drink; I'll be right back." Eric said as Adam picks up the pile of pictures and begins flipping through them, commenting on the people in the photos. When he gets to the picture of me, he looks at me.

"Do you know what I like about the woman in this picture?"

"No," I said nervously.

"Her eyes, she has beautiful eyes," he said as he looks at me.

"Thank you," I said smiling as I break from his gaze.

Eric and Gina join us, and as we chat it becomes obvious to me that they are all exceptionally good friends. I remember that Gina was with her lover Josh today yet that does not seem to matter to her or Eric. Someone lit a joint and passes it to Gina. "No thank you, I don't smoke or drink," she said.

"I should be getting home soon; thank you for a nice evening," I said standing.

As I stand both Eric and Adam get up as well. I lean over and kiss Gina on the cheek; she smiles and kisses me back.

"Thanks for coming," she said smiling.

"I'll walk you out," Eric said.

I turn to say goodnight to Adam, and he takes my hand in his.

"Goodnight, it was very nice to meet you," I say as I look him in the eye, as he holds my hand firmly in his as he looks at me.

"Good night; it was a pleasure to meet you and I hope to see you again soon."

"Me too." I said with a smile as he releases my hand.

Eric walks me to the door; and kisses me on the cheek.

"Thanks for coming, see you tomorrow."

"Thanks for having me, see you tomorrow," I said as I kiss his cheek and I head out the door.

I think of Adam on the way home and the effect he had on me and my attraction to him. As soon as I get home, I put my pajamas on, curl up on the couch and wait for John to get home.

"Hi, how was the party?" John said as he comes in the door.

"Nice, how was work?"

"The usual," he said as he leans over and kisses my cheek. He gets a beer from the fridge, sits down on the couch, turns the TV on and sips his beer. He lights up a joint, takes a hit then offers it to me.

"No thanks," I said as he takes another hit and places it in the ashtray. I lean my head on his shoulder as he puts his arm around me, and I slowly drift off to sleep.

"Chelsea, wake up. Let's go to bed," John said as he gently shakes me.

"Ok," I reply as I get up from the couch and we head to the bedroom. I snuggle up to him when we get into bed.

"Good night, I love you," he said as he kisses my forehead.

"Good night, I love you too," I reply feeling disappointed.

The next morning, I remember that Eric's birthday is this week and wonder what to get him. I want to do something different, and I think about sending him a birthday gram. I open the phone book, turn to birthday, find an ad, and call the number.

"Hi, I want to send a birthday gram."

"Ok, what do you have in mind?" the man on the phone asks.

"What are my choices?"

"Is it for a woman or a man and of what age?"

"It's for a man; he is in his late twenties."

"Ok, we have clowns, singing dancers, strippers."

No, no, I am thinking as he spouts off the choices.

"We have a Dominatrix."

"Dominatrix, what does that entail?"

"A woman in a sparsely dressed black leather outfit with fishnet stockings and high heels will handcuff him and tease him with a whip."

"Perfect." I had never heard of a dominatrix before, but I think Eric will like it and the show should be fun. We discuss the price, and I give him the time, date, and location.

As soon as I arrive at work on Monday, I tell Gina about the birthday gram dominatrix and her six o'clock arrival. "I know his birthday was last week, but I wanted to wait for you."

"Oh, thank you. That sounds like fun," she said with a smile.

"Hey, I would like to invite Adam, do you have his number?"

"Great idea, he'll love it," she said with a laugh as she gives me his number and I head to the payphone to call him.

"Hello," Adam said as he answers the phone.

"Hi, it's Chelsea."

"Hello Chelsea," he said as he sings my name, and I can tell he is smiling.

"I am having a birthday gram come to the restaurant for Eric's birthday. A Dominatrix is going to come and handcuff him and playfully whip him. Do you want to come and watch?"

"Yes!" he exclaims, and I hear the excitement in his voice.

"Great, she will be here at six."

"I will be there."

"Come to the bar."

"Ok, you take care," he said as he hangs up the phone.

I arranged for the woman to come in the bar door. Just before six I call Eric into the bar, where the staff is already waiting. She enters the bar at exactly six o'clock. She is tall, voluptuous with long dark hair and blue eyes. She is wearing a sleeveless form fitting leather and lace body suit that is tied tight up to her breasts, so they pour out at the top. Fishnet stockings, thigh-high boots, a leather cap and a choker collar complete the outfit. She is carrying a small leather whip with leather tassels on the end of it. As she walks into the bar she calls out.

"I am Jade, and I am looking for Eric, where is he?"

We all point to him as he buries his face in his hands. She struts over to him, faces him, and puts both her hands on his shoulders and rubs them up and down his chest. "You've been a very bad boy and I'm going to punish you!" she said as his face turns red, and she pulls a pair of hand cuffs out from behind her back. He is standing in front of a bar stool, and she cuffs his hands behind him to the back of the stool. Once she has Eric cuffed to the chair, she continues to rub her body against his as she buries his face in her breasts as the crowd laughs and claps.

I scan the bar looking for Adam and I find him sitting at a table near the door. He is smiling but he is not looking at the show, he is looking at me. I smile back and I feel my cheeks blush as we stare at each other. A crack of a whip on the bar stool returns my attention to the show.

"Oh, baby I think you're enjoying this," she said as she takes her whip and playfully whips Eric with the tassels. Then she turns, bends over, and wiggles her behind for him.

"Do you like that baby?" she said as she turns around and rubs up against him as she kisses both his cheeks leaving red lipstick marks on each cheek.

"Happy birthday, Eric, you better be a good boy, or I will come back and discipline you!" she said as she uncuffs his hands and takes a bow as everyone claps.

"Thank you very much; that was great," I said as I approach her and pay her.

"You're welcome; glad everyone enjoyed it."

"Pay backs are a bitch you know," Eric said smiling.

"You loved it."

"It was fun but, I'm going to get you one day."

"I'm looking forward to it," I said as I turn around and bump right into Adam.

"Oh, sorry I did not realize you were there; did you like the show?" I said stepping back.

"Yes, I enjoyed it very much. You looked like you enjoyed yourself," Adam said.

"Yes, it was great."

"Thanks for inviting me, I was wondering if you would like to have a drink with me this week?"

"Sure, how about on Wednesday?" I said excited about seeing him again.

"Great, I will pick you up at five."

"Ok," I said as I pull my order pad out of my apron pocket, write my address on a piece of paper and hand it to him.

"See you Wednesday."

"Yes, see you Wednesday," he said as he steps forward to take the paper, bringing his face close to mine. A wave of excitement comes over me as he looks into my eyes and smiles. His hand holds mine for a moment before he takes the paper. I watch him as he turns and leaves the bar wondering what Wednesday will bring.

Chapter 2

I wake up happy that John and I are off for the day. I quietly get out of bed since John is still sleeping. I go to the bathroom, brush my hair and teeth, then head out to the kitchen and make coffee. I fix my coffee and take the cup out to the living room. I sit on the couch and grab a magazine from the coffee table to read while I drink my coffee. I am on my second cup when I hear John coming out of the bathroom. I hear him fixing his coffee in the kitchen and I look up from my magazine as he walks into the living room.

"Good morning. Did you sleep well?" John said.

"Good morning, no I had another nightmare."

"I'm sorry sweetie, are you ok?" he said as he kisses me.

"I'm ok," I said as I set my cup down on the coffee table and stretch my arms.

"What would you like to do today?" John asks.

"I was thinking about going to Cafe Du Monde for beignets, doing a little shopping at the French Market and then having a muffuletta for lunch at Central Grocery. How does that sound to you?" I said hoping he will want to go.

"That sounds good to me let's get ready."

"Ok great I will get in the shower now," I said as I get up off the couch. I stop when I am in front of him and he leans down and gives me a kiss on my lips, as I put my hand up behind his neck he pulls away.

"Come on let's get going," he said as he playfully taps my bottom with his hand. I laugh even though I am disappointed and head to the bathroom. In an hour we are both showered, dressed and ready to go. We decide to take the streetcar instead of driving, so we do not have to worry about parking in the French Quarter.

We walk to St. Charles Avenue to catch the streetcar; it is a beautiful day to be outside and the streetcar is there in a couple minutes. There are other people at the stop; we wait as they get on then we step on and deposit our fare. We sit halfway back on a wooden seat; where the window is open and there is a nice breeze as the trolley starts to move. I enjoy looking at the beautiful nineteenth and twentieth century mansions and magnificent old oaks that line St. Charles Avenue.

As the trolley curves around Lee Circle, I see a statue of General Lee set on top of a tall pedestal. It is set in the middle of the circle surrounded by grass with stairs coming from each direction leading up to the base of the statue.

"A bartender at work told me this is a perfect place to watch the Mardi Gras parades; they set up bleachers and barricades and people sit there and watch the parades. He told me all about the crowd, costumes and that most people wear masks and that the people on the floats throw beads and doubloons. If you do not catch the doubloon and it lands on the ground, you do not pick it up with your hand. You step on the doubloon with your foot and then you reach down and pick it up; otherwise, your hand will get stomped."

I did not know much about Mardi Gras and have not given it any thought although it is coming up. It is January 1986, and the carnival season is upon us.

We arrive at Canal Street, exit the trolley, and walk towards Decatur Street. Decatur Street runs parallel to the Mississippi River with the French Quarter on the other side. We pass the old Jax Brewery which has just been renovated. It is now full of shops, bars featuring live jazz bands and restaurants that overlook the river and Jackson Square.

We walk over to where a large crowd has gathered at an arena area of steps that lead to the river to see what the crowd is looking at. On the sidewalk below are four guys putting on an acrobat dance show; they are telling jokes and facts about New Orleans while performing. They are quite good, so we stop and watch the show. At the end of the show, they pass a hat for tips, given the crowd they should make good money. Four shows a day would be a lucrative business.

"That was fun. Let's get to Café Du Monde," John said as he takes me by the arm.

"Yes, let's go. I'm ready for some beignets."

We walk up one block to the café and join the line. It is not long, and I can smell the coffee as we wait. The outside of the building has a green and white canopy; there is indoor and outdoor seating. There are rows of tables and chairs with tabletop menus and napkin holders on them. As guests get up from a table people in line go over to the table and sit down. Since it is late morning, we only wait about ten minutes before there is a table.

"Great, here's a table Chelsea," John said as he sees people getting up; he heads towards the table as I follow. We are only there for a moment when the waiter comes over and quickly clears and cleans our table. The waiters are all dressed in white long-sleeved shirts, black bow ties, black pants with a white apron and white paper hats with Café Du Monde written on it.

He greets us as he cleans the table. The menu is simple:

coffee, café au lait, hot chocolate, water, juice, and beignets. We know what we want so we order as he clears.

"We would like two café au laits and an order of beignets please," John said.

"Be right up," the waiter said with a smile.

He is back quickly and places the steaming cups of café au lait and a plate of three fluffy fried pastries covered with powdered sugar in front of us.

"Thank you, that looks delicious," I said.

"Do you need anything else?"

"No thank you," we said in unison as we each take a beignet and place them on the plates, he put in front of us.

"Yum!" John exclaims as he bites the fried, sugary treat.

"This is so good," I said as I sip my café au lait.

As we share the third beignet the waiter comes by, and John gets the check and hands the waiter cash.

"Keep the change."

"Thank you," he said as he puts the check and cash in his apron.

We leave the café and continue to walk up Decatur Street. Decatur street is full of restaurants, bars, dance clubs, live music, vintage boutiques, and souvenir shops. We come upon an out-door bar and restaurant where there is a jazz trio playing, and we stand there for a minute to listen. Then we continue walking just past it to the French Market.

The French Market is a covered outdoor market that spans about five blocks. It features local produce, artwork, handmade crafts, and retail items. We walk by tables of fresh produce, and I look at the fruit. Since we both work the dinner shift, we eat din-ner at work. We go out to eat on our days off since New Orleans is full of delicious cuisine. With breakfast being the only meal, we eat at home that is all I need, and I get bananas, oranges, straw-berries, and grapes. John pulls his wallet out as the man working the stand puts my fruit in a bag.

"Thank you," John said as he pays for the fruit. As we walk, we come to a meat stand, and we stop to look at the selection of meats.

"We should keep this place in mind for when we want to cook something at home," I said.

"You mean when I want to cook something at home. I can't remember the last time you cooked dinner," John said laughing.

"Cooking wasn't the reason you married me," I said with a smile as we stop at a stand that has a vast selection of hot sauces.

"I need this for my eggs, I'm almost out," John said as he buys a bottle.

"Ewe, I can't stand the smell of that stuff," I said as I wrinkle my nose.

We walk by a couple of stands selling Mardi Gras masks and umbrellas; I stop and look but do not buy anything. We pass ta-bles selling records, books, clothes, and artwork. I stop at a table selling charcoal prints. I leaf through the prints of New Orleans scenes as John walks over and we look at them together.

"These would look nice in the living room," I said.

"Yes, they would. Why don't you get some."

I choose three matted prints of different French Quarter scenes; John pays for them and waits as the clerk puts them in a bag.

"Ok, are you ready for lunch?" he spoke.

"Yes I am."

We head over to Central Grocery, an old fashioned small Italian grocery store famous for their muffuletta sandwich. We walk in and pass the shelves stocked with imported pasta, olive oils, cheeses, and jars of all kinds of specialty items. We approach the counter and order a muffuletta, which consists of imported salami, ham, Swiss, provolone, mortadella cheeses, and a special olive salad, on fresh Italian muffuletta bread.

We take our sandwich and two Barq's root beers and head to the back of the store where there are long counters with wooden stools, and we take a seat on the end. There are napkin holders on the counter. I grab some napkins as John opens the deli paper that our sandwich is wrapped in.

"Oh, this is so good," I said as I finish my first bite.

"Yes, it is," John said as he takes another bite. "What do you want to do after lunch?"

"I was thinking about going across the street to where that jazz trio was playing and having a drink. How does that sound to you?"

"Whatever you want," he said.

We finish our lunch and head across the street towards the sound of the live jazz music. It is late afternoon and there is a nice crowd. We find a table near the walk-up bar and sit down.

"What would you like?" John said to me.

"A beer, I guess. Any kind, it doesn't matter to me."

"Ok, I'll be right back."

I enjoy the music as he gets our drinks. He returns a few minutes later with two Dixie beers and puts them on the table. I pick up the bottle and look at the label.

"It's a local beer brewed right here in New Orleans," he said as he picks up the other bottle and holds it up for me to ring our bottles.

"Cheers!" we said in unison.

The trio is quite good, playing lots of songs about New Orleans. We enjoy the music while having a couple of beers. When we are ready to go John goes up to the trio and puts money in the jar they have set out for tips.

"Thank you very much!" the band leader said.

"You're welcome," John said as I gather our packages and we head out to the street.

"Well, what now?" John said.

"I don't know, um how about we walk back to the streetcar and head home. We can get dinner near home is that ok?"

"Sure, that's fine with me."

We head towards Canal Street passing Jackson Square. Some shops are still open but most of the artists have packed up for the day. We get to Canal Street just in time to catch the streetcar. I take a seat on the car so I can see the mansions on the other side of St. Charles Avenue.

When we get home, I put the fruit in a bowl and line the prints on the bookshelf so I can look at them and decide what kind of frames to get. I go to see if John is ready to go back out and I find him on the couch with his shoes off.

"What are you doing? I thought we were going to go get a drink and have dinner."

"I'm tired. Would you mind getting us something to-go?"

"No, I guess not," I said thinking we did spend all day out.

"Great, thanks."

"How about salads and barbeque shrimp from Pascal's Manale?" I spoke.

"That's perfect."

I am back in no time; John has the table set and follows me to the kitchen.

"Smells good. Do you want a glass of wine?"

"That sounds nice."

He pours us each a glass of wine while I put the food on plates. I take in the aroma of the shrimp as I carry our plates to the table, and we sit down to eat.

"This is delicious," I said as I take a bite of the spicy shrimp.

"Yes, excellent choice, sweetie."

We enjoy the rest of our dinner and the wine. After dinner we quickly clean up and go into the living room to watch TV. He sits down on the couch, and I sit down next to him, I put my arm around him and lean over to kiss him. He gives me a quick peck on the lips and sits back.

"What do you want to watch?" he said changing the channels.

"It doesn't matter," I said sadly, as I sit back on the couch.

I wake up the next morning surprised to find John in the kitchen making breakfast. He has coffee made and is chopping ham and cheese for omelets. There is a bowl of beaten eggs on the counter and there is bread ready to go in the toaster.

"Good morning."

"Good morning," he said as he hands me a cup of coffee, leans over, and gives me a quick kiss on the cheek.

"Looks good."

"Sit down and enjoy your coffee, I will have breakfast ready in a couple of minutes."

I see the table is already set. I sit and sip my coffee as he cooks our breakfast. A couple of minutes later he is at the table and places a plate in front of me.

"Thank you, that looks delicious," I said as I look down at my plate and see an omelet, toast, and a portion of the fresh fruit we bought yesterday.

"You're welcome. It does look good if I do say so myself."

"Yummy," I said as I take a bite.

"What are your plans for today?"

"Oh, the usual cleaning and laundry. I will go out later for a bite to eat."

"Sounds like a plan," he said as he enjoys his omelet.

"Thanks for breakfast," I said when we finish, and I take our plates in the kitchen and start to clean up.

"You're welcome. I am going to jump in the shower and get ready for work. I need to leave early today. They are filming the movie *No Mercy* in the French Quarter. Some streets are closed off and it takes me longer to get to work."

"Ok," I said as I wash the dishes. When I finish the dishes, I head to the bedroom to change the sheets. John is just finishing dressing as I walk into the room.

"Have a wonderful day. I love you," he said as he kisses me.

"Love you too."

I watch him walk out of the room as I continue to strip the bed. I spend the rest of the day cleaning and doing laundry. I shower and dress before going out for a late lunch. I get a burger to-go and eat it on the outside patio. I brush my teeth and fix my hair just before five. At exactly five o'clock the doorbell rings. I open the door and find Adam standing there smiling.

"Hello."

"Hello, come on in while I grab a sweater," I said as he steps in the house, as I get a sweater from the coat rack.

"Ready to go?"

"Yes, I am," I said as he turns and opens the door for me. We both step outside and I shut and lock the door behind us. I step out and see a black BMW parked in front of my door. I walk around to the passenger side and Adam follows me, he opens the door and holds it as I get in.

"Thank you," I said once I am in the car.

"You're welcome."

"How are you?" he said when he gets into the car.

"Good and you?"

"Very well, thank you."

We drive away to the outskirts of the city and pull up to Copeland's Restaurant, a casual New Orleans chain restaurant.

"Table for two?" the host asks us as we walk in.

"Yes please," Adam said.

"Follow me," he said as he takes us to a booth. "Someone will be right with you," he said as he places two menus on the table as we both slide into the booth.

"I would rather have a drink at a table then the bar," Adam said as he pushes the menu aside.

"Fine with me."

"Would you like something to eat?"

"No thank you," I said as the server comes over to the table.

"We're just going to have drinks," Adam spoke.

"Ok, what can I get you?" she said as she waits to write down our order.

"I will have a white wine spritzer."

"I would like a rum and Coke," Adam said when she turns to him.

"Ok great, I will be right back with your drinks," she said as I look around at the decor.

"This place is nice."

"Yes, it is. I enjoy the food here," Adam said.

The server returns with our drinks. "Thank you," we both said as she places our drinks in front of us.

"Enjoy, let me know if you need anything else," she said.

As I sip my drink, I notice Adam is wearing a perfectly ironed short sleeve beige collared shirt. He looks at me as he sips his drink, and his eyes hold my gaze. He has this effect on me that makes me nervous and excited at the same time.

"So, Adam what do you do for a living?" I ask thinking how odd it is that I do not know that by now.

"I manage my investments."

"Oh," I said not knowing what that means.

I tell him that I was born in New York, and I am from a big family. I have moved around a bit with John and have not lived here long. That the city makes me nervous, but I am trying to get accustomed to it. He tells me he was born in Louisiana, is an only child and that he moved to New Orleans a couple of years ago. He loves the city and all its culture, festivals, music, and restaurants.

"You will too someday," he said as he sips his drink.

"I hope so," I said as I sip my drink. "So, why is a nice handsome guy like you single?"

"Because I choose to be. Is there anything wrong with being single?"

"No," I said just as the server approaches the table.

"Would you like another drink?" the server asks.

"No thank you, I'll take the check please."

She places the check on the table as Adam reaches for his wallet. He puts the money on the check as he glances at it.

"I will be right back with your change."

"Would you like to have another drink at my house?"

"Ok," I said after a moment.

"Great!" he said with a smile.

The server comes back with his change. He picks up the money and leaves a tip. He stands and waits for me as I slide out of the booth, he holds his hand out for me, and I place my hand in his as I stand.

It is a short drive from the restaurant to his house. We turn on to a quiet cul-de-sac and pull into the driveway of a ranch style white brick house with big windows, black shutters, and a well-manicured yard. He parks the car under the car port. We get out of the car and walk up the path to his front door. He unlocks the door and holds it open for me as I step inside; he follows and turns to the alarm pad and punches in the code.

As he does that I turn and see a large open room. There is a small living room area set in front of a big bay window with a light green couch and matching drapes. It connects to a dining area with a formal table and china cabinet. There are paintings on the walls with brass lamps over each one.

I follow him as we walk through two swinging doors into a large kitchen. The kitchen is primarily white with a couple of black decorative tiles on the walls above the counters and there is a black glass lamp hanging from the ceiling over the sink. To the left is a wooded table and six chairs. The rooms are very neat and orderly; nothing is out of place. We walk through another doorway into a large living room.

There is a couch, end tables and coffee table to the right and a large TV on a stand across the room. On one wall is a large print of a big mansion in a beautiful garden. On the other side of the room there is a sliding glass door covered by drapes. On the same wall is a print of a lion. The lion is on a dock and his body is facing the water. The lion's heads turned showing his profile and the lion's blindfolded. I am staring at the print thinking about its meaning when Adam voice interrupts my thoughts.

"Have a seat while I fix us a drink."

I walk over to the couch, go around the coffee table and sit down. On the table is a neat pile of magazines, an ashtray, lighter, a small wooden box, a tin of Altoids peppermints and coasters.

Adam comes back in the room with our drinks and hands me a tall glass that looks like Coke.

"Thank you."

"You're welcome," he said as he sits next to me.

I sip the drink and realize it is rum and Coke, but it is not that strong. We each have a couple of sips of our drinks then Adam puts his drink on a coaster and takes my drink from my hand and places it on another coaster. He pushes the table away from the couch, stands up and moves in front of me.

He lifts my chin and leans down but instead of kissing me on the lips he turns my head and sensually kisses my neck. His kiss arouses me, and I feel myself getting wet. No one has touched me like this in a long time and it feels good. His mustache is so soft and feels so good on my neck. As he kisses me his lips move slowly up and down my neck as I lift my hands to his shoulders.

"Oh," I moan aloud, and he stops and looks at me with a smile.

He grabs a sofa cushion, puts it on the floor in front of me and gets on top of it on his knees. He leans in and brings his mouth to mine. As his tongue enters my mouth my tongue meets his and I moan again. He kisses the other side of my neck, and he slowly, sensually kisses me from my ear to my collar bone. His hands are at my waist, and he takes my blouse in each of his hands and pulls it up. I lift my arms up as he pulls my blouse over my head.

I lower my arms to his shoulders and slowly slide them to the back of his neck. He stops and looks at me for a moment before kissing me again. He unhooks my bra as he is kissing me and brings his hands to my breasts, his thumbs circle my nipples, and they harden from his touch.

"Oh" escapes my lips as he pulls my bra off and moves his hands to my back. He steadies me as his mouth comes down to my breast, his tongue barely touches me as it dances lightly around my nipple. "Ahh," I sigh. I throw my head back, as he takes it into his mouth and his mustache brushes my skin as he sucks my breast.

He gently pulls away and quickly grabs the rest of the couch cushions and puts them on the floor on each side of him. Then he reaches his arm behind his head and pulls his shirt off as I admire his well-toned tan chest and arms. He puts his arms around my waist and under my legs and pulls me to the floor onto the cushions. He moves to my feet, reaches up to my waist, and pulls my pants down, I lift my behind as he slides them off and my panties come off at the same time. He stands and takes off his shorts and I see his erection. Then he drops down on his hands and knees between my legs.

"Ah!" I moan as his hand runs up my leg from my ankle to the top of my inner thigh and his mouth follows. As he slowly kisses my thigh the brush of his soft mustache excites me, and I feel my heart pounding. I run my fingers through his hair, and he suddenly stops and takes both of my hands in his and puts them over my head, looking me in the eyes before he continues. He quickly moves back down between my legs; his lips are on my mound kissing my bush; I am wet and throbbing. He spreads my legs further apart as his tongue enters me.

"Oh yes that feels so good!" I moan aloud as he slowly slips his tongue in and out of me. Excited and wanting more, I raise my bottom as he pushes his tongue inside me.

"Yes, yes, yes." I moan as he moves his tongue in a circular motion over my clitoris. His tongue is darting in and out of me faster and faster as I move my hips to meet him. I grip the cushion under my head as his tongue licks my clitoris faster and faster. I thrust my pelvis up and down to meet his tongue as I moan louder and louder.

"Ah, ah, ah, ahhhh," I moan as my pelvis thrusts forward and I let out a long continuous moan as my body shakes as I come. I giggle as my behind drops down on the cushion.

Adam lifts himself on top of me and swirls his tongue around my nipple as his hand caresses my other breast. He picks his head up and kisses me as he thrusts himself deep inside me.

"Oh, that feels so good," I moan as I lift my bottom to meet his thrusts; his skin feels so good against mine. He slowly glides himself in and out of me as I slide my hands lightly down his back. He stops for a moment and stares into my eyes. Then he pushes himself deep inside me. "Ahh," I moan.

His rhythm picks up and he moves in and out of me faster, I keep with his timing as I push myself up to him. He feels so good as he pushes himself deep inside me. We move together faster and faster. I arch my whole body forward and I come again; his body pushes my body down, thrusts himself deep inside me one last time as he comes.

I giggle and catch my breath; he lays on top of me for a moment. He rolls over next to me and brushes the hair from my forehead. I feel wonderful and guilty at the same time. Well, it is not like I am going to make a habit of this I think to myself.

I wonder for a moment why we stayed here instead of going to his room. Not that it mattered, I quite enjoyed the spontaneity. I wonder what time it is and think I should be getting home soon as Adam starts to get up.

"Would you like a glass of water?"

"Yes please," I said as I get up to gather my clothes.

"Here you go," he said as he hands me a glass of water.

"Thank you. Where is the bathroom?" I ask as I take a sip of water.

"Through there to the left, second door on the right," he said as he points the way.

"Thank you," I said. As I walk through the doorway, I notice all the framed degrees on the wall above the TV which impresses and intimidates me.

When I return to the living room, I see Adam has put all the cushions and the table back in place. He is dressed and is sitting on the couch; he stands as I enter the room. I walk over to the table and take another sip of water as I look for my purse.

"I should get going soon, do you mind?" I ask.

"No, whenever you're ready."

"I'm ready," I said as I pick my purse up from the table.

He extends his arm as to lead the way; I walk by him, and he follows shutting the lights as we go. He sets the alarm as we leave the house. We follow the path back to his car and he opens the car door for me.

"Well, back to work for me tomorrow," I said as we head towards uptown New Orleans.

"Do you like working there?"

"Oh yes, it's a fun place to work. I like my co—workers and Eric is a great boss. Have you known him and Gina long?"

"A couple of years, good people."

"Yes, they are," I said.

"I hope you have a great evening," I said as he pulls up to my house. I unhook my seat belt and lean over and give him a quick peck as he turns his head and faces me.

"You too, see you."

He waits until I am in the house to pull away. It is nine o'clock, so I quickly shower, put on my pajamas, and order a pizza. I eat two slices and put the rest in the fridge, then I curl up on the couch and watch TV.

"Chelsea, Chelsea, wake up," I hear John saying as he gently shakes me.

"Oh hi, I must have dozed off," I said as John leans over and gives me a kiss.

"Did you have a good day?"

"Yeah, how was work?"

"Good," he said as he heads into the kitchen.

"There's pizza in the fridge."

"Great," he said as I hear him pop open a beer and head to the bathroom. I get up and put the oven on to reheat the pizza while he showers, so it is ready when he returns.

"Thanks," he said as he sits on the couch. He lights up a joint and takes a hit; then he eats the pizza while we watch TV.

"I'm tired, I'm going to bed," I said after a while.

"Ok, good night, I'm going to watch a little more TV."

"I love you," I said as I lean over and give him a kiss.

"Love you too, sleep good."

Chapter 3

I sleep in the next morning and when I wake up, I see that John is already out of bed. I hear him in the kitchen as I head to the bathroom.

"Good morning," I said as I enter the kitchen.

"Good morning," he said as he hands me a cup of coffee and kisses my cheek.

"Thanks," I said as I lean against the counter.

"Are you hungry?"

"A little bit. Can I help?"

"No, I got it. Go sit down."

I see he has already started to prepare breakfast and the table is set so I sit down and sip my coffee. In a couple of minutes, he places a plate of scrambled eggs, toast, and fruit in front of me.

"Oh, looks good. Thank you."

"You're welcome, enjoy."

After breakfast he heads off to shower for work and I clean the kitchen. I am ironing my uniform when he returns dressed in his dress pants and jacket.

"Ok I'm off, see you later tonight," he said as he kisses me.

"Ok, have a good day, love you."

"Love you too."

I finish ironing our clothes for the week and watch TV before it is time to take a shower. My mind drifts off to yesterday and I get excited as I think about Adam. "Ok stop it." I tell myself as I feel myself getting wet. I jump in the shower and get ready for work leaving early enough so I have time to get a bite to eat before my shift. Eric is at the host station when I walk into work.

"Hey Chelsea, how are you?"

"I'm good thanks, how are you?"

"Good."

I walk over to the host station to check the seating chart and see where my station is. As I scan it Eric leans down and whispers in my ear.

"I hear you had fun yesterday," he said with a smile.

I blush, I know they are good friends, but I did not realize Adam would tell him. Not to mention so quickly and I wonder exactly what he said.

"Yes, I did," I said with a little laugh.

"Good I'm glad; I had a feeling you two would hit it off."

"Yeah," I said thinking we sure did hit it off. I head to the server station to do my side work and check my tables. I see that Anna is already there setting up.

"Hey Anna, how are you?"

"Good, how are you?"

"Ok, what station are you in?"

"Three, you?"

"Two."

"Oh good, let's go see if the specials are up yet."

"Ok."

We head to the kitchen just as the specials are coming up. Eric is there pulling the plates out of the window onto the counter, and we all gather around as he goes over the specials.

"Ok, tonight we have spicy shrimp and sausage jambalaya served over rice, crawfish and pasta alfredo served with broccoli and a beef kabob served with a potato and vegetable. They all come with a salad; prices are on the special board. Whoever sells the most, gets a free drink tonight," he said as we all grab forks to taste the food.

The restaurant fills up three times and the shift goes by fast. As Anna and I start to clean up, Emma comes into the server station.

"I won the special contest," Emma said.

Emma is a striking beauty about my height with short blond hair and blue eyes. She is very independent and attends college like the rest of the girls at work.

"Are y'all heading across the street for a drink after work?" Emma said.

"How about going somewhere else tonight?" Anna said.

"I'm game," I said.

"I don't want to be out long. I'm just going to get a drink or two across the street. You two enjoy," Emma said.

"I know a place in the Irish Channel, Pat King's Gin Mill. Is that ok?" Anna said as she turns to me.

"Sounds good to me."

We finish cleaning up and say good night to the other girls as they head across the street. Then we make our way to the Gin Mill, a small local bar on Magazine Street.

As we step through the wooden doors, I see a long bar with a large ornate wooden mirror behind it and shelves lined with liquor bottles and red round bar stools.

There is a juke box on the opposite wall at the end of the bar and a doorway past that which I assume is the bathrooms. It is not fancy and can use a paint job, but it looks clean. There is a half dozen people at the bar and two bartenders behind it. We take two stools on the end close to the door. A woman who looks to be in her forties with long straight hair, no makeup and a nice smile comes over to us from behind the bar.

"What's your pleasure, treasure?" She said in a thick southern drawl as she places two coasters in front of us.

"I'll have an Amstel light, please."

"Sounds good; make it two, please," Anna said.

She is back in a moment with our beer, and I put a twenty on the bar. She puts the beer in front of us but does not take the money.

"I'm Pat the owner; Laura is going to take care of you ladies tonight. She'll take your money as soon as she counts out the drawer; enjoy your evening," she said with a nice smile.

"Thank you," we said in unison.

She walks over to Laura as she finishes counting out the drawer, scribbles something on a piece of paper and turns around.

"Good night, everyone."

"Good night, Miss Pat," the regulars call out.

"Good night," we said in unison.

"Hi ladies, I'm Laura, I will be taking care of you tonight. Do you ladies need anything else right now?" she asks as she picks up the twenty.

"Do you want to do a shot?" Anna said.

"No, not tonight," I said while thinking, I still feel uneasy in the city and since I did not know this bar or neighborhood, I did not want to do a shot although I did not tell Anna that.

"Ok," she said sounding disappointed.

"Thank you, ladies," Laura said as she returns with the change from the twenty and places it on the bar.

The girl that was sitting to the right of us is back from playing songs on the juke box. "Can you turn the music up please, Laura?" she said as she gets back on her stool.

"Sure," Laura said as she walks over to the register and turns a knob on the wall and music fills the bar.

We are on our second beer when an elderly man at the other end of the bar throws up on the bar, flings backwards, then he and the bar stool crash to the floor.

"Ok, time to go," I think to myself, and I turn to Anna to say let's get going, just as a young man who is standing over the man on the floor calls out.

"I need help here; I think he is having a heart attack!"

Anna jumps up and runs over to the men as the young man gently removes the bar stool from under his legs and starts mouth to mouth. Anna drops to her knees to start chest compressions as she calls out to Laura.

"Call 911!"

At that exact moment "Manic Monday" by The Bangles comes on the juke box. Laura runs over to the phone and dials 911. I figure a person on the other end asked what was going on because she starts to say.

"A man threw up," she said as she starts crying and stuttering.

"He's dying," she said as she cries uncontrollably, as the juke box blares.

"Chelsea!" Anna yells.

"Handle that!" she said as she turns her head towards Laura.

I have been watching the scene as if watching a movie in slow motion and Anna's voice snaps me into action. I jump off the barstool and zip up the bar. As I pass Anna, she calls out to me between compressions.

"Tell them he is not breathing and has no pulse."

Laura is holding the phone out for me when I get behind the bar and as I take the phone, she falls to the ground sobbing. The juke box blares as I reach for the phone.

"Hello, a man who appears to be in his late sixties threw up and collapsed to the floor. He is not breathing and has no pulse; CPR is being performed."

"Ok, what is your location?" asks the woman on the phone.

"We are at Pat King's Gin Mill on Magazine Street."

"Do you have an address?"

"What's the address?" I said, looking at Laura.

"The thirty-two hundred block of Magazine Street," Laura sobbed.

I repeat the information to the woman on the phone. Trying to concentrate as the song blares from the juke box.

"Do you know the side streets?" she spoke.

"Um, what no, I don't. Do you know the side streets?" I asked Laura.

"What?" she cries.

"Oh God, does anyone know the side streets?" I yell out to the bar.

"Can someone go look?" I yell out when no one replies.

"Don't you have a map?" I ask the woman on the phone as one of the guys goes to check the side streets.

"No, I don't."

"Are you kidding me?"

"Give me a break; I'm new at this," she said to me just as I hear the sirens approaching the bar.

"Well, I'm sure the guy on the floor is new at dying," I said, and I hang up the phone in frustration.

"Can someone go outside and flag the ambulance down?" I call out.

"I'm on it," the girl who played the juke box said as she jumps up and runs outside.

The end of "Manic Monday" rings out of the juke box as I

walk over to the knob on the wall and turn the volume to the juke box off.

Just then the paramedics rush in with a stretcher followed by the guy who went to check the side streets and the girl who flagged them down.

"Ok, we'll take over," one of them said.

As they start CPR I come out from behind the bar and walk over to Anna.

"Are you ok?"

"I think he's dead; I felt him go cold," she said holding back tears.

"Come on, let's sit down," I said as I put my arm around her, she stood frozen for a moment watching the paramedics.

"You ready to call it?" one said to the other.

"Yeah, he's gone."

"Oh no," escapes my mouth.

"SHIT!" Anna yells.

I pull her away towards our seats as they put him on the stretcher and cover him. I hear them asking Laura if she knows his name as they draft their report. The whole bar is quiet as they roll him out. The taller of the two paramedics stops at our stools as he is walking out.

"You did good, truth be told but he was probably gone the second he hit the floor," he said while looking at Anna. I put my arm around her as she buries her face in her hands. After a second, she looks at me.

"How about that shot now?"

"You got it; whatever you want I am buying."

"No, I'm buying. Thank you both for everything. I'm sorry I lost it. I never saw anyone die before, much less someone I know. Fred was a regular and a super nice guy," Laura said as she rushes over to us.

"I am so sorry; I know what you mean, I am shaken up myself. I have never seen anyone die either," I said.

"Well, I'm ready for a shot; how about a snowshoe?" Anna said.

"Ok, what's that?" Laura asks.

"I'm not sure what it officially is but I make it with peppermint schnapps and vodka," Anna said.

"Ok, you got it," Laura said.

As Laura is making our shots the guy who was performing CPR with Anna, comes out of the restroom, walks to the door and waves.

"Good night, everyone, I got to go, thanks," he said looking at Anna as he goes out the door.

Laura comes back with a chilled pitcher of shots and pours three. We each drink one and she lifts the shaker to pour another.

"I'm good for a minute," I said putting my hand over the glass.

"Me too," Anna said as Laura walks away to take care of the other customers.

"I'm ready to go; I can't sit here and get drunk," Anna said.

"I hear you; let's go," I said as we leave cash on the bar.

"Good night, Laura," we call out as we slide off our stools.

"Good night, thanks again for everything," she replies.

"Take care," Anna said as we walk out of the bar.

"Are you ok, Anna?" I said once we are outside.

"No, but I just can't talk about it right now."

"I understand, call me if you need me," I said as I scribble my number on a piece of paper.

"Ok thanks," she said as she rips the paper in half and writes down her number.

"If you need anything," she said as she hands it back to me. We hug each other, say goodnight and head home.

I am just getting out of the shower when I hear John walking through the house. He opens the bathroom door as I am drying off.

"Hey, I'm home. How was your night?"

"Not so good. After work Anna and I went out for a drink and this guy at the bar had a heart attack and died. Anna gave him CPR with another guy, while I was on the phone with 911 because the bartender was having a meltdown," I said as I move towards him.

"Oh, sweetie, I'm so sorry," he said as he wraps his arms around me and kisses the top of my head.

"Are you ok?"

"I have never seen anyone die before. Sure, relatives have died, and I went to the funeral, but I never saw anyone die."

"I am proud of you for trying to help. While you dress, I will fix you a drink and roll us a joint," he said as he caresses my cheek.

I dress, towel dry my hair and head out to the living room. When I get there, I see a rolled joint on the table as John comes from the kitchen with two bottles of beer.

"Here you go."

"Thanks," I said as I take a sip and head to the couch.

He lights the joint, takes a hit, and hands it to me. I take a hit and hold it in for a moment before exhaling slowly. John takes another hit and hands it back to me.

"Will you be ok if I take a quick shower?"

"Sure," I said as I take another hit and put the joint in the ashtray.

I am just sitting there staring off into space thinking about how one minute Fred was enjoying a beer at the bar and the next he falls to the floor and dies when John returns. He glances at the TV and sees that I have not turned it on.

"Hey, sweetie how about we go snuggle in bed?"

"That sounds good to me," I said as I get up, shut off the lights and head to the bedroom. We crawl into bed, and I put my head on his shoulder, and he strokes my hair until I fall asleep. I wake up every hour all night long. At seven I decide to get out of bed and make coffee. I am lying on the couch trying to fall back to sleep when John gets up at nine.

"Good morning, how long have you been up?" he said as he walks into the room with a cup of coffee.

"Good morning, since seven."

He sits on the couch next to me, leans in and gives me a kiss.

"Are you ok?"

"Yes, tired. I didn't sleep well."

"I'm sorry, how about some breakfast?"

"Nothing for me."

"You have to eat something."

"Ok, just toast then."

"Well, that's better than nothing."

He heads to the kitchen and comes back with a plate of toast and jelly and a fresh coffee. I sit up on the couch and eat the toast as he sits next to me and eats an egg sandwich.

"I'm going to take a shower. Are you going to be alright?" He said as he leans in, kisses my head and scoops up the plates.

"Yes, I think I will lay back down and try to get some sleep."

"Good."

I get up off the couch as he heads to the bathroom. I slip into bed and close my eyes trying not to recall the details of last night. I open my eyes when John enters the room dressed and ready for work.

"Ok, I'm going try to have a good day. I love you," he said as he leans over and kisses me.

"Don't worry; I'll be ok. I love you too. Have a good day."

I watch him leave and I drift off to sleep. A ringing phone wakes me up and I glance at the clock as I roll over to answer it. Wow, eleven-thirty; I cannot believe I slept that long.

"Hello."

"Hey, it's Anna. Did I wake you?"

"It's ok. I need to get up anyway. Are you ok?"

"Yeah, I didn't sleep well."

"Join the club; that's why I went back to sleep for a little while. Do you want to talk about it?"

"No, I don't. I wanted to know if you want to get something to eat before work?"

"Sure, sounds good. I need to take a shower. Where do you want to go?"

"I'm thinking we need comfort food, so how about the Piccadilly Cafeteria?"

"Ok, where is that?"

"I will pick you up. Can you be ready at one? If you bring your uniform, we can go right to work and dress there. Then I will bring you home tonight, ok?"

"Sounds great. See you at one."

"Ok see you," she said as we both hang up the phone.

I get up, make the bed and head to the shower. I shower, dress, fix my make-up, hair and get my uniform ready for work. I put on a blue V-neck tee, white shorts, and sandals. I am ready on time and a minute later I hear a horn beep outside. I stick my head out the door and see Anna's car.

"One second." I call out as I run back in, grab my stuff, lock the door, zip down the steps, and jump in her car.

"Hey, how are you?"

"Hungry."

"Me too. Obviously, you have been to this place before," I said as she pulls away.

"Yes, it's great. You name it they have it."

"Sounds good to me," I said as I look at Anna and see her hair is down in an unruly mess. She is wearing a wrinkled concert tee, a long cotton skirt that does not match and sandals. Well, she wanted to be comfortable I think to myself as we head towards the highway.

The host seats us in a booth and the server quickly comes to greet us. She tells us about the serving line and gets us a drink. Just like high school there are stacks of trays and rolled silverware for you to grab as you slide your tray down the line.

Anna was not kidding; they have everything you could want. There is an abundance of soups, salads, and breads to choose from to start with. As I look at all the pre-plated salads and breads an elderly lady behind the line smiles as she says, "May I get you anything?"

"I'll have a shrimp and corn soup, please."

"I'll have one also, please," Anna said.

"Thank you," we both said as she dips our soup into cups, and she places them on the counter.

"Looks good," I said to Anna.

"You're welcome," the lady said.

We each reach for a piece of corn bread and make our way down the line. As we head down the line, I notice a board on the wall with the menu and prices. I cannot believe how inexpensive this food is. As we reach the entrée section, I see about thirty different items to choose from. Every kind of chicken, fish, pork, beef, and pasta you could want and of course, there are southern specialties as well.

"I'll have the blackened shrimp and pasta, please," I said.

"May I have the crawfish etouffee?" Anna said.

A server plates up our entrees and places them in the window. We grab them and head down towards the side dishes. There is a vast choice of side dishes as well. Since I am having pasta, I decide to get a vegetable. I am about to ask for the green beans when Anna turns to me.

"Get the carrot souffle. Trust me it is so good."

"Ok, can I have the carrot souffle please?"

"Make it two, please."

We stop at the dessert choice. I am about to pass when I see chocolate pecan cream pie.

"Oh boy, how are we going to work after eating all this? We are going to need a nap."

"We'll get some coffee with dessert and walk it off at work," Anna said with a laugh.

We pay the cashier and head to our table to enjoy our food. The food is tasty, and we sample each other's entrees. Anna was right about the carrot souffle.

"Wow that is delicious!" I exclaim as I take a bite of the carrots.

"I told you," Anna said with a smile.

"You were right when you called this comfort food. This is just what we needed today."

"Wow, we better get going," Anna said as she looks at her watch and we both get cash out of our purses to leave a big tip for the server before heading to work.

We arrive at work with just enough time to change. We check our stations and go to the server station to set up. Ashley is already there setting up. Ashley is a sweet petite girl with long wavy auburn hair and bright green eyes. She is younger than the rest of us and in her first year of college. As we enter the station Emma is right behind us.

"Hey, did y'all have fun last night?" Ashley said.

"No, a guy had a heart attack at the bar and died," I stated.

"What!" Emma said.

"I really don't want to talk about this," Anna said.

"I'm sorry."

"No, I'm sorry. You have a right to talk about it if you want to, Chelsea."

"Don't worry about it; let's talk about something else. We had lunch at Piccadilly Cafeteria today. It was great," I said trying to change the subject.

"Oh, I love Piccadilly. My mom and I go there all the time," Ashley said.

"It's ok; not one of my favorite places," Emma said.

"I'll check everyone's sugars," Anna said as she leaves the station with a basket of sugar packets.

"Are you both ok; what happened?" Ashley and Emma both ask as they turn to me as soon as she is gone.

"It was very upsetting. She did CPR on him; she told me later that she felt his body go cold. Let's talk about something else before she comes back; I do not want to upset her anymore by talking about it."

"What about you, are you ok, Chelsea?" Emma asks.

"I'm pretty shaken up, but I'll be ok."

"Well, I'm here if you need to talk."

"Thanks, Emma," I said.

As we get to work setting our stations Eric calls us to the kitchen to go over the specials. Thankfully, the evening goes by quickly and before we know it the shift is over.

"Do you guys want to get a drink across the street?" Emma said.

"No thanks, I just want to go home," Anna said.

"Yeah, me too," I said happy the day is over.

The rest of the weekend flies by and before I know it is Monday morning. John just left for work, and I am sitting in the living room drinking coffee when the phone rings.

"Hello," I said as I pick up the phone.

"Hi, this is Gina."

"Oh hi, how are you?"

"I'm ok, has John left for work yet?"

"Yes, he has. What's up?"

"Adam asked me to call to see if it is ok to call you."

"Yes, he can call me."

"Ok, I will call him and let him know. I'll see you tonight at work."

"Ok thanks, see you tonight, goodbye."

"Bye," she said as she hangs up the phone.

I hang up the phone, sit back on the couch then a minute later it rings again. I sit on a stool at the counter since the phone cord does not reach far.

"Hello," I said as I pick up the phone.

"Hello, Chelsea. It's Adam. How are you?" he asks as he sings my name.

"I'm ok. How are you?"

"I'm good. I was wondering if you would like to get together on Wednesday," he said as I hear the excitement in his voice.

"Yes, I would like that," I said without hesitation thinking this is perfect. We will get together occasionally and just have sex; nothing complicated.

"Great. Is one o'clock, ok?"

"Yes, that's perfect."

"Ok great. I will pick you up at one."

"Ok, I'll see you then."

"You take care," he said as he hangs up the phone.

"Ok bye," I said as a wave of excitement comes over me as I hang up the phone. I try not to think about him for the rest of the day until Gina asks me about him at the end of the shift.

"So, are you going to see Adam on Wednesday?"

"Yes," I said as my cheeks get flushed, and I wonder why does he have this effect on me?

"That's nice; have fun."

"Thanks, I hope you enjoy your days off as well."

"I will; see you next week."

"See you," I said as I walk out the door.

Chapter 4

$\mathcal{I}$ wake up feeling refreshed Tuesday morning, glad that we are off. John is still asleep, so I quietly slip out of bed, so I do not wake him. I hear the rain hitting the kitchen window as I am making coffee. I am on my second cup when I realize how late John is sleeping.

I go back to the bedroom to check on him. He is still sound asleep, so I go back to the living room and put the TV on. I turn to the morning news and the weather report is calling for rain all day. "Well, that stinks," I say out loud. I am making myself a piece of toast when I hear John coming down the hall.

"Good morning, sleepy head," I said as he walks into the living room.

"Good morning. Sorry I slept so late; I don't feel too good."

"Oh, I'm sorry. What's wrong?"

"I have an upset stomach; I was up most of the night."

"Oh no, would you like a hot tea and toast?"

"That would be great, thank you."

I make him a cup of tea and toast and bring it to him in the living room. I put my hand to his forehead to see if he has a fever.

"Well, I don't think you have a fever."

"I don't feel like I have a fever; I just don't feel well. I think

I will eat this and go back to bed. I am sorry for ruining our day off."

"You didn't ruin anything; I'm going to run to the store and get some food and something for your stomachache."

"Ok thank you."

"I will be back soon; go back to bed. Do you want anything in particular? I am going to get soup, crackers, and ginger ale."

"No, that's good. Thank you; be careful."

"Ok, I will be back soon, love you," I said as I blow him a kiss.

"Love you too," he said with a smile.

I head out in the rain to Winn Dixie on Tchoupitoulas Street and get everything on my list and a bottle of Pepto Bismol. When I get back to the house, I find John still asleep, and I decide not to wake him. I put everything away and then I make myself lunch. I am just finishing cleaning up when John comes in the kitchen.

"Hey, when did you get back?"

"A little while ago. How do you feel?"

"A little better I guess."

"Would you like a bowl of soup and crackers?"

"Sounds good."

I bring him a bowl of soup and crackers; he eats everything and lies down on the couch. I find a movie on TV and pull the afghan off the back of the couch and cover him. I clean up the dishes and join him on the couch to watch the movie. John falls asleep halfway through the movie. I watch the rest of the movie and am doing the wash when he wakes up.

"I guess I fell asleep."

"That's ok. How do you feel?"

"Better thanks."

"Are you hungry?"

"A little bit; can I have some toast please."

"Sure." I said as I head to the kitchen and make us both something to eat, happy that he is feeling better.

I wake up and see that John is already out of bed and I find him in the kitchen making breakfast.

"Well good morning. How are you feeling?" I said as I enter the kitchen.

"Good morning, I feel much better. Are you hungry? I'm starving."

"Oh, I am so glad you feel better. Smells good," I said as I give him a kiss, and get a cup of coffee, as the smell of bacon frying fills the air.

"It will be ready in a minute."

"I'll set the table," I said as I open the silverware drawer.

"Ok great."

"That looks wonderful, thank you," I said as he puts the plates on the table.

"You're welcome. What are your plans for today?" he said as he takes a bite of eggs.

"Oh, I have some cleaning to do, and I will probably go out for a bite to eat later," I said feeling horrible for lying while thinking, I do not want to hurt John.

"That sounds good. At least it's not raining."

"Yeah," I said as we finish eating.

I clear the dishes and clean the kitchen while John showers and dresses for work. I am in the living room when he comes in dressed and ready for work.

"Ok, I better get going."

"Ok, see you tonight. I love you."

"Enjoy your day, love you too." he said as he leans in and gives me a kiss.

I spend the rest of the morning cleaning the house and at noon I jump in the shower and put on a sun dress and sandals. Five minutes to one I am waiting for Adam at the door thinking I would not mind if we did not go out for drinks. Adam pulls up at exactly one o'clock, I pull the door shut behind me, skip down the stairs and jump into his car.

"Hi, how are you?" I said as I get into the car.

"Hello, I'm good. How are you?" he said as he turns and looks at me with a smile.

"I'm ok, how was your week?"

"Great, how was yours?"

"Good," I said skipping the details of Fred dying in the bar.

"I was thinking we could have a drink at my house instead of going out right now."

"That's perfect!" I said smiling.

"It's a beautiful day; I'm glad it isn't raining."

"Yes, we had enough rain yesterday."

We arrive at his house in no time at all. He waits for me to come around the car and follows me up the path to the door. He holds the door open for me as I walk in.

"Let's go into the den."

"Ok."

"Have a seat while I get us something to drink."

"Ok, thank you," I said as I sit on the couch.

He comes back into the room holding two drinks that look like Coke. He hands one to me and sets his on a coaster.

"Thank you."

"You're welcome," he said as he goes back to the kitchen.

I take a sip of the Coke and realize it is rum and Coke, but it is not too strong. He returns with two shot glasses full of a brown liquid and sits next to me on the couch.

"Have you ever had Jägermeister before?"

"No, I haven't."

"Well, here you go," he said as he holds the glass out for me.

I take the glass from his hand and sniff it thinking it does not smell particularly good.

"Cheers!" he said as he holds his glass up to mine.

"Cheers!" I said as we ring our glasses and drink the shots.

"Wow!" I said making a face.

"Did you not like it?"

"It's ok. I usually drink something fruitier," I said as I set the shot glass down and take a sip of the rum and Coke to get the taste out of my mouth.

"Are you ok?"

"Yes, I'm fine."

When we finish our drinks, Adam looks at me and speaks. "Take all your jewelry off and put it on the coffee table."

"Ok," I said thinking that is a little strange as I take my rings and earrings off and place them on the table.

"Come with me," he said as he stands up.

I stand and walk around the coffee table; he comes behind me and places his hands on my shoulders. He steers my body towards the doorway as he marches behind me.

We enter his bedroom and I see a door to the left of me that I assume is a closet. There is another door a couple of feet away that is open, and I can see it is the bathroom. There are two windows on the other wall and a chest of drawers behind me. Two nightstands grace each side of his bed in the center of the room.

His bed is a beautiful eighteenth century French provincial caramel colored king size bed that you would see in a museum or antique store. The headboard looks to be about three feet high with a post on each end and an ornate gold design below each post. There is a string of gold leaves embossed on the headboard like garland. The footboard is also quite high, and it wraps slightly around the foot of the bed. It does not have posts like the headboard but does have the same gold design on each end. In the center of the footboard is an embossed circle of the same gold leaves that are on the headboard.

There is a white chenille bedspread on the bed and there is something red coming up from below each corner of the bed and lying diagonally across the bedspread a couple of feet from each corner. I see that it is a red Christmas ribbon that you would use to wrap a gift and I realize his intentions.

"I can't let you tie me up on the second date!"

"Yes, you can," he whispers in my ear. He is still behind me; his hands are still on my shoulders. He drops his hands and moves from behind me to beside me.

I keep my attention on the bed, but I can see out of the corner of my eye he is looking at me. Watching me, waiting as I decide. I have never been tied up before. Obviously, there is a big trust factor involved in letting someone tie you up, much less someone you hardly know. But something told me that even though I do not know this man very well, it is not his plan to tie me up and hurt me.

Thinking that, I decide I am getting what I want from this relationship so if he wants to play tie me up why not let him. It could be fun, and nice to not be in control for a change.

"Ok," I said as I turn towards him, and a big smile comes across his face as he steps towards me.

"Take off your clothes and lay in the center of the bed with your legs together and your arms at your side."

He watches me as I undress, not moving until I am lying in the center of the bed. He looks at me for a moment from the foot of the bed, as his tongue licks his lips.

He comes over to the left side of the bed, picks up my hand and stretches my arm towards the ribbon. As he begins to tie the ribbon around my wrist, I realize at once he is not playing; he has done this before. I am not scared though; actually, I am excited. He checks the tightness of the ribbon making sure it is not too tight around my wrist and does not hurt. There is no slack as I try to pull it towards me, and I am not able to get my wrist out. I wonder for a moment if this was why we did not come in here last time.

"Did you," I start to say, as he raises a finger to my lips.

"Shh."

Did he have this planned? Did he save the first time I saw his bed to add to the effect? I wonder to myself.

He moves to the end of the bed and gently picks up my ankle and spreads my leg with my toes pointed to the corner of the bed. A wave of excitement comes over me as he touches my ankle and ties the ribbon around it. He glides his hand up my leg to my upper inner thigh and slowly caresses its way down to my toes.

"Ooh," escapes my lips.

He moves around to the other side of the bed and picks up my wrist. I watch him as he swiftly ties my wrist with precision taking care that it is not too tight. He caresses my cheek with the back of his hand and runs his fingers down my neck over my shoulder and up my arm until he reaches the ribbon around my wrist. As he stands his fingers dance lightly across my skin from just under my arm down the side of my breast, my stomach across my hip, thigh, and shin until he reaches my ankle.

"Ooh," I moan with pleasure as his fingers move down my body.

He picks up my ankle and spreads my leg to the corner of the bed and ties my ankle with the ribbon. He places his hand on my mound, and I push my bottom up. He caresses my mound for a moment as he watches me, and I sigh with pleasure. "Oh."

He slides his hand to the inside of my thigh and his fingers slowly move down my leg. As he does this my leg shakes with excitement from his touch. His eyes are on me, watching my reaction to his touch.

He moves to the bottom of the bed and stands there with his hands on the foot board looking down at me, reviewing his work. I turn my head from side to side and wiggle my body in excitement.

I see his erection in his pants; he is excited, and I can tell he likes seeing me tied spread eagle. My petite body leaves ample room on the bed; he gets on the bed on his knees and moves himself above my body. An arm on each side of me, his legs are straight in between mine as he holds himself above me. Not touching me as he looks intently into my eyes.

I am excited, wet and my heart is pounding. He lowers his face to mine and his tongue darts into my mouth, my tongue hungrily meets his. He cups my chin in his hand and turns my head as he kisses the side of my neck. I like the softness of his mustache as it caresses my neck, as his lips move down towards my collarbone. He kisses my collarbone until he reaches my shoulder, then he slowly kisses his way up my neck to behind my ear. I turn my head offering him my neck as he does this. His mouth glides down my neck below my chin as I raise my chin up to the ceiling.

He slowly kisses his way down the center of my chest as I arch my back and push my breasts forward. My nipples are hard and waiting for him. I cry out with pleasure wanting more as his lips move lightly around my breast. I let out a moan as his tongue flicks in and out of his mouth around my nipple. He circles my nipple with his tongue before he lightly licks it.

"Ah," I cry out as I push my chest forward as his mouth swallows and sucks my nipple.

"Oh, yes," I moan as he takes his hand and cups my other breast. He takes my nipple between his finger and thumb and gently squeezes it. As I move my hands, I feel the ribbon against my wrist holding me back and it excites me as I want more.

He kisses his way to my other breast and brushes his mustache lightly across my nipple before he devours it in his mouth. I moan with pleasure as I fight the restraints wanting to grab him. As his hand lightly caresses the side of my calf moving slowly up my leg and inner thigh until it reaches the very top.

My leg shakes uncontrollably, and I wiggle with excitement. His mouth moves slowly across my chest kissing his way down my stomach past my bellybutton to my mound as he delicately kisses me.

"Oh, yes, yes," I moan wanting more as his tongue enters me and slowly slides up inside me. I moan loudly and push my bottom forward as his tongue lightly flicks my clitoris. He teases me as he barely touches me with his tongue. I am so excited that I am pulling on the ties, trying to move my arms as I arch my body forward trying to reach him.

He pushes his tongue deeper inside me and I moan with pleasure as he slowly circles my clitoris with his tongue. I move my bottom up and down in rhythm with his tongue as he thrusts it in and out of me faster and faster. I shake my head from side to side as my arms and legs pull at the ties. I realize I am not moaning aloud with pleasure; I am screaming. My heart is pounding, and my inside is throbbing against his tongue.

"Ah, ah, ah, ah, ahhhhh," I scream as his tongue circles my clitoris faster and faster, as my screams get louder and longer, as I get closer to coming. My whole-body jerks forward and stiffens as I explode with pleasure, and I hear myself growl like an animal. I collapse on the bed as my legs twitch and shake uncontrollably.

My body glistens with sweat and my screams subside into soft cries of satisfaction and then instead of my usual giggle I burst out laughing. Adam lifts his head and looks at me as he lets out a devilish laugh. I smile as I close my eyes and catch my breath as I hear him get up and leave the room.

He strides back into the room, and I hear him put something on the nightstand. I open my eyes and see he is holding a glass in front of me.

"Would you like a drink of water?"

"Yes please," I said thinking he is going to untie me. As he holds the glass to my mouth, I lift my head and take a sip. The icy water tastes good as my mouth is dry from screaming.

"Thank you."

"Would you like more?"

"Yes please," I said as he holds the cup to my lips, and I take another sip.

"That's enough, thank you," I said as I lay my head back on the bed as he set the cup on the nightstand.

I hear water dripping and turn my head and see he is wringing out a washcloth above a bowl of water. He sits on the bed next to me and gently wipes my face with the cool cloth brushing my damp bangs from my forehead. The cool water feels good against my warm skin as he continues wiping the cloth over my neck.

He gets up, rewets the cloth, sits back down and continues to wipe my chest. I watch him as he does this, and I see he is smiling. My nipples get hard as the cloth slides over my breasts, and I moan softly as he continues to wipe my arms and hands. He looks up at me, gives me a devilish smile then wets the cloth again and continues to slide it across my stomach and hips.

"OH," I cry out with pleasure as he puts the cloth between my legs. He looks up at me and smiles, I can tell he is enjoying my reaction. He watches my face as he moves his fingers and the cloth inside me. I move my pelvis up and down as I moan and bite my lip wanting more.

"Oh no," I cry when he removes his fingers and the cloth as he gets up to wet the cloth again. He wipes my legs and I giggle when he wipes my feet. He places the cloth in the bowl and begins to undress.

I watch him as he pulls of his shirt, and slips off his shorts, I see his erection and I smile as I look up and see he is smiling. He gets on the bed, holds himself above me, and looks into my eyes as his mouth comes down on mine. I meet his tongue with mine as his hand finds my breast and his finger circles my nipple.

"Oh yes," I said as he lowers his body onto mine. I feel his erection against me. Waiting, wanting him inside me as I push my pelvis up to him. He pulls back teasing me more as he lowers his head to my breast and playfully bites my nipple.

"Oh God, don't stop," I beg as he sucks it into his mouth. I am wet and throbbing again and I try to move my arms to pull him to me. The ribbon stops me and that excites me even more.

"Oh, please don't stop! Yes, yes!" I said as he lowers himself between my legs again, I feel him just barely touching me as I push myself up toward him again. He holds back for another moment. Then he rubs his hard cock against my throbbing mound.

"Oh God, please don't stop," I cry out trying to pull my arms, wanting to pull him into me as he thrusts himself deep inside me.

"Ahh," I moan with pleasure as he looks intently into my eyes, as he moves himself slowly in and out of me.

He feels so good I know I will not last long before I come again, and I moan with delight as I move to meet his thrusts. Our pace quickens and my heart pounds as he pushes his hard cock inside of me harder, faster, and deeper.

"Ah, ah, ah," I hear myself beginning to scream louder as my arms pull against the ties.

"Oh, oh, oh, ooooh," I moan as my head shakes back and forth. Then I let out a long scream as I come again. I hear his breath quicken as he moves in and out of me before he trusts himself deep inside me one last time as he comes.

We both breathe heavily as he lays on top of me and I giggle with delight, as he looks up at me and smiles. He moves from on top of me, gets off the bed, reaches into the nightstand, and pulls out a pair of scissors.

"Don't move," he said as he slips the scissors between my wrist and the ribbon and cuts it off me. He picks up my arm and slowly lowers it to my body.

"Is your arm ok; does it hurt?"

"I'm ok," I said as I look at the red marks and indentations on my wrist from the ribbon.

"That will go away soon," he said sensing my nervousness and sounding like the voice of experience. As he cuts the ribbons off my other arm and ankles, checking each one to make sure they are ok.

"Ok, time to take a shower," he said.

"Ok," I said as he holds out his hand and I place my hand in his as I get off the bed.

I follow him into the bathroom, there are towels lying folded on the vanity. He pushes the shower curtain back and turns on the water checking the temperature with his hand.

"Perfect," he said, and he holds out his hand.

"Thank you," I said as I take his hand and I step into the shower thinking how nice of him to start it for me. I am surprised when he steps in behind me.

"Turn around face me and put your head back under the water."

I follow his instructions as he puts his hands up to my head and runs them through my hair. Once my hair is wet, he reaches for the shampoo bottle, squirts some in his hand; then he begins to gently work the lather into my hair. When he finishes washing my hair, he gently tilts my head under the water and begins to rinse the shampoo out.

He wets a washcloth and wraps it around a bar of soap. I reach for the cloth when it is soapy, and he gently pushes my hands aside and begins washing my face taking care not to get soap in my eyes.

"Close your eyes," he said as he takes the shower head off the holder and rinses my face. He places the shower head back in the holder and begins washing my shoulders, arms and hands taking care to wash each finger.

"A girl can get used to this," I said.

"I'm going to take very good care of you," he said as he begins to wash my chest.

"Arms up," he said. As I hold them up, he washes me, and I laugh as the cloth tickles me.

"Turn around," he said. As I turn around, he washes my back and bottom. He wraps his arm around me and pulls my body against his as he reaches around with his other hand and washes between my legs with the warm cloth.

"Oh," I moan as he moves the warm cloth between my legs.

"Turn around," he said as he releases me. When I turn around, he drops to one knee and pats his other knee with his hand.

"Put your foot up here," he said, and I put my foot on his knee and he washes my thigh, calf and foot carefully washing each toe.

"Ok, switch."

I switch and he washes my other leg, foot, and toes, I put my foot down when he finishes. He stands, takes the shower head off the holder again and begins to rinse me. He sprays my shoulders, arms, and chest. I raise my arms as he sprays underneath washing the soap away. He holds the spray out in front of me rinsing me down to my toes.

"Turn around," he said. I turn around again, and he rinses my back, arms, bottom, and legs; he pulls me against him again and puts the sprayer in between my legs.

"Oh," I sigh as the warm water washes the soap away.

He releases me and I turn around as he hangs the shower head back up.

"Ok all done. Start drying off; I will be out in a minute."

"Would you like me to wash you?"

"No thank you, I can wash myself," he said with a smile.

"Ok," I said, and I step out of the shower and begin to dry off.

"There's a robe hanging on the back of the door if you need it."

I see two blue robes hanging on the door, a man's cotton robe and a women's silk robe. When I look closer, I see an Asian design on the back, and I wonder about the women who have worn that robe. I leave the robe and go into the bedroom and begin to dress. I look at the ribbon on the bed as I dress, and I think of the effect tying me up had on me. Adam enters the room and interrupts my thoughts and I blush as I think of how he made me feel.

"Do you have time to have dinner with me?"

"Sure," I said thinking no sense going home and going to eat by myself; besides, I am starving.

"Great, I will be ready in a couple of minutes."

We are both dressed and ready to go in a couple of minutes and head out the door.

We arrive at Copeland's Restaurant and Adam holds the door open for me and we approach the hostess.

"Table for two?" the hostess asks.

"Yes, please," Adam said.

"Follow me," she said. "Someone will be right with you," she said when we get to the table. She places the menus on the table as Adam holds a chair out for me.

"I am starving," I said as I review the menu.

"Yes, I am very hungry as well," he said as he quickly looks at the menu, closes it and lays it back on the table.

"What are you going to have?"

"I am going to have a French dip, fries and a Coke."

"I think I will have a burger, and a Coke sounds good."

The server takes our order, and we sip our Cokes while we wait for our food. Our meals come out quickly and we both dig in and satisfy the appetites we worked up.

"Would you like dessert?" he asks as we finish our meals.

"Oh no, thank you; I'm full. That hit the spot."

"What are your plans for the rest of the week?" he said as we drive towards my house.

"I have to work, nothing exciting. What about you?"

"I have work to do and errands to run. I am going to stop by the restaurant and see Eric and Gina on Monday. Will you be there?"

"Yes, I'll be there," I said as we approach my house.

"Ok great, see you then."

"See you then," I said as I lean over and give him a quick peck on the lips and get out of the car.

He waits until I get in the house before he pulls away as I turn and wave. Since I am in for the evening, I put my pajamas on. I check the marks on my wrists and ankles; they are still there but lighter.

I see that it is seven thirty so it will be a while until John gets home. I pour myself a glass of wine, curl up on the couch and put the TV on. My mind wonders to what happened today and my reactions. I have never been tied up before and I am shocked at how much it excited me. I wonder was it being tied up that excited me or was it being tied up by Adam? Would being tied up by John or anyone else have the same effect on me? Something told me it would not.

I decide to read in bed and grab the book I just started, The Glory Hole Murders, a great murder mystery that is set in New Orleans, and I turn off the TV and head to bed.

I wake up disoriented for a moment I look at the clock and see it is three-thirty. I must have fallen asleep. I roll over and see John is asleep next to me. I quietly slip out of bed to go to the bathroom. My heart skips a beat and I look down at my wrists. I see that the marks are gone, and I feel relieved. I go to the bathroom, wash my hands, and slip back into bed.

I woke up early the next morning from a nightmare. I see John is still asleep, so I go out to the kitchen and make coffee. While it is brewing, I start to get breakfast ready. John walks in just as I am about to pour a cup of coffee.

"Good morning."

"Good morning," I said as I give him a kiss.

"You were sleeping so soundly when I got home, I decided not to wake you."

"Sorry, I must have fallen asleep."

"Did you have a good day?"

"Yeah, how was work?" I ask as a wave of guilt comes over me.

"Good, busy, lots of people coming into town for Mardi Gras. I am glad we'll both be off on Fat Tuesday and will be going to our first parades together.

"Yeah, me too, since we'll be working and miss all the parades this weekend."

"Smells good; what's for breakfast?"

"Scrambled eggs, bacon and toast, my specialty," I said laughing.

"Yes, one of the three things you can cook," he said with a laugh.

"That's not true. It's one of the five things I can cook."

"Sandwiches and salads don't count."

"Grilled cheese sandwiches count," I said with a smirk.

"Oh yes, you're a regular chef."

"That's right," I said as I bring our plates to the table.

"Looks good, sweetie. Thank you very much."

"You're welcome," I said with a smile.

"I got to get to work early today. I have a lot of work to do, we're going to get slammed this weekend," he said as he eats his breakfast.

"Well, that makes for a long day."

"Yeah, but that's ok. Being off on Tuesday will make up for it," he said as he gets up and brings his plate to the kitchen.

"I'll get the dishes; you get ready for work."

"Ok thanks, sweetie," he said as he gives me a kiss on my cheek. Then he heads to the bathroom as I start the dishes. He is back in no time dressed and ready for work.

"Ok I'm ready to go. I love you. Have a wonderful day. See you tonight," he said as he kisses me on the lips.

"Ok, don't work so hard. I love you," I said as he walks to the door.

The days fly by and we are so busy. On Saturday as I get to work the daiquiri place in the shopping center of the restaurant catches my eye. A daiquiri for the girls while we are setting up our stations would be nice. I am just walking in when I hear Anna call my name.

"Hey, Chelsea, wait up," she said as she rushes to the door.

"Hi, how are you? I am just getting us daiquiris."

"Good idea," she said as we approach the counter.

"What can I get you?" the girl behind the counter asks.

"Can I please get four, virgin strawberry," Anna cut me off mid-sentence.

"Virgin, you're funny. We'll take one virgin and three regular strawberry daiquiris please," she said to the girl, then turns to me.

"They're not that strong."

"Who's the virgin for?"

"Ashley doesn't drink."

"Oh, I didn't know that."

"That's why we call her the smart one of the bunch."

"Listen, I want to talk to you about something. I heard you are having an affair with Eric's friend, Adam, is that true?" Anna asks as she looks at me.

"Where did you hear that?" I said, knowing it had to have come from Eric.

"Emma overheard Eric and Gina talking about it. She said something to me because she is concerned. Are you?"

"I do not want the entire world to know about this. I am not proud of myself. I love John very much but there are private issues that I am not going to go into."

"You don't owe me an explanation and I know this is none of my business, but you should stay away from that guy. I don't like him, he's strange."

"It's no big deal; we just got together a couple of times."

"I hear he likes to tie women up and have sex with them. That is why Emma told me; that is why we are concerned about you."

The look on my face gave me away.

"Oh my God, you let him tie you up! That is crazy. Did you have a safe word?"

"A safe word, what's a safe word?" I ask inquisitively.

"A word you say when you can't take anymore."

"No, I didn't have a safe word. He did not hurt me; he's really very good to me."

"Of course, he is good to you because you let him tie you up. Very few women would let him do that to them. Did it occur to you that's why he is single?"

"This is not as crazy as you think; we are two consenting adults having casual sex. So, he tied me up one time; he didn't hurt me," I said, not telling her that I enjoyed it.

"I do not know why you are with him anyway. If you want to have casual sex with someone there are tons of guys out there. You can have anyone you want. My concern is as this relationship progresses and it will. Considering you have been together twice, and he already tied you up. Hurting you physically is only one concern this type of relationship will affect you emotionally and mentally. You may be having fun now because you're having sex with someone different, but I am telling you this guy has a dark side for which you are not prepared."

"Listen, don't worry. I'm not going to let him do anything crazy, ok?" I said, trying to calm her down as the girl brings us our drinks and I pay for them.

The look on her face lets me know this conversation is not over. We walk into work, check our stations and head to the server station. Emma and Ashley are already there setting up.

"We got daiquiris," I said as I put them on the counter.

"One for you, Ashley, and here's yours, Emma."

"Oh, I love strawberry, thank you," Ashley said.

"Delicious, thanks," Emma said as she takes a sip.

We set up our stations together. Anna fills everyone's sugar. Emma puts out fresh creamers and ketchup. Ashley stocks the server area and I make sure each place has silverware, a napkin and placemat. It is easier and faster when we work together as a team. Eric calls out that the specials are up, and we head to the kitchen where I notice there is a message on the specials board. "If you take the second line, be to work on time."

"What does that mean?" I ask Emma.

"It means if you follow the music and go to the parades, be sure to get to work on time."

"Oh, well, I haven't been to any parades yet but I'm looking forward to Fat Tuesday!"

"Oh, your first Mardi Gras. You're going to love it."

We taste the specials and get to work. As the night goes by, I decide to ask the girls if they want to have a drink after work. Eric finds me towards the end of the shift before I have a chance to ask them.

"Chelsea, I need a big favor. Three girls called off tomorrow morning. Can you please work the day shift?"

"Ugh breakfast, that's so early," I said knowing I do not have a choice; I have to help him.

"Please, you are the only one who will do it. Plus, you will be off on Sunday night."

"Ok, what time?"

"Great, thank you, six-thirty. I will leave a note and tell the girls to set up your station. You're the best," he said while hugging me.

"Yeah, yeah," I said as I walk away.

"Well, I'm on day shift tomorrow," I said to the girls.

"Yes, I heard. Eric asked me to come in early," Ashley said.

"I guess I'm going straight home tonight."

"We'll miss you," Anna said.

"Just think, you will get to take the second line," Emma said.

I do not realize what she means by that. I finish setting my tables, cash out and say goodnight.

I get home, quickly shower, set the alarm, and get my uniform ready for tomorrow. John gets home just as I am getting into bed.

"Well, you're going to bed early tonight."

"Yeah, I have to work the day shift tomorrow. Three girls called off."

"Oh, that stinks."

"Tell me about it," I said as I give him a kiss.

"Good night. I'm going to have a beer and watch some TV."

"Ok sleep good. I love you."

"Love you, too, sweetie."

Chapter 5

I wake up before the alarm goes off and quietly get out of bed, so I do not wake John. I go to the bathroom and head to the kitchen kicking myself that I forgot to set the coffee pot last night. The coffee pot is set up with a banana in front of it and a note from John.

"Good morning, sweetie. I set the coffee pot for you. I will miss you this morning; I hope you have a wonderful day. Love John."

I flip the note over and grab a pen while the coffee is brewing.

"Good morning, honey. Thank you for getting the coffee ready. I cannot wait to see you tonight, I love you!"

I shower, dress, dry my hair and put on my makeup. I bring a change of clothes so when I get a bite to eat after work, I am not advertising that I am a server and have cash on me. I grab the banana to eat on the way.

I get to work a couple of minutes early and I check the chart for my station. It is bigger than normal since we are shorthanded. My tables are all set up, so I go to the kitchen to look for the girls. Sandy and Alice are already there.

"Good morning, everyone," I call out as I enter the kitchen.

"Good morning. Thanks so much for coming in," Sandy said.

Sandy is in her thirties, my height with black hair pulled back in a ponytail and light blue eyes. She has worked at the restaurant since it opened years ago.

"No problem."

"Yes, thank you. We really appreciate you helping," Alice said. Alice is also in her thirties; she is tall with short blonde hair and deep brown eyes. She has also worked here for years. They have the kitchen all set up as well and Alice quickly goes over with me where everything is.

"Now I am not trying to insult you but don't forget this is breakfast, so the food comes up quick. "If you need help just yell," Alice said.

"No worries, you're not insulting me," I said just as Miss Jane the expediter walks into the kitchen.

"Ok ladies, I reckon you better get out to your stations."

"Yes Miss Jane," we said in unison.

Miss Jane is a petite, sweet, gray-haired woman who looks to be in her seventies but works circles around everyone in the place.

"Thanks for helping, Chelsea. Let me know if you need anything."

"Ok I will," I said as I head out to my station.

The place fills up and we get slammed. In no time at all, I am in the weeds. Breakfast goes fast, thank goodness for Miss Jane. She is a gem. She trays up our plates, makes the toast and keeps the coffee brewing. Everyone works together and the shift goes by fast.

Ashley comes in early, and we set the stations for the night shift. I change into shorts, sneakers and a short-sleeved V-neck shirt that ties at my waist. I am cashing out when Emma and Anna get to work.

"Ok ladies, have a good night."

"Yes, you too," Anna said.

"Have fun, see you tomorrow," Emma said.

"Goodnight, Eric," I said as I pass the hostess station.

"Thanks again, Chelsea. Enjoy your evening. Laissez les bons temps rouler."

"It means let the good times roll," he said seeing the inquisitive look on my face.

"Oh, thanks. See you tomorrow," I said as I head out the door.

I am heading down St. Charles Avenue, when I get to Napoleon Avenue; barricades stop me from going any further.

"Why are there barricades here?" I ask the police woman standing there and she looks at me like I have three heads.

"Because the parade is coming," she said as she points across the street. As I look across the street I see tents, ladders and people lined up on the sidewalk and the neutral ground behind the barricades drinking and waiting for the parade.

"What time will the parade be here?"

"Bacchus will be here in less than an hour," she said referring to the name of the parade.

"Thank you, officer."

"You're welcome."

I know John and I had planned to go to our first parade together but since I am here, I decide to stay. I see a bar called Fat Harry's across the street and decide to get a drink. The bar like the sidewalk is wall to wall people. I wait in line to order a drink and I finally make my way to the bar.

"What can I get you?" the bartender asks.

"I'll take a bottle of Budweiser, please."

"You can only have a drink on the street if it's in a can or cup; no glass."

"Oh, sorry. I'll take a can, please."

He is back with the can of beer in a second holding up two fingers as he sets it down. I hand him three ones, pick up my beer and go out to the street. I join the people having fun drinking while waiting for the parade.

People are wearing costumes like it's Halloween, and others are wearing crazy outfits of purple, green and gold colored hair, masks, and clothes. Most are standing; others are sitting on camping chairs. Families are on blankets on the neutral ground, a New Orleans term for the street median. Children are sitting in seats on top of specially made ladders with their parents standing behind them.

I decide to watch from the sidewalk, so I will not have to keep crossing the street for a drink or to use the bathroom. The sidewalk is full of people, but I see a spot by a tree, and I stand there. I notice a couple to my left who look to be in their mid-thirties.

"Hi, I'm Allison and this is my husband, Paul," she said to me.

"Hi, I'm Chelsea."

"Where y'at Chelsea," Paul said.

"Are you by yourself?" Allison asks.

"Yes, I just got off work. I did not realize there was a parade until I got to the barricades, and I decided to stay. I have not lived here that long; this is my first Mardi Gras and my first parade."

"Wow, well, you're going to love this. Bacchus is one of the best and biggest parades. It's my favorite," Allison said.

The crowd gets larger as the parade time gets closer. People are standing shoulder to shoulder and several feet deep behind the barricades. There is not a barricade where I am standing and the crowd swells all around me. Someone tries to come between Allison and me and as they do, she protectively puts her arm around me and pulls me towards her.

"We're together."

"Oh sorry," the guy said as he moves over.

"No problem."

"Thanks," I said as I hear the crowd around the corner screaming.

"Ok, here they come!" Allison exclaims.

Rounding the corner is a team of horses pulling a wagon and I quickly realize they are Clydesdales. The team of eight horses and wagon stops right in front of me, and I am in awe of these magnificent animals. I have seen them on TV but never up-close. They are massive with beautiful white faces, shiny coats, and white hoofs each wearing a shiny decorative rein. The team pulls a Budweiser wagon holding two Dalmatians and drivers. As they start to move Allison grabs my arm.

"Look, here comes the king of Bacchus," Allison said as she points to the elaborately decorated float heading towards us.

"Wow, that looks like John Ritter!" I exclaim.

"It is John Ritter; he's this year's king. The king is a different celebrity each year," Allison explains.

"Throw me something, mister," she yells out as she raises her arms above her head.

As John Ritter tosses a handful of doubloons down to the crowd, we each stomp on one and then reach down and pick it up. I look at the coin with a picture of a bearded man drinking from a goblet with BACCHUS MARDIGRAS NEWORLEANS written on it. I stick it in my pocket as I see a marching band approaching. They have the crowd rocking with their beat as people dance to the music. They move on, and another float follows.

"This is the Title float; it bears the title and theme of the parade," Allison explains.

I read "New Orleans We Love You" on the side of the float.

The riders are all dressed in colorful sequined costumes with masks and hoods on their heads. They toss out beads as they go by. Allison catches one and turns to me and puts it around my neck.

"Happy Mardi Gras."

"Thank you," I said as I look down and admire the purple plastic medallion showing Bacchus the God of wine attached to a strand of purple beads.

Next is a high school marching band. I am impressed how great the kids play and another beautifully decorated float follows.

"This is the officer's float; it carries the officers of the krewe," Allison explains.

The hooded masked men throw doubloons to the crowd as the float rolls by. Next comes another great high school marching band that stops in front of me. I sway to the music as the band members blow their horns and tap their feet to the music before moving on.

"Ok, get ready; here we go," Allison said.

I see a float coming towards us, a tugboat, The Port of New Orleans. It is a double decker float with flashing lights all around it. There are dozens of hooded masked riders on each level and each side of the float.

The riders shower us with handfuls of beads and doubloons as the crowd all reach up to catch the throws. People bump into each other since we are so close together but are polite and friendly. I catch my first strand of beads and I'm hooked. I put them around my neck, reach my arms up in the air and beg for more.

As I watch the float go by, I see a woman standing up against the barricade to the right of me. As the float rolls by she lifts her shirt and bares her breasts. A rider on the float rewards her with a long strand of white beads. A police officer is in front of her in a flash.

"Hey, that is not tolerated here. There are children present, this is the family section. If you want to do that take yourself down to Canal Street. If you do that again I will take you to jail understand?"

"Yes," she said shaking her head.

As I look around, I see a large police presence. The officers are not harassing anyone for being intoxicated or silly. They are holding the crowd back when they get too far into the street when not held back by a barricade.

They are picking up throws that land in the street out of reach and giving them to children. They are safely helping people cross the street in between floats. It is obvious they have experience dealing with crowds and I feel safe.

"Hey, do you want to get on Paul's shoulders you will catch more throws?" Allison said to me, and I notice quite a few girls in the crowd on top of their guy's shoulders.

"No that's ok, thanks anyway."

"Ok, let me know if you change your mind," Paul said.

The next float is a huge lion's head with animals all around it, a tribute to the Audubon Zoo. Next come floats paying tribute to New Orleans. A clown, space, Andrew Jackson, a steamboat, an oil worker, a cemetery, and the French Market. I am in awe of these impressive floats.

"This is one of the most incredible things I've ever seen," I said to Allison.

"Greatest free show on earth!" she said with a wink and a smile.

I catch a strand of white beads as the guy next to me catches the same strand. I am about to let go when he releases his grip.

"You can have them."

"Oh, thank you," I said, and I put them around my neck.

The riders are generous and throw stuffed animals to the children as their parents behind them on the ladders put the throws into bags. They throw frisbees, cups and doubloons by the handful.

A rider throws a whole sleeve of cups; Allison and I each catch one. As the cups land on the ground everyone scrambles to get them. It is a cool plastic reusable cup with BACCHUS written on it with a picture of the God of wine surrounded by grapes and a goblet. I will bring a bag with me to the next parade I go to, I think to myself as I lay my cup at the base of the tree.

"Here you go," Paul said as he hands Allison and me a beer.

"Thank you," I said, and I reach into my pocket for money.

"Oh no, that's on us," Paul said with a smile.

"Thank you," I said as I take a sip of the nice cold beer.

The next float coming my way needs no introduction. It is King Kong; the massive ape is alone on the float and to my surprise the crowd is throwing its beads at him.

"Why are they doing that?" I ask Allison just as she throws a strand of beads at Kong.

"It's tradition."

"Well, you all can throw your beads at him; I'm not throwing any of mine."

"That's because it's your first Mardi Gras and you have bead greed. I bet you will next year," she said with a laugh.

Queen Kong follows, and she is alone on the float just like Kong, with a big bow on top of her head and she is wearing a bikini top and matching skirt and, just like Kong, the crowd pelts her with beads. Next is Baby Kong holding a bottle, wearing a cap and a diaper.

"Oh, how cute," I said as the float goes by.

The next float has a big Saints football player on it. As I reach my arms up, I catch a strand of beads with distinct size, shape, and color beads.

"Look at these," I said to Allison.

"Oh my, glass beads. You are a lucky girl. They are hard to get. Look at this, Paul, glass beads at her first parade."

"Nice."

"You keep them," I said to her.

"Oh, bless your heart, I have a strand at home. It's good luck that you caught these," she said as she hands them back to me and I put them around my neck.

The next float is an exceptionally large friendly looking dinosaur called Bacchasaurus. Its head moves up and down, while the riders are standing up high inside its back. As it goes by, I see its long moving tail.

"Oh, wow, look at this," Allison said as a huge alligator comes towards us.

Bacchagator has a long snout with piercing red eyes; his mouth is open showing his large teeth. He is a double decker float with dozens of riders in his exceptionally long body followed by his long tail.

"That is the biggest float I have ever seen. That bad boy is new this year. He is unbelievable," Allison said as he goes by.

After Bacchagator comes another great marching band and floats saluting, creole cooking, Bourbon Street, Lafitte, King Louis, Satchmo, and voodoo. By the end of the parade the crowd is covered with beads.

"Well, that's it. The fire truck signals the end of the parade," Allison said as the firetruck comes down the street.

"Well, goodnight. Thank you for everything Happy Mardi Gras," I said as I gather my throws.

"Goodnight; Happy Mardi Gras to you," they both said as Allison gives me a hug. I hug her back thinking how nice it was to meet such great people for my first parade.

As I walk down St. Charles Avenue, I notice Orleans Parish prisoners starting to clean up the piles of garbage, beer cans and beads left behind. I decide to pop into Que Sera and get a beer and something to eat. I get a beer at the bar and order two shrimp cocktails to go. I take my beer to the patio which has cleared out a bit since the parade has ended. I am amazed how quickly and efficiently the crew cleans up the mess. I sit and sip my beer watching the cleanup while I wait for my food before going home.

I get home and put my pile of throws on the counter, the food in the fridge and I jump in the shower. I am just opening the to-go box when John walks in.

"Hey sweetie, how was your day?" he said just as he notices the pile of beads.

"You went to the parade?" he said, and I can hear the disappointment in his voice.

"Yes, I am sorry. I had no intentions of going; I did not even realize there was a parade tonight. But there was a barricade right in front of it. Seeing the crowd made it hard to walk away and go home. Please don't be upset with me."

"I guess it would have been hard to go home after seeing that.

Only you can stumble on your first Mardi Gras parade. Did you enjoy yourself?" he said with a laugh.

"Oh yes, it was incredible."

"We'll let us see what you got," he said looking at the throws. "Looks like good stuff."

"Yes, I cannot wait until Tuesday to go to more parades. I got us shrimp cocktails. Are you hungry?"

"Yes, let me take a quick shower first."

I have the shrimp set on plates on the table with two beers when John gets out of the shower. After we enjoy the shrimp John gets up to watch TV.

"I'm tired; I'm going to bed. I love you," I said as I kiss his cheek as I pick up a couple of beads to hang on the bedroom mirror.

"Goodnight, love you too," he said as I head to the bedroom.

I am still thinking about the parade as I walk into work the next day and see Gina smiling behind the register.

"Hi, how are you?" I ask as I put my purse under the counter.

"I'm fine, how are you?" Gina asks.

"I'm good," I said as I head to the kitchen to punch in.

I call out hello to everyone as I punch in. When I return to the host station, Eric is there with Gina.

"Hey, Chelsea, how are you? Did you have fun at Bacchus last night?" Eric asks.

"Oh yeah, that was incredible. I can't wait until Tuesday."

"I'm glad you had fun. Adam mentioned he was going to stop by tonight when I spoke to him earlier."

"Yes, he told me that the other day. I guess he'll come by when he is done working."

"Working, what are you talking about? Adam doesn't work." Eric said laughing.

"He told me that he manages his investments."

"Yes, that translates to he is independently wealthy."

"I did not realize that, not that I would know by how he acts. Anyway, that doesn't matter to me," I said with a laugh.

"No, I guess the only thing that matters to you is that you are ok with being tied up," he said as he and Gina giggle.

"I cannot believe he told you; that should be private, and the girls overheard you two talking and now they know."

"I am sorry the girls overheard us. But as for Gina and me keep in mind we have known Adam for years and the women he has dated and are aware of his sexual interests."

"Well, I would like to keep things quiet in the future, please," I said blushing.

"Ok, I won't tell you what he tells me," Eric said laughing.

"Oh, great; thanks," I said as he heads towards the kitchen.

I review the seating chart to check the stations. There are always eight servers on mid-week and ten on the weekends. I check the specials board and of course since it is Monday the special is red beans and rice, just like every restaurant in New Orleans. As I begin to organize the menus the door opens and a well-dressed elderly woman with impeccable make up and stunning jewelry approaches the host station.

"Hello, my dears. Someone told me there are some charming dress shops near here. Can you please tell me where they are?"

"Oh, yes; they are two blocks up when you go out the door," I said as I point in the direction of the shops.

"Thank you very much," she said with a smile, and she walks out the door and turns towards the shops.

"Didn't she look just like Mrs. Howell from *Gilligan's Island*?" I said to Gina.

"I was just about to say that to you."

Moments later Eric comes running towards the host station from the bar.

"You will never guess who is in the bar having a drink."

"Mrs. Howell," I said laughing.

"How did you know?"

"She came in here a couple of minutes ago asking about the dress shops up the block. She obviously went in the bar entrance for a drink. Will you watch the door for me while I get her autograph, please?"

"Yes, hurry up. I want to make you and Gina dinner before we get busy."

I go to the bar and wait while she finishes signing an autograph for a customer. I feel bad for disturbing her and I am about to turn to leave when she looks right at me.

"May I help you, dear?"

"Yes, please; can I get your autograph?" I said shyly.

"Of course, dear," she said as she writes here name on the paper I handed her as I think how gracious she is.

"Thank you very much," I said looking at her autograph and her lovely penmanship as I read "Best Wishes Natalie Schafer."

"You're quite welcome," she said, and she turns her attention to her companion as I return to the host station and get back to work.

When I get back to the host station, I know it is five o'clock without even looking at my watch when the door opens and Henry walks in.

Henry is a tall grey-haired gentleman in his late sixties. He is always dressed in a suit, tie, and a hat. He is a regular who comes in for dinner every night at precisely five o'clock. He will only sit in the last booth right by the kitchen door coffee station. Heaven help the hostess who does not save him his booth because he will stare you down the whole time, he waits for it.

"Hello, Henry, how are you?" I said as he approaches me.

"Good evening, Chelsea, very well and you?"

"I'm ok, are you ready for dinner?" I said as I pick up a menu.

"Sounds good," he said as he follows me to his booth.

When we get to his booth, I place the menu in front of him as he sits down. Knowing he wants coffee I step into the kitchen and grab a coffee pot. I pour the fresh steaming coffee into the cup in front of him.

"Oh, nothing like a cup of Community Coffee. Did you know it's made right here in Louisiana and that most restaurants in New Orleans serve it?"

"No, I did not know that, but it is good coffee. The chicory coffee is a little strong for my taste. Ashley will be with you in a moment; enjoy your dinner."

"Thank you."

"Ok, I am off to make you ladies dinner," Eric said when I return.

"Oh good, I'm starving. I haven't had anything since this morning before I worked out," Gina said.

"What's for dinner?" I ask.

"It's a surprise," Eric said with a smile.

The staff can order food off the menu for half price, but when Gina works, he cooks for the two of us. He also occasionally cooks for a handful of regulars. He really enjoys cooking and is quite good at it. He returns with two plates of shrimp and pasta primavera. We sit at a table in the station behind the register and Eric works the register and seats the guests while we eat.

"This looks wonderful," I said as I look at my plate.

"Oh, it is delicious," Gina said as she takes her first bite.

"Thank you, do you like the lemon zest in it?" Eric asks.

"I love it," I said as I take another bite.

We enjoy our dinner and get back to work just as Henry comes to the register to pay for his dinner.

"See you at nine," Gina said referring to when he will be back for dessert and coffee.

"See you later," he said as he heads out the door.

The shift goes by fast although we are not that busy since it is the night before Mardi Gras. We are all happy that since the Riverbend is not on the parade route, we are all off for Mardi Gras Day. Since Mardi Gras Day is a holiday all schools, government offices and most businesses in New Orleans are closed.

Eric and Adam walk up front from the bar area and sit at the table behind the register.

"Hello Gina, hello Chelsea," Adam said with a smile.

"Hi, how are you?" Gina said.

"Very good, and you?"

"I'm ok."

"Hello, Adam, would you like a menu?" I said as I approach the table.

"No thank you; can you sit for a minute?"

"Sure, I'll watch the door," Eric said before I could answer, and I sit down as he gets up.

"How are you? How was the rest of your week?" Adam asks as he smiles at me.

"I'm doing well. I had a wonderful time at my first parade last night how are you?"

"I am fine; glad you enjoyed your first parade. What are your plans for Fat Tuesday?"

"John and I are going to the parades."

"That's great. I'm sure you will have a wonderful time."

"I'm sure we will. What are your plans?"

"I'm spending the day with Eric and Gina."

"That sounds like fun."

"Can we get together on Wednesday?"

"Sure," I said blushing as a vision of last week comes to mind.

"Great, I will pick you up at one o'clock," he said smiling.

"Ok great."

"I was shopping at the Riverwalk today and I got this for you," he said as he pulls a small brown velvet pouch from his pocket and hands it to me.

"Thank you," I said as I take the pouch and open it.

Inside is an interesting, shaped brass lighter. It reminds me of a scuba tank with a ring on the end.

"It's a World War Two vintage brass lighter."

"It's very nice, thank you."

"You're welcome."

"I better get back to work," I said and as I stand up Adam stands as well.

"I hope you have a happy Mardi Gras, Chelsea."

"Thank you, I hope you do too."

"Goodnight Gina; I'll see you tomorrow."

"Goodnight; see you tomorrow."

Eric walks Adam out as I return to the hostess station. The restaurant is almost empty except for a couple of tables and Henry is in his booth having his pie and coffee. Everyone is cleaning up and getting ready to close when Eric calls everyone up front.

"In honor of Mardi Gras tomorrow I want us all to celebrate together with this king cake. As you know, there is a plastic baby inside. Tradition says the lucky one who gets the baby in their piece, buys the next king cake, or hosts the next party. I hope all of you have a safe and happy Mardi Gras. Remember if you take the second line be to work on time," he said as he starts to cut into the large round ring cake topped with icing and purple, green, and gold coloring. After everyone has a piece and we are all enjoying the delicious cake it only takes moments until we all hear.

"I got the baby!" Ashley calls out.

"Then you buy the cake next year," Eric said.

"Ok," she said laughing.

We all finish our cake, clean up and wish each other a happy Mardi Gras. A couple of the girls go across the street for a drink, but I decide to go home.

"Good night, happy Mardi Gras," I said as I walk out the door.

"Happy Mardi Gras," Eric and Gina said in unison.

Chapter 6

"Chelsea, wake up. Its Mardi Gras Day!" I hear John shout as I open my eyes.

"Good morning!" I said with excitement as I think, instead of only seeing one parade, we will be parading all day!

"Let's get up and get going. We're not going to make it to Zulu but if we hurry, we can catch Rex," he said referring to today's parades.

"Ok, let me have a quick cup of coffee and then I will get in the shower."

"Great I will make breakfast while you are in the shower. It is going to be a beautiful seventy degree today."

We shower, dress, and eat breakfast in record time. I grab a large canvas bag and transfer some things out of my purse that I will need, leaving room for our throws. I find a purple V-neck shirt to wear with capris, and we are both wearing comfortable sneakers. We know we will be walking all day; since the parades are on St. Charles Avenue there is no streetcar today.

We walk up to St. Charles Avenue, and I am in awe by the scene. It looks much like it did the other night at Bacchus with tents, chairs and ladders set up, but an even larger crowd. Most people are in costume and if they are not in costume, they are wearing purple, green and gold. Like the other night it is mostly families and children. I see grills with people barbequing and coolers everywhere. The party has started, and I see people are already drinking.

I want to stay here with the local families, but John wants to go to the Quarter, so we decide to watch the parades as we walk towards Canal Street. Since it is daylight, I can see so much more than the other night, and I cannot believe the crowd up and down the street. I did not give it much thought the other night to how long the parade route is. The parade route starts on Magazine Street then turns onto Napoleon Avenue; from there it turns onto St. Charles Avenue. It rolls down St. Charles Avenue and ends up on Canal Street.

So over seventy blocks of people shoulder to shoulder twenty to thirty people deep, that is a whole lot of people. We are just in time for the second parade Rex; Rex the King of Carnival is one of the oldest parades of Mardi Gras and is the source of many of the Mardi Gras traditions celebrated today. One of the most notable is the official Mardi Gras colors being purple, green, and gold. Unlike Bacchus using celebrities to be their king, Rex bestows that honor to a local resident who is active in civic and philanthropic activities.

King Rex rolls down St. Charles Avenue sitting high up on his float under a large crown, waving to the crowd. We make our way to the street as the next float comes our way.

"Throw me something mister!" we yell with our arms in the air, as the riders shower the crowd with beads and doubloons. I catch a purple, green, and gold strand of beads with a gold crown in the center of it.

"Look, John," I said as I turn to John and show him the beads, just as he is stomping on a doubloon. He bends down and lifts his foot to get the doubloon.

"Those are nice beads," he said as I lift my arms and put them around his neck.

"Thank you."

"Happy Mardi Gras."

"Happy Mardi Gras to you," he said as he kisses my lips.

"Look at this doubloon," he said as he opens his hand.

I see the silver doubloon; it states Rex King of Carnival with a picture of King Rex wearing his crown. As I look up, I see another beautiful float. We are ready with our arms in the air as it comes towards us. Just as it does John jumps in the air and catches a strand of beads.

"Wow, look at these, they look different," he said as he holds the beads out for me to see. They are a long strand of wooden beads painted yellow, black, and white.

"They're beautiful," I said as he places them around my neck.

"So are you."

"Thank you," I said as I give him a kiss.

"You're welcome my love."

Another float approaches us, and we are lucky to catch a frisbee and a cup and I am happy that I brought a bag. We walk towards Canal Street in between floats, which is not an easy feat as the sidewalk is full of people. We walk closer to the houses as people gather close to the street.

As we are walking, I notice people have their doors, balconies and fences decorated with purple, green, and gold wreaths, banners, flags, masks, and beads. Just like you would decorate for Christmas. Our goal is to be on Canal Street to see Comus, the final parade of the day and then hit Bourbon Street.

"Would you like your face painted?" a woman said to me as I walk by just as she is finishing her current costumer.

"Oh, no thank you," I said noting what an excellent job she did.

As we walk, I realize there must be a hold up, that the parade has stopped, and we have caught up to King Rex's float. Rex's float has stopped in front of a beautiful mansion and bleachers. I hear someone toasting Rex and thanking him for all he has done for the city and how deserving he is to have the honor of being Rex bestowed on him. I hear Rex say that the Krewe of Rex has raised money for the children of New Orleans and the public schools. How wonderful that they raised all that money I think as we continue to walk, until we finally reach Canal Street.

"Oh, my goodness, look at this," I said to John.

I see the crowd of people shoulder to shoulder packed behind the barricades up and down Canal Street. There are not any tents or chairs like uptown. It is wall to wall people; being so close to the French Quarter this is mostly tourists. I see lots of girls on top of guy's shoulders, and they are lifting their shirts in exchange for beads. Although I see a great police presence, they do not stop the girls like they did uptown; then I see there are hardly any children here. The party is in full swing here and this crowd is already feeling no pain.

"How are we going to get to the other side of the barricades to get to Bourbon Street?" I asked.

"We are going to walk up Canal until we pass the end of the barricades and then walk back down."

"I wish we would have waited and come down here later instead of fighting this crowd. The way this crowd is, crammed up against the barricades, we will never get close enough to catch anything from Comus."

"I'm sorry, sweetie. I didn't realize it would be like this."

"I know, let's just get to the other side," I said as we walk to the end of the barricades, cross the street and head back down Canal.

"Hey, Chelsea, do you want a Lucky Dog?" John asks.

I turn and see a cart in the shape of a hot dog and a bun on wheels with an umbrella over it. The vendor is dishing up hot dogs and drinks to the crowd of customers around him.

"No thanks; I would like to sit down for a drink and some lunch when that's possible."

"I know just the place away from this crowd in the Quarter, Johnny Whites. Let's go there before we go to Bourbon Street and get a late lunch, ok? It's where all the locals go for a drink after work."

"Ok, sounds good to me," I said as we see floats from Comus rolling on Canal Street as we head towards St. Peter Street.

After walking twenty-five blocks through the crowds, it is nice to have some breathing room as soon as we step off Canal Street. Since the parade is still going on and the streets are not that crowded, we get there quick. The bar has a good crowd, but it is not full. There are seats at the bar but not two together.

"You sit here," John said as he pulls out a bar stool for me.

"Ok," I said as I start to sit on the stool.

"We can move down if you want," the girl sitting next to me said.

"Thank you; that would be great," John said as he sits on the bar stool as the girl moves down.

"Thank you so much," I said to the couple.

"You're welcome," they reply in unison.

"Oh, I am so happy to be sitting down," I said to John.

"Now all we need is a drink and some lunch," John said.

It is a cozy casual bar that is open twenty-four-seven. I see a sign on the wall that reads, WE NEVER CLOSE.

"Happy Mardi Gras, what can I get you?" the bartender said.

"Happy Mardi Gras. I would love a Budweiser, and can I have a shrimp po-boy dressed, please?" I said, not needing a menu.

"Yes, would you like fries with that?"

"Yes, that would be great."

"Sounds great. I will have the same thing, and can we buy the couple next to us whatever they are drinking," John said.

"Sure can," she said as she quickly sets our beer in front of us.

"Happy Mardi Gras," John said as he raises his beer bottle.

"Happy Mardi Gras," I said as we ring our bottles together.

"Thank you, happy Mardi Gras." The couple next to us calls out as they raise their glasses.

"Happy Mardi Gras," we said in unison.

The bar has a nice crowd, and we enjoy our drinks while we wait for our food. The juke box is playing lots of Mardi Gras songs as a group of the patrons sing along. When the "Mardi Gras Mambo" comes over the juke box the whole bar begins to sing.

"Here you go. Can I get you anything else?" the bartender said as she put our food in front of us.

"We'll each have another beer and I'll take the check," John said.

"Coming right up."

"Thank you."

Our lunch is delicious; we enjoy the po-boys, beer, and music. When we finish, we pay the bill, and we are ready to hit Bourbon Street. We make the short walk to Bourbon Street and on the corner, there is a woman with a big cart selling flowers.

"Oh, look John," I said pointing to a flower headpiece.

"We'll take one," John said to the lady as he hands her money.

"Oh, thank you," I said as she places it on my head.

"Looks great," John said as we turn and join the crowd on Bourbon Street.

The street is full of people as they slowly shuffle shoulder to shoulder up and down the street. I see the windows of all the businesses on the street have protective caging covering them. The balconies are full of people holding beads out for the people on the street as they hold their arms up hoping to catch them. We get two beers in to-go cups and look up at the people on the balconies.

A man on the balcony is dangling a long strand of white beads over the balcony as the people on the street are holding their arms up hoping to catch the beads. He points to a woman on the street.

"Show your tits!" he yells to the women.

"I will!" another woman yells.

"Come on, show your tits!" he yells to the woman as the others on the balcony join in.

"Show your tits!" They chant as the people on the street join in. Then the whole crowd is chanting.

"Show your tits! Show your tits!"

After the crowd chants this a couple of times, she lifts her shirt and the crowd roars as the man on the balcony drops the beads.

As we continue to walk, I see a guy with no shirt on and his chest and back have purple, green, and gold paint on it. He is trying to climb up a street pole and each time he falls off, he gets up and tries again. People are dancing in the street, as others are trying to catch beads from the people on the balconies. Lots of women are showing their breasts for beads. I see someone throwing up on the corner as Mardi Gras songs play from every bar we pass. It is near midnight, the street is full of people, and everyone is still partying.

"Let's go in here; one of the guys at work said this is a perfect place to be at midnight. It's about midnight, let's go in and have a drink," John said as he points to a bar called Le Booze. The bar is a rectangle shaped bar with windows across the whole front so you can see Bourbon Street while you sit and have a drink.

"Sounds good to me," I said as we enter the bar and get two seats facing the street.

"Look at that," John said as he points to a line of police officers on horseback on the street outside the bar.

At exactly midnight one officer holds a bullhorn up to his mouth, and we hear him shout. "Mardi Gras is over please clear the street and go home!" he said and repeated as the horses slowly move forward. To my surprise people move out of the way and the crowd leaves the street. A clean-up crew with a large water hose follow as they begin to clean up the garbage and to hose down the street. What a perfect place to end the day I think as we finish our drinks and head home.

The next day I am only waiting at the door for Adam for a minute as he arrives precisely at one.

"Hi, how are you?" I said as I get in the car.

"Great. How was your Mardi Gras?"

"Oh, my goodness it was fabulous," I said as I begin to chatter on about Rex, the toast and the crowd chanting show your tits. He listens intently as I go on like he has never been to Mardi Gras when I burst out laughing.

"What's so funny?"

"I just realized I'm telling all this to someone who has been to Mardi Gras many times."

"That's ok. I like seeing you delighted; I am glad you enjoyed your first Mardi Gras."

"I did. How was your day?"

"Great, we all had an enjoyable time also," he said as we drive towards his house.

We arrive at his house and as we enter the living room, I see the sofa bed is open and all made up.

"I thought we could have a drink and watch a movie while I give you a body massage,"

"That sounds wonderful!" I said with a sigh.

He fixes us each a rum and Coke that we sip as we sit on the end of the sofa bed, then he lights a joint and we each take a couple of hits. When we finish our drinks, he places our glasses on the coffee table in front of us.

"Take off your jewelry, then take off all your clothes and lie on your stomach in the middle of the bed," he said.

"Ok," I said as I take off my jewelry and place it on the coffee table. Then as instructed I take off all my clothes and lie in the middle of the bed.

He crosses the room, turns the TV on and puts a movie in the VCR. He takes off all his clothes, grabs a bottle from the end table and sits next to me on the bed. I hear the oil squirt out of the bottle and his hands rubbing together. The movie starts and I am amused as I realize its soft porn.

He turns my head, so I am face down and I feel his hands gently rubbing the warm oil over the back of my neck. I feel his fingers rubbing deeply into my neck moving in a circular motion in the center up to the base of my skull and down to the top of my back. He massages each side of my neck working his fingers deeply but gently into my skin.

"Ahhh," I moan as he works his fingers down to the top of my back and he massages them across to my shoulders. He gets on his knees and straddles me on my hips without putting his weight on me as he massages his fingers into the center of my back as he slowly moves them down my spine.

When he gets to my behind, he slowly works his fingers into my back while going up to my neck. He squirts more oil onto his hands, and he places a hand on each shoulder. He rubs each shoulder for a couple of minutes. Then he puts both hands on my right shoulder. Rubbing in a circular motion before deeply pushing his thumbs around my shoulder blades.

"Oooh, that feels so good."

He moves his hands to my left shoulder, rubbing in a circular motion before he pushes his thumbs deeply around my shoulder blade. I giggle as I hear the poor dialogue of the porn movie, as the bad plot unfolds. But I guess people do not watch porn for the acting and I am enjoying myself, so I do not care what is on. He works a hand into each of my shoulder blades as he pushes into my back his cock presses against my butt.

"Oh," I moan.

His fingers run down my spine again; then he massages the right side of my back moving his hands and fingers over my body.

His hands cross over my back to my left side as his fingers massage from the center of my back to my side. He lifts himself from my body and sits next to me and I hear him squirt more oil into his hands.

He moves his hands to my shoulder and massages my right arm. He slowly works his fingers into the muscle as he picks up my arm and runs his hands up and down my forearm. He holds my hand in his as his fingers massage my palm and knuckles simultaneously. He massages each finger from the knuckle of my hand to my fingertip. Then he deeply works his thumbs into my skin from my wrist to my inner elbow. He slowly works his fingers up my arm until he reaches my armpit and I laugh as he tickles me.

"Oh, this is just what the doctor ordered," I said as he moves to the other side of me and begins to massage my left arm. Taking great care to give it the same attention as he gave my right arm.

I hear him squirt the oil into his hand again. Then he places both hands on my bottom one on each cheek as he rubs them in a circular motion.

"Oh, yes that feels good," I said as I wiggle a little.

He stays the course and works his fingers and thumbs into the back of my thigh slowly moving from my upper inner thigh down to the back side of my knee.

"Oooh," I moan as he touches my upper inner thigh and I try to roll over as he gently holds me in place. His fingers move to my calf as his fingers deeply work the muscle from my inner knee to my ankle.

"Oh, that feels wonderful!" I exclaim.

"Glad I stopped you from rolling over?" he said with a laugh as he bends my leg at the knee and begins to massage my foot. He holds my foot in one hand as he massages the bottom of my foot with his other hand, and I burst out laughing as he tickles me.

He tightens his grip on my ankle as his fingers move to my toes, carefully, slowly massaging each toe. He moves to the other side of the bed and begins to massage my other leg giving it the same detailed attention. When he finishes massaging my leg, he pats my behind.

"Ok, roll over." As I roll over, I sit up and lean forward to kiss him. As I do this, he puts a hand on each shoulder.

"Lie down, I'm not done," he said softly.

I lie on my back, and he brings his hands to my face. Then he slowly, gently begins to massage my face starting with my forehead. His fingers lightly trace over my eyebrows and eyelids. He runs two fingers from my forehead up and down my nose bridge. Moving to my cheek bones just below my eyes, he puts a hand on each cheek and gently moves his hands in a circular motion. He moves them across my mouth and chin as he continues to massage my face. It feels good and is very relaxing.

He tilts my head back as he moves his hands onto my throat and lightly massages the front of my neck working down to my collar bone. He gently moves his finger across my collar bone from the base of my neck to my shoulders. He moves his hand to my right breast as he massages his fingers all around my nipple but does not touch it. He stares into my eyes and watches my reactions as he does this.

"Ohhh," I moan as my breath escapes me and I arch my back pushing my breasts out, offering them to him. He moves his hand to my other breast and massages his fingers all around my other nipple.

"Ohhh," I cry out and I put my arms on his to pull his hands to my nipples. He gives me a stern look as he pulls his hands away and he takes my arms in each of his hands and pushes them to my sides.

"Don't move!" he said. Then his face softens as he stares into my eyes, as his index finger and thumbs squeeze each nipple.

"Oh," I moan as I move my head back and lick my lips. He squeezes my nipples a little harder for another moment as I moan again. For a moment I hear the couple from the porn movie having sex.

Then his hands move from my nipples as he massages my

stomach and sides until they reach my bikini line. He spreads my legs as he moves and sits in between them, facing me. He places a hand on each of my upper thighs and holds them there as his thumbs run up and down inside my thighs just outside my vagina.

"Oh God, don't stop!" I moan as I push my pelvis up.

He moves his hands to the top of my right thigh as he moves his fingers deeply into my muscle, massaging me from the top of my thigh to my ankle. My leg quivers as I use all my power not to move. I want to grab him and pull him to me. I point my foot out as he runs his finger over the top of my foot. He turns his body and moves his hands to my other thigh and begins to massage me until my leg is quivering, and I am whimpering.

I am wet and throbbing and I quiver as he moves his hands to the top of my mound. Rubbing his fingers all around my mound as I push myself forward. His hands gently push me down as his fingers are at the top of my mound; then he begins to rub them in a circular motion just outside of my vagina right on top of my clitoris.

"OH, YES, YES!" I cry out as he slips a finger inside me, and he slowly massages my throbbing clitoris. He slides down until his face is between my legs and he parts my vagina with his fingers and slides his tongue inside me.

"OOOOH," I moan loudly, and I push myself up wanting him deeper inside me.

He flicks his tongue in and out of me as I moan with pleasure. I push my bottom up wanting more; he holds back teasing me with his tongue. I cry out wanting to pull him to me, but my hands do not leave my side. I hear a soft hum as his tongue licks my clitoris as something enters my vagina and pushes deep inside me. The vibrator pulsates inside me as his tongue simultaneously licks me.

"OH MY GOD!" I scream as I move my knees up slightly as he thrusts the vibrator in and out of me. I am bucking my bottom up and down faster and faster as he plunges the tool inside me.

The vibrator makes every part of my vagina pulsate. My head is shaking back and forth as I throw my arms above my head and pound them on the mattress. My screams are getting louder and louder as his tongue flicks my clitoris faster and faster. He pushes the vibrator deep inside me as I let out one long continuous scream as I come. My whole body is shaking, and I hear myself growl like an animal followed by laughter as he gently pulls the vibrator out of me.

I am giggling with pleasure as he gets off the bed, leaves the room and is back in a moment with a glass of water. I sit up as he hands me the water and I take a big gulp. I hold the glass for a moment and take another small sip before handing it back to him.

"Thank you."

"You're welcome," he said as he set the glass on the table beside the bed.

He sits crossed leg next to me on the bed and I sit up and move towards him. I reach my hand out towards his cock as I move my head in that direction. He takes my hand in his as he cups my chin with his other hand as he looks at me. "What are you doing?" he said softly.

"I am going to please you," I said as I look up at him.

"You already do," he said as he gently pushes me back on the bed. He lays down next to me on his side with his head resting in his hand as he runs his other hand lightly up and down my arm as he looks at me. "Pleasing you gives me immense pleasure. Taking care of you pleases me, all you must do is follow my instructions and enjoy yourself, do you understand?"

"Yes," I said as I look into his eyes.

"Good." he said as he leans down and kisses me. His tongue swirls in my mouth as his soft mustache brushes my face. He slowly kisses me down to my breast and circles his tongue around my nipple teasing me before he takes it into his mouth.

"Oh," I cry out with pleasure as he sucks on my hardened nipple while he takes the other one in his hand and circles his finger around and around until it too is hard. He kisses his way to my other breast and takes it into his mouth.

"Oh yes, that feels so good."

He moves himself above me and pushes my legs apart with his. He lowers his body down to mine and pushes his hard cock against me without entering me. I spread my legs further apart and push my bottom up wanting him inside me. He takes my arms and holds them above my head, while looking into my eyes.

"Ahh," I moan as he slowly enters me, and I push my bottom up but he holds back making me wait a moment before he plunges himself deep inside me.

"OH YEEES!" I cry out.

He presses his body to mine as he slowly moves his hard cock in and out of me. I arch my back and thrust my pelvis forward as his body meets mine while he holds my hands above my head. He lets go of my hands and moves his hands on each side of me as he pushes himself deeper inside me. He moves himself in and out of me faster and faster and I meet his thrusts as I push my pelvis forward while keeping my hands above my head. We are both breathing harder and faster, and I am moaning louder and louder as my head shakes from side to side.

"Yes, yes, yes!" I call out as I come, and he pushes his cock deep inside me and moans as he comes.

His body falls on top of mine as we both catch our breath and I giggle with delight as he moves next to me, and we lay in silence.

"Time to take a shower," he said as he gets up off the bed and holds his hand out for me.

"Ok," I said as I sit up, take his hand, and follow him to the bathroom.

He pulls the shower curtain back and starts the water. He again holds out his hand, I put my hand in his and step into the shower and he steps in after me.

"Stand under the water and tilt your head back," he said as he runs his fingers through my hair making sure it is wet. He reaches for the shampoo, pours it into his hand, and begins to lather it into my hair.

"Close your eyes," he said when he finishes washing my hair and tilts my head under the water and rinses the shampoo out.

He reaches for the washcloth and puts the soap on it and begins to wash my face, ears, and neck.

"Close your eyes," he whispers as he rinses the soap away.

He washes my chest and arms before turning me around washing my back and bottom. He pulls me towards him as he washes in between my legs with the warm soapy cloth.

"Turn around," he said, and I turn to face him.

He drops to his knee and pats it with his hand without saying a word and I pick my leg up and put it on his as he washes me. When he finishes with that leg, I switch to my other leg for him to wash. He reaches above me and gets the shower head and rinses the soap from my body. He holds my body close to his as he puts the sprayer between my legs.

"Oh, that feels good," I moan as he caresses my cheek before he releases me.

"There is a towel on the vanity for you to dry yourself, I will be out in a moment," he said as he pulls back the curtain and holds out his hand for me to take to step out of the shower.

"Thank you," I said as I step out of the shower and begin to dry myself off. I grab the silk robe from the back of the door and put it on before I head out to the living room to dress. I am fixing my make up when Adam enters the room.

"Are you hungry? I would like to make you dinner," Adam asks.

"That sounds great. Can I help?"

"No thank you, I will take care of everything."

"Ok, do you want the bed stripped?"

"I will take care of that later. Come into the kitchen while I cook," he said as I follow him into the kitchen and see the table is already set. I did not notice that earlier.

"Sit down. Would you like a glass of wine?"

"Yes please," I said as I sit, and I realize he has the place settings at each end of the table instead of next to each other.

He pours us each a glass of wine and holds his glass up in front of me and I hold my glass up to his.

"Shall we make this a weekly standing date?" he said with a smile.

"Yes!" I said smiling.

"Happy Wednesday," he said as he looks into my eyes.

"Happy Wednesday," I said as we ring our glasses together and sip the wine.

"I marinated chicken breasts this morning. They won't take long on the grill, and I am making baked potato."

"Sounds great. What vegetable are we having?"

"I don't care for vegetables so I'm not making any."

"So, you don't eat any vegetables?" I say with a chuckle.

"No, I don't," he said with a devilish laugh as he prepares dinner.

"I can't believe you don't eat any vegetables," I said shaking my head.

"Ok, dinner is served," he said as he put a plate in front of me.

"Thank you, that looks wonderful." I said as he sits across from me and watches as I take my first bite.

"It's delicious."

"Thank you, I'm glad you like it," he said with a smile as he takes a bite of his chicken.

"So, what are your plans for the rest of the week?" I said wondering what someone who does not work, is not married, or have children does all week?

"Doing my usual daily workout, working on the computer, I also must cut the grass and change the oil in my car. What are your plans?"

"Just working the rest of the week; nothing exciting," I said surprised that he cuts his own grass and changes his own oil.

"Let me put the dishes in the dishwasher before we go," he said as he clears the dishes and wipes the table when we finish eating.

"Ok, let me get my purse," I said as head into the living room to get it.

"Are you ready to go?"

"Yes," I said as I follow him out to the car. "Thank you," I said as he holds the car door open for me as I slide into the seat.

"You're welcome."

"So, Chelsea, tell me your fantasy," he said as we pull out of his driveway.

"Well," I begin to say as he interrupts me.

"Wait a minute. I don't want to hear a fantasy about a specific man or anything to do with anal sex, ok?"

"Ok, no problem. My fantasy doesn't include either," I said with a chuckle.

"In my fantasy I am in the Smithsonian Museum of Art. My lover and I are walking through the rooms looking at the beautiful art. We come upon an altar, and we get on top of it, and he ravages me. I change the setting occasionally; sometimes it is an Egyptian room or Asian setting and sometimes I am in a room with Greek statues. Well, it is a great fantasy when I close my eyes and imagine it as I masturbate, since it obviously will never happen," I said laughing.

"Well, that's interesting. Certainly not your average fantasy, and definitely not what I was expecting to hear."

"Now tell me your fantasy."

"Oh, I'm going to show you my fantasies," he said with a smile.

A mixture of excitement and nervousness comes over me as I wonder what they are. I lean over and give him a quick kiss when we get to my house.

"Enjoy the rest of your week. See you Wednesday," I said as I unhook my seatbelt.

"You, too. See you Wednesday."

I get out of the car, walk up the steps, turn and wave knowing he would wait until I get in the door before leaving. I watch him wave as he pulls away.

A little over a month goes by and I see Adam every Wednesday and there seems to be a pattern to our Wednesdays. I notice if we have a day of erotic sex and he ties me up, the next Wednesday he takes me out to lunch or he gives me a body massage while we watch a movie followed by sex and then the pattern repeats.

Chapter 7

The girls and I are quick to clean up on Saturday night so we can get to Tipitina's and see the Neville Brothers. We all brought clothes to change into, and John and Mike are meeting us there. I am happy that John agreed to come and meet my friends. We cash out and change in the bathroom. It is nice to dress up in a skirt and heels to go dancing.

Tipitina's is a great bar on the corner of Napoleon and Tchoupitoulas where you can see all kinds of live music. It has a large room with an open floor in front of the stage. Over the stage is a huge picture of Professor Longhair. The bar originally opened as a place for him to play and "Tipitina" is the name of one of his songs.

I am extremely excited to be seeing the Neville Brothers, a famous group from New Orleans who play rhythm and blues, jazz, and soul music. The girls have all seen them perform before and love them. They are already playing when we walk in, and the bar is wall to wall people. I hear them announce "This is one of Professor Longhair's songs," as they begin to play "Go to the Mardi Gras."

"Let's get a drink first," Emma said as soon as we walk in.

"Ok, what does everyone want?" Anna asks as we approach the bar.

"I'll have a beer," I said.

"Cranberry juice please," Ashley said.

"Michelob," Emma said.

"That works for me," I said as I move to the music.

Anna orders our drinks, and we take them to the upper level that overlooks the stage. There is a nice crowd moving to the music and we have a much better view of the stage. In addition to the guitar and drums there are bongo drums keeping the beat going as they hit bells and chimes making beautiful music. The upper level is a perfect place to keep an eye out for the guys as we sip our drinks and sway to the music.

"Oh, look; there's Mike. Let's go back downstairs," Anna said.

We head downstairs and meet Mike at the bar. Mike is Anna's height, medium build, with brown curly hair and a round friendly face.

"Mike, this is Chelsea; and you know everyone else," Anna said.

"Hello, ladies. Hello Chelsea. Nice to finally meet you," Mike said.

"Yes, nice to finally meet you too. Perfect timing here comes John," I said as John comes towards me.

"Hi," John said as he kisses me on the cheek.

"Everyone, this is my husband, John. John this is Emma, Anna, her fiancé Mike, and Ashley."

"Hi, nice to meet everyone," John said to the group.

"Nice to meet you," they said in unison.

"Let me get a beer; does anyone else need anything?" John said.

"I'll take a Bud," Mike said.

"Oh, look there he is." Emma said smiling.

"There who is?" Ashley said.

"Rich, we met him at Madigan's the other day, and we mentioned coming here. He has eyes for Emma," Anna said.

"Good for you, Emma. He's a hunk," Ashley said as we all look at the six-foot-two, muscular, blond hair hunk in a tight T-shirt and jeans as he spots Emma and heads our way.

"Hi, how are you?" Rich said as he smiles at Emma.

"Good, glad to see you. These are my friends," Emma said as she introduces everyone, just as "Johnny B. Goode" starts to play.

"Let's dance." Ashley said as we all move to the dance floor.

The girls are right; the band is great. I love the music and the sound of their voices. They play songs about New Orleans which the crowd loves. We dance together in a group, and I can see that Emma and Rich are hitting it off.

"Time for a beer break," John said.

"Sounds good. Want to get a beer with us, Rich?" Mike said.

"Ok," Rich said although I do not think he wants to leave Emma.

"This is a song by the Meters. It's called "Hey Pocky A-Way" the band leader said.

"I love this song," I yell out to the girls as we dance.

We take a break and join the guys at the bar for a quick drink to cool us down. Emma and Rich are talking quietly to each other and look like they are done dancing for the night.

"Ok, let's get back on the dance floor," Ashley said.

"Ok, come on, John."

"You go ahead; I'm comfortable here."

"I'll sit this one out also," Mike said.

Anna joins us on the dance floor and the three of us dance the rest of the night away. Emma comes over to say goodnight before she leaves with Rich, as the evening winds down and we join the guys at the bar. When the band finishes playing, they pass a big empty Kentwood water jug around the bar for tips, and we all put money in.

"Wow, they were great," I said.

"I knew you would love them," Ashley said.

"Ok, time to go. See you ladies tomorrow," Anna said.

"Goodnight," we all say as we walk out together and head home.

I wake up happy to be celebrating St. Patrick's Day with John today in the Irish Channel. Just like everything else in New Orleans, St. Patrick's Day is celebrated with parades and block parties.

We have breakfast, shower and dress in green shirts and head to Parasol's bar for the block party and parade. We get there at noon and the street is full of people. John goes into the bar to get us a beer while I find a spot on the street to watch the parade. There are crowds of people; most are standing. There are tents and umbrellas set up with people picnicking under them.

"Wow, you were gone a while," I said as John joins me on the street.

"The bar is packed," he said as he hands me a plastic cup of green beer.

"Well, you're just in time. The parade is starting."

Walking groups dance down the street handing out beads and flowers. They're followed by bands playing Irish music and the crowd is singing along. Floats roll down the street throwing green beads, doubloons, potatoes, carrots, cabbages, and Moon Pies and I laugh as I catch a carrot.

"This is fun," I said as John jumps in the air and catches a strand of green beads.

"Here you go," he said as he put the beads around my neck.

"Thank you," I said as I kiss his lips.

"I'm going to get us some lunch and a couple of beers while you try to find us a spot to eat, ok?"

"Ok, great idea."

I am sharing a picnic table with other parade goers when John returns with cups of beer and two roast beef po-boys. We enjoy the music as we eat our food and watch the crowd. We get another beer and walk around while enjoying the festivities. The party is still in full swing when we leave.

"That was a great St. Patrick's Day party," I said.

"Yes, it was," John said as we head home.

On Wednesday, I am waiting at the door when Adam pulls up at exactly one o'clock.

"Hi, how are you?" I said as I get into the car.

"I'm great. How are you?"

"I'm wonderful. Where are we going?" I said as I notice he is driving in a different direction than usual.

"Well, since it will be Easter in less than two weeks, I am taking you to see some Easter eggs."

"Oh, where is that?"

"You shall see," he said.

We arrive at City Park and the New Orleans Museum of Art. We head right to the room where the eggs are on exhibit. Outside the room is a sign "The Faberge Eggs from the Matilda Geddings Gray Foundation Collection." The eggs are the Imperial Faberge Easter eggs originally created for Czar Alexander and his son Nicholas as gifts for their wives. The room has pedestal displays of the eggs covered by glass which is quite nice as you can get right next to them at eye level.

"Oh, my. I have never seen anything so beautiful," I said as I look at the first egg.

The Imperial Napoleonic Egg, a beautiful egg of emerald panels and yellow gold with diamond and ruby designs. Inside each egg is a surprise; the top of this egg opens to a satin and velvet lined interior. The surprise is a six-panel miniature screen of watercolors of different regiments surrounded by emeralds and diamonds. I am in awe of this beautiful work of art. I am so captivated by its beauty that I just stand there and admire it for a while.

Adam is standing beside me as I admire the egg. He moves behind me and wraps his arms around me. I am surprised as we never touch each other in public. He crosses his arms over my chest and his body is touching mine. His hands are under his arms, cupping my breasts, as his fingers begin to caress my nipples. To anyone watching it looks like he is just hugging me as he leans in and whispers in my ear.

"I am surrounded by beautiful works of art as my lover ravages me," he said as his fingers continue to circle my now hardened nipples and his mustache brushes my neck.

"Oh," I said as a soft moan escapes my lips as I try to keep my composure.

The couple admiring the egg to my left moves on to the next egg. Adam moves his arms and takes my hand and moves us to the next egg.

The Danish Palaces Egg is a stunning pink enamel with diamonds, emeralds, sapphires, and gold. The surprise is a ten-panel screen that has pictures of the Empress's favorite retreats. The gold framed pictures are beautiful; there is a cottage, castle, mansion, villa, and yachts and I imagine what it must have been like to vacation at these places.

As I am admiring the egg, Adam stands behind me and puts his hands on my waist.

"Do you like this egg?" he whispers in my ear.

"Oh yes, look at these beautiful places," I said as Adam's hands slide down my waist to my hips as he begins to caress the top of my thighs in a circular motion.

"What are...." I said as Adam cut me off.

"Shh, relax, no one can see my hands," Adam said as I realize his hands are behind the pedestal. Then he slowly moves his hands to the inside of my thighs and slowly caresses me.

"Oh my," I whisper as I lick my lips and take a breath as I stare at the egg.

"Are you ready to look at the next egg?"

"Yes," I said as he moves his hands from my thighs.

We walk to the next pedestal and see the egg it holds. The Imperial Caucasus Egg is as beautiful as the others. The red opulent egg decorated with diamonds, pearls, crystal, and ivory is stunning. It sits in a gold stand and has four oval doors that are open. Inside each door is a picture of a hunting lodge in the mountains.

"Look at this stunning egg," I said to Adam as he comes behind me.

"Oh yes, it is stunning," he said as his hands move back to my inner thighs and his fingers slowly caress me.

"Oh, that feels good," I whisper as his fingers slide in between my legs and move lightly over my vagina.

"Oh!" I exclaim as he pushes his hand up and rubs it over my vagina. I am wet, and throbbing and I can hardly contain myself.

"Shall we look at the last case?" he whispers in my ear as his lips softly brush my neck.

"Oh yes," I said, and I take a breath as he moves his hands and steers me towards the last case.

The last case holds a basket, The Lily of the Valley Basket. The basket has individual stems decorated with pearls and diamonds. The stems are set in the basket of gold with long green leaves that look so real.

"I love this basket; it is so beautiful."

"Yes, it is," Adam said as he moves behind me again.

This display is near the door to the exhibit room, and we are visible from all angles. Realizing this, Adam wraps his arms around my arms and chest again as a couple on the opposite side of the glass admires the basket.

"Look at the detail of each blossom; aren't they lovely?" Adam said as his fingers circle my nipples.

"Oh yes," I said as I exhale my breath.

"Would you like to see more of the museum, or shall we go?" he said as he squeezes each nipple between his finger and thumb. My nipples are hard, I am wet and throbbing and I want him now.

"Let's go," I said breathily.

"You sure?" he said with a chuckle, and we quickly exit the museum.

"Did you enjoy that?" he said once we are in the car.

"Yes, I did. The eggs were nice too." I said with a giggle.

"I thought you would enjoy both," he said with a devilish grin.

"Isn't it nice that someone would donate those treasures so everyone can see them," I said recalling the sign at the entrance.

"Yes, it is," he said as he watches me as we drive towards his house.

We arrive at his house, and I cannot wait to get inside as I am extremely excited. I jump out of the car and walk quickly by him up the path to the door.

"I see you are in a hurry," he said with a laugh as he follows me to the door.

He unlocks the door, punches in the code, and turns on the light as I enter the house. We walk through the room towards the kitchen door, and he stops in front of the dining room table. As I look at the table, I notice the center piece and chairs are not there and that there are silk scarves coming up from all four corners of the table.

"We come upon an altar, we get on it and my lover ravages me," he whispers in my ear.

"Oh my."

"Take off your clothes and jewelry and I will help you onto the table," he said as he looks at me with a smile.

I quickly undress, drape my clothes over the couch and place my jewelry on the end table. I see he has a step stool in the corner, he brings it next to the table and holds out his hand. I place my hand in his as I step onto the stool and sit on the table.

"Slide into the middle of the table and lie down with your arms at your side and your legs together."

I lie in the center of the long table in the commanded position. He stands next to the table behind my head and as I look up, I see he has a silk scarf in his hands and as he lowers it to my eyes, he whispers to me.

"It is a great fantasy when I close my eyes and fantasize as I masturbate," he said as he ties the scarf over my eyes.

He adjusts the scarf to be sure that I cannot see. Then he takes my arm and extends it over my head towards the corner of the table and the scarf. He ties the scarf around my wrist taking care to make sure it is not too tight; the silk feels good against my skin. I hear him move down the table and I jump a little when he touches my ankle and moves it towards the scarf. He is quiet while he ties my leg with the scarf. When he finishes, his hand caresses my inner upper thigh down to my ankle.

"Oh," I moan as my leg jerks from the excitement of his touch. I hear him move around the table and I feel his hand on my other ankle as he spreads my leg towards the scarf. As Adam ties the scarf around my ankle a wave of excitement comes over me. He slips his finger between my leg and the scarf to make sure it is not too tight as I try to wiggle my leg.

I hear him move and can tell he is beside me as he lifts my arm above my head. My excitement heightens as he ties my wrist with the scarf. I hear him move towards the end of the table and I twist and pull on the ties in anticipation of his touch. He is quiet and I know he is looking at me tied up, spread eagle, and blindfolded, and I know he likes me like this. I hear him take his clothes off and I take a deep breath in and exhale slowly thinking I like it too and he knows it.

As I lie waiting, something brushes across my lips, and I lift my chin and open my mouth. I jump as the same soft strands brush my nipple until it hardens; he moves it to my other nipple as I push my chest forward. I cry out as he dances the strands down my body and my legs. Then he presses a hard object to my mound, and I push my hips up. He takes it away and I hear him climb on the table. He is quiet for a moment as he holds himself over me. I lick my lips and raise my chin as I wait for him. His mustache brushes my neck and I moan aloud with pleasure.

"Oooh."

I turn my head wanting more as he kisses my neck. His mouth moves down my neck across my throat and up the other side. He stops kissing my neck, and suddenly he is quiet, not touching me or moving, although I know he is still above me.

I try to move my arms, but the scarves stop me, I arch my back and push my chest forward but do not feel him. I turn my head from side to side trying to find him, I lie back on the table and wait for him.

Suddenly his tongue lightly flicks my nipple. I jump as it touches me. I know my reaction excites him and he continues to tease me making me want him, making me wait for him.

"Oh no," I cry out as he moves his mouth from my nipple, and I push my chest forward wanting him to take me in his mouth. I feel his tongue dance across my other nipple as I moan aloud with pleasure, as he takes me in his mouth.

"Oh yes!" I moan louder as he sucks my breast. I pull my arms unsuccessfully trying to grab him as I push my chest and pelvis forward. His body moves and I cry out.

"Please don't stop!" I beg as he kisses his way down my chest over my stomach to my mound.

"Oh God yes, don't stop," I plead as his fingers spread my vagina open and his tongue enters me.

"OOOOOH YES!" escapes my mouth in a long continuous moan. I thrust my pelvis forward to meet his tongue as he lightly licks my clitoris before he slowly circles it with his tongue. I know it will not take me long to come as he has been teasing me all day.

"YES, YES, YES!" I cry out as I push my pelvis up and down faster and faster to meet his thrusts.

"OH MY GOD!" I yell as he hold my hips down as his tongue thrashes against my clitoris faster and faster. I push my chest forward, as my arms pull on the scarfs.

"AH, AH, AH, AH, AH, AH, AHHHH!!!" I scream as I shake my head from side to side as my hands pound on the table. My legs shake uncontrollably as I have an explosive orgasm. My scream turns to a growl and I breath heavily as I laugh aloud with delight.

"Ha, ha, ha," escapes Adam's mouth with a devilish tone. He lifts himself above me, wanting me, as he too has been waiting all day. He pushes himself against me, I feel his hard cock slide just inside me as it touches my clitoris and I moan aloud as my body jerks with pleasure.

"Ooh yes, yes, yes!" I cry out as I push my body forward, wanting him inside me.

He pulls back slightly, and I feel him just outside me for a moment. Then he trusts himself into me with a hard, deep thrust pushing my body back onto the table.

"Ooooh," we both moan as he enters me. He begins to slowly move himself in and out of me as I push my pelvis forward to meet his cock, as I pull my hands against the scarfs.

"Yes, yes, yes," I yell out as he rams himself deep inside me. Our pace quickens and I push my bottom up to meet him. I feel his hand on my hardened nipple as he is squeezing it between his fingers. I hear him moaning softly for a moment as he comes until I drown out his moans.

"Oh, oh, oh, oh, oh, ooooh," I moan aloud as my body collapses, as my moans subside to a whimper.

"Oh, my goodness," I said breathily as I giggle as Adam lets out a loud devilish laugh. We lay quietly for a couple of minutes as we both catch our breath. He moves from my body, climbs off the table, and leaves the room.

"Would you like a sip of water?" he said when he returns.

"Yes please," I said thinking he would remove the blindfold.

"Lift your head," he said as I hear the ice in the glass close to my mouth. I lift my head to meet the glass and take a sip, and the water drips down the sides of my mouth and Adam immediately wipes it away.

"Would you like more?"

"Yes please," I said as I take another sip. Then I put my head down and I hear him set the glass on the end table.

"Ok, time to take a shower," he said as he carefully removes the blindfold. I blink my eyes as they adjust to the light. As he unties the knots in the scarves that binds my hands and feet, he checks each one to make sure I am ok.

"Let me help you up," he said as he holds out his hand. I place my hand in his as I sit up. I slide to the end of the table as he helps me step down on the stool.

"Be careful," he said softly.

"Ok," I said as I step off the stool.

We head to the bathroom; Adam runs the water, checks the temperature, and holds out his hand when it is ready. I place my hand in his as I step into the shower. I no longer need instructions. I know exactly when to close my eyes, put my head back, turn around and pick up my arms and feet as he washes me. I step out of the shower and start to dry off. I grab the robe off the back of the bathroom door, I dry my hair and go into the dining room to get my clothes. I am just finishing dressing when Adam walks in.

"I will be ready in a moment. Are you hungry?"

"Yes," I said as I put my jewelry on while I look at the table. I doubt I will walk by this table in the future without a vision of today coming to mind I think to myself.

"Do you want me to help you clean this up?" I ask.

"No thank you; I will take care of it later," he said with a smile as I pick up the leather-bound wand with long leather tassels.

"It's a flogger; I'm glad you liked it."

"Yes, I did," I said with a smile.

We finish dressing, head out the door and down the path to his car. We enjoy dinner at Houston's Restaurant, an upscale restaurant chain before heading to my house. Adam puts the radio on as we drive, and the song "Don't Stop" by Fleetwood Mac comes over the radio.

"Oh, I love this song, I love the whole album," I said.

"What album is that?" Adam asks.

"*Rumours* by Fleetwood Mac," I said as I sing along.

"Oh," he said as a smile comes over his face.

"Have a great night," I said as I give him a quick kiss when we get to my house.

"You take care." he said as I get out of the car.

Thursday morning after John leaves for work I am ironing my uniform when the phone rings.

"Hello."

"Hi, it's Anna. How are you?"

"I'm ok. What are you up to?"

"I was wondering if you want to have lunch and go see a movie before work?"

"Sure, what's playing?"

"*Dream Lover*. It came out a couple of months ago, but this one theater only charges a dollar for already released movies. We can have lunch at La Crepe Nanou before the movie."

"Sounds good to me."

"Can you be ready in an hour?"

"Sure, do you want to meet at the restaurant?"

"I'll pick you up. Bring your uniform."

"Ok, see you in a bit."

"Ok bye," she said as we both hang up the phone.

I am ready to go a few minutes early and decide to wait outside since it is a beautiful day. When Anna pulls up, I hang my uniform in the backseat before I get in the front.

"Hey, great idea, lunch and a movie. I have never been to this restaurant," I said as I fasten my seat belt.

"You're going to love it; I always go there before I go to the movies."

We are there in no time, I love the cozy atmosphere although the tables are a little close together. We order quickly since we are going to the movie. I enjoy the onion soup and Anna has the escargot while we wait for our crepes.

"So, what did you do yesterday?" Anna asks.

I stop eating for a moment and look up from my soup. Before I can say a word, Anna chimes in.

"Oh God, I can't believe you are still seeing him."

"Let's not talk about him, ok?"

"Gladly; did I tell you I am going to move in with Emma?"

"No, but it's a great idea."

"Yeah, we are excited about it except the packing part. I need to get going with that."

"I can help you if you want," I said as I finish my soup.

"Great, thanks. Let's start soon. I want to be out at the end of the month."

"Ok, oh look, here comes our lunch," I said as the waiter brings our crepes.

"Here is the crepe a la Crabbe, and here is the crepe bourguignonne," he said as he places the plates in front of us.

"Oh, they both look delicious."

"This is so good; would you like to try mine?" Anna asks.

"Yes, here try some of mine," I said as I put a portion of my crepe on her plate.

"Oh, yours is so good. I'm going to get that one next time," Anna said.

"Hey, we better hurry or we will be late for the movie," I said as I look at my watch.

We finish our crepes, skip dessert and head to the movie. We enter the theater and rush to the counter to get our tickets.

"Can I get two tickets for *Dream Lover*?" I said to the lady behind the counter.

"Wait a minute. Did the movie start already?" Anna asks.

"Yes, it just started about six minutes ago," the lady replies.

"Forget it. We're too late." Anna said.

"Are you kidding? It's probably still the coming attractions."

"No, I don't go into a movie once it has started."

"Wow, I wish you would have mentioned that earlier. Ok, what would you like to do instead?" I said shaking my head.

"We can go to Magazine Street and do a little shopping."

"Ok, sounds good to me," I said not minding the change of plans.

Magazine Street is full of all kinds of great shops with a mixture of new and used items. You can find vintage clothing, records, jewelry, antiques, art galleries, bars, and restaurants. We walk up the street hitting a couple of shops until it is time to go to work. I wish we had more time. The shops are so great; you can easily spend the entire day here shopping and having lunch and I cannot wait to come back. I am lucky and find a vintage flapper dress, feather headband and long black gloves. Now I am ready for Mardi Gras next year.

"Hello everyone," I said as we enter the server area.

"Hey, what's up?" Anna said.

"Not much. What are you two up to?" Emma said.

"Not much; we went to lunch and did some shopping on Magazine Street," Anna said.

"We were supposed to go to the movie, but we were late,"

"Oh no; guess you didn't go," Ashley said.

"I see you know about that rule."

"Of course, we do," she said with a laugh.

"No big deal, now I know for next time."

"So, the other day, Rich and I saw the movie *Nine and a Half Weeks*. It is about a couple who have a S & M relationship; it reeks of you and Adam," Emma said with a chuckle.

"Very funny, Emma."

"Hey, who wants to go to Cooter Brown's after work tonight and get oysters and play a couple of games of pool?" Ashley said.

"Sounds good to me," I said grateful that the subject changed.

"Let's go, ladies. The specials are coming up," Eric calls out to us. I follow him out of the server station and as we head to the kitchen he leans down and whispers in my ear. "So, I hear you enjoyed the museum yesterday," he said with a smile.

"Yes, I did," I said smiling while thinking they really tell each other everything.

The rest of the girls are right behind us. We all taste the specials and get to work. The evening goes by quickly and before we know it, we are walking into Cooter Browns.

Cooter Browns is a great sports bar with a huge beer selection, a great bar menu and of course raw oysters. The bar is a cozy local bar, near work in the area known as the Riverbend. Just the place for us to unwind, have a beer and catch up with each other. We order a round of drinks and oysters and settle at a table close to the pool table so we can play a couple of games when we finish eating.

"So, how is it going with the hunk?" Ashley asks Emma.

"Great, he is so sweet."

"I bet he is. Do you see this getting serious?" Ashley said.

"Oh, I guess it could get serious. It's still too early to say. Right now, I'm just having fun."

"He's a great catch, nice handsome guy, excellent job, and lots of fun," Anna said.

"Well, I'm a great catch too!" Emma exclaims.

"Yes, you are Emma, and there's nothing wrong with just having fun," I said thinking Rich is a great catch, but they shouldn't rush into anything.

"Speaking of fun, who's up for a game of pool?" Ashley said.

"I am," I said raising my hand.

"I got winners," Anna said.

Chapter 8

"Well, I am off to work," John said as he grabs his motorcycle helmet.

"Oh, you're taking the bike to work today I see."

"Yeah, I haven't had the old girl out in a while, so I thought I'd take her out for a spin."

"Well, it's a beautiful day for a ride even if it is only to work."

"What time are you leaving for Anna's to start packing?"

"Probably in a half an hour."

"Well, y'all sure left that to the last minute."

"I know. We started talking about it a couple of weeks ago and here we are with just days left in the month. Since this Sunday is Easter, we need to get going," I said as I follow him to the back door.

"Well, happy packing. I love you," he said as he kisses me on the lips.

"I love you too. Please be careful," I said as I watch him walk out the back door.

He walks by our patio table, chairs and barbeque grill and heads towards his bike which he parks just beyond the patio. He puts his helmet on, straddles the bike, and starts it up.

Instead of turning around and driving onto the street off the patio, he heads down the narrow alley between our house and the neighbors towards the front of the house waving as he pulls away. I finish getting ready and leave for Anna's house. I stop at the deli down the block from her house and get egg sandwiches and coffee. I hear movement inside as I approach her door and I shift the food to one hand as I knock with the other.

"Hey, thanks for coming. Come on in," she said as she holds the door open for me.

"No problem. Are you hungry?" I said as I place the food and coffee on the counter.

"Yes, I'm starving. I've already started on the kitchen," she said as I hand her a coffee.

"Great. Where would you like me to start?" I said as I unwrap an egg sandwich.

"How about the bedroom closet and dresser. I have some suitcases in there, you can fill them first. If there is not enough room for all my clothes there is a box in there as well," she said as she takes a bite of the sandwich.

"Ok, sounds like a plan," I said as I sip my coffee.

After we finish eating, I head into the bedroom to start on the closet. I see Mardi Gras beads hanging across her dresser mirror and I smile. I grab the large suitcase, open the closet, and cannot believe what I see. A closet full of beautiful, expensive clothing, most of them still have tags on them. There are designer jackets, sweaters, dresses, pants, and blouses. I walk back out to the kitchen to find Anna.

"Whose clothes are those in the closet?" I ask.

"They're mine," she said laughing.

"Where did you get all those expensive clothes and why don't you wear them?"

"My mother buys them for me all the time because she cannot

stand to see me in the rags, she claims I wear. I don't wear them because they're not my style. Please feel free to take whatever you want."

"I wish they would fit me, but I am one size smaller than you. What a shame to let those beautiful, expensive clothes go to waste. Obviously, you came from money. I never would have guessed that. I grew up poor from a big family; we wore hand me downs," I said with a laugh.

"Believe me I wish she would stop buying them. You are lucky to have a big family; I bet that was fun growing up. I just have one brother."

"Yes, it was fun growing up in a big family," I said with a smile.

We get back to packing and get quite a bit done in a few hours. After packing her clothes, I move on to her knickknacks and books as she packs the sheets and towels and her bathroom stuff. We have everything packed, and I cannot believe how much we accomplished in one day.

"Thank you so much. Now let's get something to eat before work. Where do you want to go? My treat."

"You're welcome. That's what friends are for. Any place is fine with me. You pick."

"How about Ye Olde College Inn. They have great po-boys."

"Ok, sounds good to me."

Ye Olde College Inn is another great local place that opened in the thirties, famous for their po-boys and breaded veal cutlet. We relax while we wait for our oyster po-boys and sip our Cokes.

"Sucks that we have to go to work," I said.

"We could have gotten this done yesterday if you weren't tied up," she said with a chuckle.

"Very funny. We went for a walk in City Park and out to lunch.

City Park is fabulous with its magnificent old oak trees covered in moss, beautiful statues, and sculptures. Obviously, you have been there," I said laughing.

"Yes, it is lovely. Glad you went don't think that changes what I think of him," she said as the server brings our po-boys, and I give her a smirk as I take a bite.

"Good morning. Happy Easter," I said as I walk into the kitchen and give John a kiss.

"Happy Easter to you. Are you hungry? Since we both must work today, I am making you a special Easter breakfast."

"Oh, how sweet. Thank you so much. What are we having?"

"It's a surprise. Sit down and have some coffee; breakfast will be ready soon," he said as he hands me a cup of coffee.

I see that the table is already set, and we are using our good china. There are two monkey dishes with fresh fruit and two glasses of orange juice already on the table. I sip my coffee and watch him as he plates up our breakfast.

"Breakfast is served, my love," he said as he places our plates on the table.

"Oh, wow, eggs Benedict. My favorite. Thanks, this looks delicious."

"I am glad you like it, I wanted to make you something special. I am sorry we both must work and will not see each other all day."

"Me too. Let's do something special on Tuesday," I said.

"That's a great idea. I was thinking about picking you up after work on Monday night and going out somewhere. How does that sound?"

"That sounds great. Now we have our own Easter celebration

to look forward to. Do you have any place in mind?" I said as I take a bite of fruit.

"Well, I was thinking we could go to the Quarter on Monday night for drinks, and I hear Clancy's restaurant is wonderful. Would you like to go there on Tuesday for dinner?"

"Sounds great."

"Happy Easter," he said as he raises his orange juice glass.

"Happy Easter," I said as we ring our glasses.

After John leaves for work, I call my parents and sisters to wish everyone a happy Easter before I go to work.

"Hey, Chelsea, happy Easter," Eric said as I walk in the door.

"Happy Easter to you," I reply.

"You spoke to your sisters today; I can always tell your New York accent is more pronounced on days you speak to them."

"Oh, I didn't realize that." I said with a laugh as I go to punch in and head to the server station.

"Happy Easter, everyone," I said.

"Happy Easter, Chelsea," Anna and Ashley said in unison.

"Happy Easter, everyone. I got daiquiris," Emma said as she enters the station and puts the cup holders on the counter and begins to pass them out.

"Oh, yummy, pina colada," Anna said.

"Great idea, Emma, thank you," I said as I pick up a cup.

"Thank you, Emma. This is delicious," Ashley said.

"Ashley and I have our stations all set. Let's go see if the specials are up," Anna said.

"Ok," I said as we all head to the kitchen.

The rest of the servers and Eric are already there, and he is about to start telling us the specials. "In honor of Easter today's specials are baked ham with scalloped potatoes and honey glazed carrots, lambchops cooked to order with roasted potatoes and asparagus and pancetta wrapped pork with baked macaroni and cheese and green beans. They all come with a salad. Prices and dessert specials are on the eighty-six board. Enjoy," he said as we all grab forks to taste the specials.

"These are so good. I can't decide which one I am going to have tonight," Ashley said as she tastes the specials.

"Hey, how about we go across the street tonight after work and get a bite to eat and a couple of drinks?" Emma said.

"Sounds like a great idea," Ashley said.

"I'm in," Anna said.

"Me too."

We all head out to our stations; we are busy early and then it slows down. I have the station near the kitchen, Henry is in his booth enjoying his dinner. I am glad we are open, and he has a place to go for the holiday. When I stop at the host station to bring the menus back Eric approaches me.

"Hey, Chelsea, I have been meaning to ask you. Are you interested in learning how to expedite? I think it would be a good thing for you to learn how to do and it would be great to have a backup if we are ever shorthanded."

"Sure, sounds good to me. How hard can it be to pull plates out of the window, make sure they look right and add garnish. Let me know when you want me to train."

"Ok great; I will check the schedule and let you know."

"Let's go, ladies. Let's start to clean up and get out of here," Anna said when I return to the server station.

"Already on it," Emma replies.

We finish cleaning up, cash out and are heading across the street in no time.

"Good night, Eric. I'll see you tomorrow," I said as we walk out the door.

"Good night, ladies. Have fun."

"We will," we all said in unison.

"I'll go to the bar and get us a round of drinks and order a couple of appetizers while y'all get us a table," Emma said.

"Sounds like a plan, Emma," Anna said.

"This Easter is beginning to shape up," Ashley said when Emma returns with our drinks.

"Yes, it is. Happy Easter, ladies," I said as I raise my glass.

"Happy Easter," they all said as we ring our glasses.

After a couple of drinks, some food, and a game of pool I head home to find John already asleep. I am surprised since it is not that late. He did have a long day I think to myself. I shower and nestle next to John in bed and drift off to sleep.

I wake up and see that John is already out of bed. I go to the bath-room and head to the kitchen for coffee.

"Good morning. How was your day yesterday?" I said as I en-ter the kitchen.

"Busy. How was yours?" he said as he leans down and kisses me.

"Good, we were busy early then it died down. I went out with the girls for a couple of drinks after work. I am sorry I missed you, I did not think I was out that late," I said while fixing myself a cup of coffee.

"I'm sorry; I was beat, I heard you come in and was about to get up, but I fell back to sleep."

"Are you ready for breakfast?" he said as he put scrambled eggs and toast on our plates.

"Yes, thank you. Are we still going out tonight after work?" I ask as he places our plates on the table.

"Yes, I'm going to come home, change, and then pick you up."

"Ok great," I said as I take a bite of toast.

John carries his dish into the kitchen when he finishes eating and I hear him starting to clean up.

"I'll do the dishes. Go and get ready," I call out.

"Thanks," he said as he gives me a kiss and heads for the bathroom.

I finish cleaning the kitchen and am heading to the bedroom to make the bed as John comes out of the bedroom dressed for work.

"I'm ready to go, see you tonight. I love you."

"Ok, have a good day. I love you too," I said as we kiss.

I am just finishing ironing my dress for work when the phone rings. I walk across the room and pick up the receiver.

"Hello."

"Hello, Chelsea." I hear Adam sing my name and I know he is smiling.

"Hi, how are you?" I said as a smile comes over my face.

"I'm fine. How are you. How was your Easter?"

"I had to work but it was ok. How was yours?"

"Very nice. I just wanted you to know that I am thinking about you, and I am really looking forward to seeing you on Wednesday," he said with a little devilish chuckle.

"That's nice. I am looking forward to seeing you too," I said wondering what he is up to.

"I hope you have a wonderful day; you take care," he said as he hangs up the phone.

I realize now that his Monday phone calls are foreplay for him. I imagine him setting up the ribbon on the bed or the scarves on the table and getting excited. Funny thing, now they are foreplay for me too as I wonder with excitement what he has planned. I think about Wednesday as I finish dressing and head to work.

"Hi, Gina," I said as I walk in the door.

"Hello. Wow pretty dress," she said.

"Thank you. John is picking me up after work for an evening out."

"Oh, that sounds like fun."

"Yes, a little post Easter celebration, and tomorrow we are going to Clancy's Restaurant."

"I guess we both have a fun day planned. I get to see Josh tomorrow," she said with a smile.

"Oh, look, it's Wednesday's Girl," Eric said as he approaches the podium.

"Who came up with that name?" I said with a laugh.

"I did. I think it's fitting and don't worry no one else but us and Adam will hear it," he said with a smile.

"I love it," Gina said.

"When I referred to you as Wednesday's Girl to Adam today, he loved it too."

"I'm so glad I can entertain all of you," I said laughing as I head to the time clock to punch in.

"Hello, ladies," I said as I enter the kitchen.

"Hello, Chelsea," the girls call out. I punch in and head back to the hostess station, check the special board, stations and make sure the menus are clean.

"Ok, ladies, I am going to make your dinner. I saved lambchops from yesterday. Is medium rare ok with you, Chelsea?"

"Yes, that's perfect."

Henry comes in, I walk him to his booth, get him a cup of coffee and call out to Anna as I pass the server area.

"Anna, Henry's here."

"Ok, thanks."

"Here's your dinner, ladies," Eric said as he put our plates on the table.

"This looks delicious," I said as I look at the lambchops, asparagus and roasted potato.

"Yum," Gina said after her first bite.

"So, Gina said John is picking you up and that the two of you are going out tonight. That sounds like fun."

"Yeah, I'm excited. We don't go out that often on Monday night, even though it's not the weekend. It's our Friday since we are off on Tuesdays."

"It's New Orleans; every night is a party in the Quarter," Eric said.

"The Big Easy!" Gina exclaimed.

"Tomorrow we're going to Clancy's. Have you ever been there?" I asked Eric.

"Yes, it's a fabulous restaurant. You're going to love it."

"I'm really looking forward to it," I said.

"I'm glad we finally get to meet John," Gina said.

"Yes, me too."

The night drags on. Since it is the day after Easter, it is not busy. At the end of the shift the place is almost empty. The girls are doing their side work, and I am wiping down the menus when John walks in.

"Hi, sweetie."

"Hi, honey. John, this is my boss, Eric, and his wife, Gina. Eric, Gina, this is my husband, John."

"So nice to finally meet you both," John said as he extends his hand.

"Nice to meet you too," Eric and Gina said as Eric shakes his hand.

"Hey, Chelsea, go ahead and get going. I'll punch you out," Eric said.

"Ok, thanks," I said as I grab my purse.

"Have fun," Eric said.

"Enjoy your days off," Gina said with a smile.

"Thanks, you too," I said as I give her a quick wink.

"Goodnight," John said as we walk out the door.

"You look beautiful," John said as we get in the car.

"Thank you, you look handsome yourself."

"Hey, sweetie, I was just thinking, how about we go home, drop off the car and call a cab? This way we are not driving after drinking and it will be quicker than the streetcar."

"Ok with me."

"Great."

I grab the phone book and start to look up taxi cabs as soon as we get to the house.

"Does it matter which cab company?"

"One of the ladies at work swears by United Cab," John said as he reaches for the phone.

"Ok, here it is," I said as I read him the number.

"Great, thank you," John said as he dials the phone.

The cab is outside in minutes, and we climb in.

"Good evening. Can you take us to Pat O'S please?"

"Sure thing," the cab driver said as he turned on the meter.

"This was a great idea; this may become my new favorite mode of evening transportation," I said as I settle into my seat.

"Oh no, I have created a monster," John said with a laugh as we head towards the French Quarter.

"That will be $5.90," the driver said when we arrive at Pat O's. John hands him money as I get out of the cab.

"Thank you, keep the change," John said.

"Oh, thank you very much," the driver said as John gets out of the cab.

There are two men standing at the door greeting customers as they walk in. "Good evening. Welcome to Pat O'Brien's."

"Good evening," we said in unison as we walk through the door.

As we walk through the carriageway the main bar is on the left. The main bar reminds me of a local neighborhood bar. It is a comfortable bar that has beer steins hanging from the ceiling, champagne bottle lamps and a juke box.

Further down the carriageway on the right is the piano bar. The piano bar has two pianos, and a performer is playing "When the Saints Go Marching In," as the crowd sings along.

We continue to the patio bar; a large outside bar with a big flaming fountain in the center surrounded by tables and chairs. There are two bars on the patio, and we choose to sit at the bar in front instead of a table.

"Good evening, what can I get you?" the bartender asks.

"What would you like, sweetie?" John said.

"I will have your famous hurricane, please," I said to the bartender.

"I will have a Corona, please," John said.

The bartender serves our drinks and explains that the souvenir glass costs extra if I want to keep it. The glass is ten inches high with a pedestal base that has Pat O'Brien's New Orleans, LA written in green on the front and Have Fun is on the back. The tall drink of fruit juices and rum topped with a cherry and orange slice looks delicious.

"Cheers," I said as I lift my glass.

"Cheers," John said as we ring our glasses.

"Oh, this is so good."

"Be careful; that looks like a 24-ounce glass, I know there is ice in it but that's still a big drink."

"It doesn't taste that strong," I said as I take a sip.

"Famous last words," John said with a chuckle.

There is a nice crowd for a Monday, and we sip our drinks as we watch the crowd come and go while enjoying the glow of the flaming fountain. Pat O's is timeless; young, old, couples, groups, locals, and tourists come and go as we enjoy our drinks.

"Would you like another drink?" the bartender asks.

"Oh, no thank you, but I would like to keep the glass," I said.

"Would you like to walk on Bourbon Street a bit?" John asks.

"That sounds great," I said as John pays the tab and I collect my glass.

We walk towards Bourbon Street and join the crowd looking at the street acts and people on the balconies as we walk.

"I bet you a dollar I know where you got those shoes," a man said to me.

"Oh," I said thinking how he can know where I got these shoes as I get ready to accept the bet.

"Yeah, she got them on her feet," John said as the guy starts to laugh as he walks away. "They tried that on me one night."

"How about we have a drink at Le Booze before going home?" John said.

"Sounds good to me. I like that bar."

We make our way to the bar and get two seats facing the street. The bar is not very crowded, and the bartender is talking to a couple on the other side of the bar. She comes over to wait on us once we sit down.

"Hi, how are you folks doing tonight?" she asks as she places two cocktail napkins in front of us.

"Just fine, thank you," John said.

"What can I get you to drink?"

"I will have a Corona. Sweetie what would you like?"

"I will have a Budweiser," I said distracted by the couple across the bar.

As the bartender gets our drinks, I finally get a good look at the couple across the bar. I instantly realize who she is; I knew she looked familiar when we walked in.

"That's Heather Weber from *General Hospital*." I said to the bartender as she serves us our beer, saying the name of her character on the show.

"Yes, it is. Just like everyone else, celebrities love New Orleans."

"She's great. Her character has been very entertaining over the years," I said.

"Yes, she's everyone's favorite villain," she said as she heads back to the other side of the bar as we take a sip of our beer.

"Are you ready to go home after this drink?" John said.

"Yes, I'm ready," I said as John reaches for our tab and puts cash on the bar.

We finish our drinks and head towards the door as we wave to the bartender. "Thank you, goodnight," we said in unison.

"Thank you, good night," she replies with a wave.

I am in the kitchen fixing myself a cup of coffee when John walks into the room.

"Good morning," I said as I give him a kiss.

"Good morning. Have you been up long?"

"No, I just got up. The coffee is ready; let me fix you a cup."

"Thank you," he said as I hand him a cup.

"What would you like for breakfast?" I spoke.

"I'll cook breakfast. How about French toast?"

"That sounds good."

"Did you have fun last night?"

"Yes, good thing I only had one hurricane though."

"Glad I warned you."

"I am too; they go down very easy," I said looking at the glass on the shelf.

"Let me start fixing us some breakfast."

"Ok, I'll set the table."

"Great, thank you."

After breakfast John goes outside to wash the car and motorcycle while I get the laundry done and clean the bathroom. We skip lunch, shower, and dress in the late afternoon for our five o'clock reservation.

"You look beautiful," John said as he opens the car door for me.

"Thank you."

"I'm really looking forward to this restaurant. The chef at work raved about it. I hope you like it." John said as he gets into the car.

"I'm sure it's going to be wonderful."

Clancy's is located uptown close to our house, so we are there on time. I purposely made an early reservation so we would not have to wait for a table. The host seats us right away, and I am pleased that the tables are not too close together. Mirrors and sketches of locals adorn the walls and the white linen tablecloths are pressed to perfection.

"Let's see what they have on the wine list," John said as he looks at the list that the friendly maître d' gave him.

"Oh, wine sounds like a nice idea," I said as the waiter greets us and John orders a nice bottle of wine.

"We're not in any rush." John tells our server Mark once he serves our wine.

"Very well then. I will give you some time," Mark said as he leaves the table.

"Thank you," John said.

"To us," he said as he raised his glass.

"To us," I said as we ring our glasses and taste the wine.

"Now, let's see what's on the menu tonight," John said as he picks up the menu.

"Everything looks so good I don't know what I am going to have," I said.

"Are you ready to order, sir?" Mark asks as he pours us more wine.

"Yes, we are. My wife will start with the soft-shell crab, and I will have the sweetbreads with Madeira."

"Very well and for your entrees, sir?"

"My wife will have the sautéed veal and I will have the filet medium rare with the red wine demi-glace."

"Wonderful selection, sir."

"Thank you," John said as we hand him our menus. We sip our wine and take in the atmosphere until the appetizers arrive.

"Oh, my goodness!" I exclaim as the soft-shell crab topped with a pile of lump crabmeat is set in front of me.

"Do you need anything else?" Marks asks as he pours more wine.

"No thank you, this looks delicious," John said.

We share the appetizers and enjoy the wine. We are delighted when the entrees are served. John's filet looks superb, but my sautéed veal topped with fried oysters and hollandaise takes the cake.

"Oh, this is like heaven," I said as I took a bite.

"So is mine."

"Try some of mine," I said as I put a bite of veal and an oyster on John's plate.

"That's to die for. The chef was right about the food."

"How is everything?" Mark asks as he comes to the table.

"Wonderful!" we exclaim in unison.

Mark returns when we finish eating. He clears our empty plates and crumbs our table as he tells us about the desserts.

"No dessert for us, thank you, but we will have an expresso, a cappuccino, a Frangelico and a white crème de menthe," John said.

"Coming right up," Mark said.

"Well, it's still early what do you want to do after this?" John asks.

"Well, do you want to go have a drink somewhere or we can rent a movie," I said knowing my options are few.

"A movie sounds like a great idea."

We sip our after-dinner drinks while we watch the bustle of the restaurant that is now completely full. John pays the bill and leaves Mark a generous tip for his wonderful service.

We stop at Block Buster video, rent *Back to the Future* and head home. The movie is good, and I am glad it makes John laugh. By the time it ends I am ready for bed.

"You go ahead, I am going to stay up for a while," John said.

"Ok goodnight, I love you," I said as I kiss his lips.

"Love you too, goodnight."

As I climb into bed, I think about Adam's phone call. I think about how excited he sounded about seeing me on Wednesday and I wonder what he has planned. I think about his effect on me and how he makes me feel as I drift off to sleep.

I am only at the door for a moment when Adam pulls up at exactly one o'clock. I close the door behind me, skip down the steps and jump into his car.

"Hello, how are you?" Adam said as I put my seatbelt on.

"Feeling good and you?"

"I feel good as well," he said as he looks at me with a smile. "It is good to see you. Did you enjoy your day off yesterday?"

"Yes, we went to Clancy's restaurant. It was wonderful."

"Oh, I am glad you enjoyed yourself," he said as we drive towards his house.

When we arrive at his house, I settle in the living room while he makes us a drink. He hands me what I assume is rum and Coke and sets his on the coaster. Then he goes back to the kitchen. He returns with two shots of Jägermeister and hands one to me.

"Happy Wednesday!" Adam said as he raises his glass.

"Happy Wednesday!" I said as I raise mine. I drink the shot and quickly reach for the rum and Coke to get rid of the taste which makes Adam chuckle.

Adam is smiling ear to ear as he watches me as we sip our drinks. He looks so excited that I cannot help but wonder what he is up to. A couple of minutes later he put his glass on the coaster.

"Take off all your jewelry and your clothes," he said.

"Ok," I said as I put my glass down and begin to take my jewelry off.

When I stand to take my clothes off, Adam stands as well and take his clothes off. He hands me the blue robe and as I put it on, he puts his robe on as well. He walks over to the sliding glass door and pulls the drapes and door open.

"Put your sandals back on and follow me."

"Where are we going?"

"To my workout room," he said as he points to the detached

garage on the corner of the property, as I stick my head out the door and look around.

"Relax. There is a six-foot fence all around the back of my property; no one can see us."

"Ok," I said as I follow him out the door and wait as he closes the door behind us. We walk across the grass and stop at the garage door.

"Turn around so I can put this on you," he said as he pulls a blue silk scarf out of his robe pocket.

I turn around and he ties the scarf over my eyes making sure that I cannot see. He places his hands on my shoulders and turns me back around and takes my hand. I hear the garage door open, and he steers me through the door. I feel a thick mat under my feet as we walk a couple of feet into the garage.

"Take off your robe and kick your sandals off, walk two steps forward and turn around with your feet together and arms at your sides," he said as I hear the door close.

I do as instructed and as I wait for his next command, he takes the robe from me. I hear the clank of chains as he takes my arm and stretches it towards the ceiling and wraps a thick chain around my wrist. I feel the coolness of the chain against my skin, and I hear a click as he locks the chain around my wrist. A wave of excitement comes over me and I take a deep breath in and let out a quick moan.

"Oh."

He brushes my cheek with his hand as he takes my other arm and extends it towards the ceiling. I feel the weight of the chain against my wrist as he locks it into place. I feel his fingers at each of my wrists as they lightly move down my arms and stop on the side of my breasts.

"Oh," I moan aloud with pleasure as his fingers continue to move down my body to my ankles.

"Pick your foot up and stretch your leg out to the side."

As I stretch my leg, I hear the clank of the chain as he wraps it around my ankle and locks it. His fingers caress my leg from the chain up to my upper thigh across my mound and down my other leg until it reaches my other ankle. My body shakes as I moan aloud with pleasure.

"Ahh," I moan as he touches me.

"Pick your foot up and stretch it out to your side," he said as I stretch my leg to the side and as I hear the clank of the chain, he pulls my leg out a little further before he wraps the chain around my ankle and locks it.

The click of the last lock heightens my excitement and I take a breath and lick my lips in anticipation. As I wiggle a little and move my arms, the chains clank. I imagine myself spread eagle, my arms locked to chains hanging from the ceiling and my legs chained to something on each side of me.

"Oh yes, I like you like this!" he exclaims as I hear him taking his clothes off and walking across the mats on the floor followed by a click.

As the song "Second Hand News" by Fleetwood Mac begins to play, I squeal with delight. As I sway my body to the music, I feel his lips on mine, and I hungrily meet his tongue with mine. His kiss leaves me breathless as his mouth travels to my neck and I cry out with pleasure. "Oh yes!" I sigh as his mustache lightly glides across my neck to the other side. As I turn my head, he slowly kisses his way down my neck.

He slowly kisses me just above my breast and I arch my back to offer my breasts to him. His tongue lightly licks my nipple and I moan with pleasure; it hardens as he takes it in his mouth.

"Oh yes," I whisper.

The music plays on as I slowly move my head from side to side in time with the music as he begins to kiss my other nipple. His wet mouth makes my nipple hard, and I moan as he sucks on it. I move my hands up enough to grab hold of the hanging chains.

"Oh yes, that feels so good. Please don't stop!" I beg as his hand cups my other breast and squeezes my nipple. His hand caresses me until it is between my legs, and he slips his finger inside me.

"Ohhh God, don't stop! Please don't stop!" I beg as he fingers my wet throbbing clitoris.

"Oh no," I cry when he stops. I hear something slide across the floor and I feel it slide in between my legs. I hear and feel him get on the object with his head between my legs. His fingers open my vagina as he slips his tongue inside me.

"Yes, oh God, yes!" I exclaim as I move my pelvis to meet his tongue.

"Don't Stop" begins to play, and I move my hips in time with the music. His tongue slowly circles my clitoris and I moan with pleasure as he thrusts his tongue against my swollen clitoris.

As he slides a finger inside me, I moan aloud. "Oh yes, that feels so good," I said as he slides another one in and pleasures me with his fingers as he licks me. I throw my head back as my arms pull on the chains as I push myself down onto his face.

"Ooh, ooh, ooh," I moan as I shake the chains as his tongue circles my clitoris faster and faster. "Oh, don't stop!" I beg as he fingers my wet vagina.

He pushes his fingers deep inside of me, in and out of me slow at first then faster, harder, and deeper. I thrust myself onto his fingers and against his tongue as I move up and down on my toes. As I move, my arms shake the chains. His tongue thrashes against my clitoris in quick thrusts faster and faster as I rock my pelvis back and forth. "Oh yes, yes, yes!" I yell out.

"AH, AH, AH, AH, AH, AHHHHHH!" I scream louder and louder until I let out one continuous scream as I shake uncontrollably, rattling the chains as I growl like a wild animal, and I come with such a force that my body stiffens then slumps and my hands hang lifeless from the chains. My knees get weak as my feet come down on the mat. I let out a single laugh and a satisfying sigh as my head hangs down. The chains are all that is holding me up.

Adam quickly moves from between my legs and removes the object. He quickly unlocks my left leg and realizes I cannot move it and helps me straighten it. It buckles when I put weight on it, he holds me up while he unlocks my other leg, and it buckles. As he unlocks my wrist, my whole-body slumps onto him once my hand is free.

He unlocks the last chain and holds me as my arm comes down. He scoops his arm under my legs and picks me up and carries me a couple of feet and gently lowers me to the mat on the floor. His fingers gently wipe my wet hair from my forehead, and I softly sigh, "Ahh."

"Would you like a sip of water?" he asks softly.

"Yes, please," I said while thinking I do not want him to leave me. He gets up and I hear him pulling a bottle out of an ice bucket and water pouring into a glass.

"Here you go," he said as he holds my head up with his hand and holds the glass to my lips.

"Thank you," I whisper as I take a sip.

"Would you like more?"

"Yes please," I said as I take another sip. He gently puts my head down, then he gets up and I hear him flip the tape over and he lays down next to me. His finger and thumb gently squeeze my skin as they move up my arm while I enjoy the music.

As the song "The Chain" begins to play his finger begins to slowly trace my lips. I open my mouth as his finger moves over my lips. Then he runs his finger down my chin and over my neck. I cry out as he cascades it up and down the center of my chest. He moves it to my nipple and circles it until it hardens; he circles my other nipple until it too hardens from his touch.

"Spread your legs," he said as he moves above me. As I do his mouth comes down on mine and he kisses me as his cock presses against my mound.

"Oooh," I moan as I feel his hard cock pushing against me. As much as I want to reach out, I know better. I couldn't anyway as my arms are so weak. I feel his cock rubbing against me, teasing me before he enters me with a quick deep thrust.

"Oh!" he moans as he thrusts himself in and out of me. Our tongues swirl together as I push my hips up to meet his thrusts. He pushes himself slowly in and out of me as I moan with pleasure.

"You feel so good," I whisper breathily.

He holds himself above me as he slides himself in and out of me faster and faster. He pushes himself deep inside me as I push my hips up with hard, fast thrusts and we both moan aloud as we come together. I giggle as my bottom collapses on the mat and Adam's body covers mine. We are quiet, and I listen to music. "Gold Dust Women" begins to play and Stevie Nicks sings.

"Ahhh," I let out a satisfying sigh and I lay still as I enjoy the music. Adam moves beside me and strokes my hair as the song plays.

"Time to take a shower," he said when the song ends.

"Ok," I said as he helps me sit up and he removes the blindfold. I blink a couple of times as my eyes adjust to the light.

I see the pad I am sitting on is a thick grey pad you would find in a gym. There are all kinds of weights and work out equipment nearby. My eyes wonder and I see the chains hanging from the ceiling and chains extending from rings coming from the floor.

In the center is a bench that you would lay on while lifting weights. I giggle and blush when I imagine myself hanging there. I wonder if the neighbors heard me scream and growl like an animal, sounds I have never made before I met Adam. I look down at my wrist and ankles; I see they are red from the chains but not too bad and I know the marks will not last.

"Here, let me help you put this on," Adam said as he helps me up and stands behind me and helps me into the robe.

"Thank you," I said as I slip my sandals on that he put in front of me, and I feel my legs ache.

"Let's go right into the shower and then I will make us dinner."

"Sounds good," I said as I follow him into the house.

I know he is pleased that I need no instruction in the shower, and we move in sync as he washes me. I can tell he enjoys taking care of me as much as I enjoy him pampering me. We shower, dress and head to the kitchen for dinner.

"I have filets wrapped in bacon, steak fries and I am making you some broccoli for dinner," he said with a chuckle.

"Thank you," I said with a smile.

"Medium rare for your steak, right?"

"Yes, thank you," I said not surprised that he knows that.

He heads to the patio to put the steaks on the grill and when he comes back, a cat is following him.

"Whose cat is that?"

"That's my cat; she is an outdoor cat."

"Oh, what's her name?" I ask as I reach down and pet her.

"I call her Cat," he said as he hands me a bag. "I got this for you for Easter."

"Oh, thank you," I said as I take the bag and open it, finding a gold box with Godiva written on it inside.

"Easter candy. Have you ever had Godiva chocolate?" he asks.

"No, I have not, thank you," I said as I open the box and look at the beautiful chocolates.

"You can have one for dessert. Dinner is served," he said as he put our plates at each end of the table which still amuses me.

"Thank you," I said as he watches me cut into my steak and take a bite.

"It's delicious," I said as a smile comes across his face.

"Thank you, I am glad you like it," he said as he takes a bite of his steak. "French Quarter Fest is coming up in a couple of weeks. Are you going?"

"Oh, I never heard of it. What is that?"

"Another fun filled New Orleans festival of food, booze and music," he said with a chuckle.

"That sounds like fun. I don't know if John will want to go."

"I am going with Eric and Gina. You can come with us if he doesn't."

"Ok great, I'll let you know."

"Try one of the chocolates," he said when we finished dinner.

I open the box and look at the paper describing the selection of beautiful chocolates and choose a chocolate raspberry; I offer him one, but he declines.

"Oh my, that is delicious," I said as I savor the chocolate as he looks at me and smiles while he cleans up.

"All cats out," he said as he opens the sliding glass door, and the cat runs out before we leave.

Chapter 9

Two weeks later, I wake up on the couch to the sound of John coming in the door.

"Hi, sweetie. How was your day?" John said as he leans down and gives me a kiss on the cheek.

"Good, how was work?"

"Ok."

"Are we still going to French Quarter Fest tomorrow?" I ask as I get off the couch.

"Yes, in fact my boss said I can come in a little late."

"Great, I can't wait," I said as I get him a beer.

"Yeah, they have been setting up all week. It will be nice to taste food from several different restaurants and hear some good music."

"Yes indeed," I said.

"I'm going to take a shower," John said as he takes a sip of his beer and sets the bottle down on the table. I put a silk nightie on while he is in the shower and am waiting in the living room when he returns. He picks up the joint from the ashtray, takes a hit and offers it to me.

"No thanks. I'm going to go to bed. Do you want to join me?"

"I am going to stay up for a bit; I will be in later. I love you," he said as he takes a sip of beer.

"Love you too," I said as I give him a kiss goodnight. Wishing he would come to bed with me; it has been a while since we have been together.

"Good morning," I said as I grab two coffee cups out of the cabinet.

"Good morning, did you sleep well?" he asks as he kisses me.

"No, I had a nightmare," I said as I fix our coffees.

"Maybe the nightmares are from all the murder mysteries you read," John said.

"Well, since they're not about murder, and since I have been having them two and three times a week since I was a child, I doubt that," I said annoyed. "We should get ready to go soon."

"Ok, sorry you had a nightmare," he said.

"I am going to shower while you enjoy your coffee," I said.

"Ok," he said as I head to the bathroom.

We are about to walk out the door when the phone rings and I walk across the room to answer it.

"Hello, it's Gina. How are you?"

"I'm good. How are you?"

"Great. Eric and I were wondering if you and John are still going to French Quarter Fest today?"

"Actually, John and I are about to walk out the door and head down there. We're going to the square."

"That's where we're going. I will keep a look out for you."

"Ok, see you there," I said.

"Bye," she said as she hangs up the phone.

"That was Gina. She and Eric are also going to the Quarter and wanted to know if we were still going."

"Oh, good. Hopefully we will see them there. We're going early enough that it shouldn't be too busy," John said.

"Yeah," I said feeling a little nervous about running into Adam with John.

We drive to the Quarter, park at John's job, and make the short walk to Jackson Square. We are just walking by the line of horse and buggies waiting for their first customers of the day right outside the square when I hear Eric call my name.

"Hey, Chelsea," I hear Eric call out as they walk towards us.

"Hey," I call out as I wave.

"Oh good. You are just getting here also," Gina said as she gives me a kiss.

"John, this is our friend Adam. Adam this is Chelsea's husband, John," Eric said.

"Nice to meet you," they both said as they shake hands.

"Chelsea, have you met Adam?" John asks.

"Yes, we met at Eric and Gina's party and at the restaurant. Nice to see you again," I said hoping my face is not red as a vision of yesterday flashes in front of me.

"Nice to see you too," Adam said with a smile.

"Let's go in and get some lunch," Eric said.

The square is set up with tents of food from a variety of French Quarter restaurants. In addition to the artists that are always here, I see a large stage and hear jazz music as the band starts to play. There is a nice crowd but since it just opened it is not that crowded.

"So, since this is your first French Quarter Fest, Chelsea and John, let me tell you a little about it," Eric said as we enter the Square.

"It is a free annual music festival; it started in 1984 to get the locals to come back to the French Quarter. It is a fantastic way to sample all these great restaurants' cuisine while listening to fabulous music. It is nice for the restaurants also; they get people to try their cuisine and hopefully go to the restaurant another time," he said as we look at all the booths in the square.

"The wonderful thing about this festival is the money made from the festival is put right back in New Orleans. This is only one part of it; there are stages and music throughout the Quarter featuring local jazz, blues, funk, folk, and gospel music. It runs from Thursday through Sunday and runs all day through the night," he said as we start to walk around.

"Well, New Orleans sure knows how to throw a party," John said.

We walk by each booth looking at the food they have to offer. I am impressed with the choice of food from the city's best restaurants. Combined with the great music and southern hospitality I can see why this is an enormous success.

The first booth is Pat O's selling their famous hurricane which we all pass on since we must work later. Followed by the Court of Two Sisters where you can sample a crawfish dish or turtle soup. Next is Antonine's one of the oldest restaurants in New Orleans; they are offering veal and baked alaska. Brossard's has an authentic crawfish boil; Brennen's has a barbeque shrimp po-boy that I know John will love. Finally, K Paul's is serving shrimp & cheddar grits.

"Wow, how is anyone supposed to choose?" I said after viewing the selections.

"You can come sample something each day," Eric said.

"I think I would like to sample something at K Paul's," I said.

"Well speaking of Paul, there he is," John said as I turn and see the famous chef himself. Paul Prudhomme looks dapper dressed in all white with a white bowler hat on his head. He flashes a big smile and waves as someone from the crowd calls out to him.

"I will get us a table while everyone gets what they want. Surprise me with something yummy," Gina said to Eric.

We all head out in different directions and meet back at the table with our selections. We enjoy our food while listening to the music.

"I got to get to work. Have fun everyone," John said once we finished lunch.

"I'll see you tonight, love you," I said while feeling self-conscious with Adam watching us.

"Love you too," John said as he kisses me.

"Goodbye," everyone said in unison as he heads out of the square.

"Let's go over to the stage and listen to the music for a while," Eric said.

"Good idea," Adam said as we make our way to the stage.

The square is full of people now. There is a large crowd around the stage where the all-female group on stage has the crowd dancing to the beat.

"This next song is a number by the Dixie Cups, a talented group from right here in New Orleans," the lead singer said as they begin to play "Iko Iko" and the crowd cheers. I sway to the music as I wonder where I can get an album from the Dixie Cups.

"I love this song," Eric said to me as he moves to the music.

"Me too," I said as I glance next to me and see Adam staring at me smiling. My attention turns to Gina as she dances in front of me singing and we enjoy the music for a while as the square fills up with people.

"I guess we better get home and get dressed for work," Eric said after a while.

"Ok, I will see you there," I said.

"Why don't you just come with us, and I will bring you to work. We can stop at your house for your uniform," Eric said.

"Actually, it's in my bag."

"Great, let's go," Eric said as he directs us from the crowd.

As we walk, I hear Adam humming a tune. At first, I thought it is a tune we had just heard, but after a moment I realize it is "You Make Loving Fun" from Fleetwood Mac. I turn my head in his direction, and I see he is watching me smiling. I giggle as my cheeks feel flush as I envision myself blindfolded hanging from chains, swaying to the music, as he lays between my legs pleasuring me and I feel myself getting excited.

We are walking on Decatur Street heading to Eric and Gina's when my thoughts are interrupted by someone across the street. I see a middle-aged woman on roller skates wearing an old fur coat as ducks trail behind her. Before I can say a word, Gina calls out.

"Oh, look it's Ruthie the Duck Lady!"

"It's who?" I ask.

"The Duck Lady, a wonderful New Orleans treasure who has ducks follow her since she was a young girl. Sometimes she skates around in a wedding dress, and she loves to drink and smoke. She is quite famous. The tourists ask about her when they come in the restaurant."

"I have never heard of her."

"She is quite a character," Eric said as I watch her skate along.

Eric and Gina just moved into a small apartment complex in the Quarter that has six apartments, a small pool, and a tall iron gate. Eric unlocks the gate, and we head around back past the pool to their unit which is quite large and very modern.

"Have a seat," Eric said as he and Gina go upstairs to change.

"Did you enjoy the festival?" Adam said as we sit on the couch.

"Yes, I did. You were right about New Orleans, the music, food, people, parades, history, culture and southern hospitality, I am falling in love with this city."

"I told you that you would."

"Hey, Chelsea, since you're going to be early how about you train to expedite for a while with Miss Jane before your shift?" Eric said as he walks down the stairs in a fresh dress shirt and slacks.

"Sure, I can do that."

"I also want to look at the schedule and see what days you can come in early and learn to bartend if you are interested. It will be good for you to learn these things so you can go on to be a restaurant manager someday."

"Yes, and since he can't get me to do those things, he will train you to do them," Gina said chuckling while walking down the stairs.

"Again, it doesn't hurt to learn something new and to have more skills," Eric said.

"I love my job, making good money, and don't want to do anything else right now, that's all," Gina said as she kisses Eric on the cheek which makes him smile.

"There is nothing wrong with being a server but having other skills doesn't hurt," Eric said.

"I agree with Eric. Learning something new and having other skills to add to your resume is a great idea," Adam said.

"I don't have a resume; I just fill out an application when I apply for a job."

"After you do this training, we will write your resume," Adam said.

"That's a great idea," Eric said.

"Ok, sounds good to me."

"We better get going. Gina, do you want me to drop you off at work?" Eric said.

"No thank you. I'll walk. I want to do some window shopping, see you tonight," she said as they kiss.

"This was fun. See you both soon," she said as she kisses Adam and I on our cheeks.

"See you soon," Adam and I said as she heads out the door.

We all walk out together, and Adam waits with me for a moment as Eric gets his car. He pulls up in front of us in a dark green two door convertible with a beige hood and matching leather seats. Adam opens the door for me and waits until I get in and shuts the door.

"Thank you, it was nice to see you," I said with a smile.

"It was nice to see you as well. You take care," he said as he kisses my cheek making me blush. "Take care, Eric."

"You, too, Adam," Eric said as we pulled away.

"I love your car; it's nice with the top down."

"I love convertibles; it is my favorite kind of car. I had fun today; I hope you liked the festival."

"Yes, I did. I was just a little uncomfortable being with John and Adam at the same time."

"Yes, I know. I don't care to see Josh when I am at Gina's job."

That must be hard I think to myself. John does not know about Adam, but Eric knows about Josh and Gina and Josh is aware of that. I know that must be difficult no matter how indifferent he acts; he loves her too much for it not to bother him. It would be different if they had an open relationship, but they don't. I do not know too many people who would be ok with this, and I wonder for a moment how it started but decide not to ask.

"So, Jazz Fest is coming up next and if you loved the music today you will love Jazz Fest," Eric said, changing the subject.

"When is that?"

"It is always the last weekend of April and the first weekend in May, so it is right around the corner. It's held at the Fairgrounds. There are countless stages of music, all kinds of local cuisine, artists, and craft vendors."

"That sounds like fun, I can't wait."

"Yeah, this year's lineup is impressive, B.B. King, Nina Simone, Stevie Ray Vaughan, Dr. John, Jerry Lee Lewis, Rita Coolidge, and The Neville brothers. There are more acts; I just cannot remember all of them; I have the list at home. We can grab the *Gambit* magazine outside of work. The lineup will be in there."

"Wow sounds great. I've never read the *Gambit* magazine."

"You should check it out. It's a free weekly magazine that advertises news and events in New Orleans."

"Ok, I will get one. Thanks." I said as we drive to work.

When we get to work, I quickly change into my uniform, and Eric tells Miss Jane to train me to expedite. He does not explain why, and I can tell by her face she is curious, and I feel awkward for a moment.

"Is there an opening that I am unaware of?" she asks.

"No, Eric just wants me to train in case we are ever short-handed. Trust me I am happy being a server," I said hoping that alleviates her worries.

"Oh, I see. Well, it will be easy to train you since you already work here and know where everything is. Let me take you to the back walk-in and storeroom. I will show you where everything comes from and goes back to at the end of the day. As you know the expediter gets out and puts away most of the items that the servers use."

I follow her to the walk-in and storeroom, and she shows me where the cart with the salad bar items are. She shows me where the creamers, desserts and other cold items are. Then she shows me the dry storage where the crackers, coffee, tea bags and other dry items are kept. Pointing out the list on the doors of both the storeroom and the walk-in where you write down and date all items taken. When we get back to the line, she shows me the check list of the set up and break down duties of the expediter for each shift.

"Of course, you already know to keep everything stocked, clean and fresh while garnishing and traying up the food."

"Yes, I think I can do it in an emergency," I said as Paula the short, pleasantly plump evening expediter walks in.

"What's going on?" she said as she puts her long dirty blonde hair in a hair net.

"Eric has her training just in case we are ever shorthanded," Miss Jane said as she and Paula look at each other.

"Oh, well, I don't know when that would be since I have never called out, not even when I'm sick," Paula said sounding annoyed as she looks at me.

"Listen, Paula, I promise you that is all this is. I am happy being a server and have no interest in your job," I stated.

"I hope if it isn't you would tell me, because you know I need this job."

"I would definitely tell you, Paula, and I assure you that's not what this is about, I am going to train to bartend also," I said knowing from the few times she has joined us for a drink that money is tight for her. That at twenty-two she is the sole support for her two younger siblings.

"I'm sorry, I don't mean to give you a tough time," she said.

"No problem, it's ok. I better get out front and start setting my station."

"Hello everyone," I said as I enter the server station.

"Hello," the girls reply.

"What was going on in the kitchen?" Anna asks.

"Eric has me training to expedite in case there is ever an emergency and Paula got upset thinking her job is in jeopardy."

"We heard her saying something to you about her job when we threw our purses on the shelf," Emma said.

"It's just in case of an emergency; he wants me to train to bartend also."

"Learning to be a bartender is a good thing to know," Emma said.

"I guess if I ever need a job that will give me more to choose from."

"You should think about taking some college courses," Emma said.

"I have thought about that since meeting all of you."

"Well, we're all here for you if you have any questions."

"Thank you, I appreciate that."

"Hey, Chelsea, can you come up front for a minute?" Eric calls out from the entrance to the server station.

"Sure," I said as I follow him up front.

"How did it go with Miss Jane?"

"The training went fine but both Miss Jane and Paula questioned why I was training. They're concerned about their jobs, and I can understand that. I explained what was going on; I do not want to have a problem with anyone."

"Do not worry about that right now. Listen, bartender training is going to take more time, so I thought we would start by having you come in early on Saturday and Sunday. Is one o'clock, ok?"

"Sure, that's fine."

"Ok great, and I have some VCR management tapes for you to watch and a book on wines that would be nice to add to your resume."

"Ok, thank you."

"Great, I will bring them in for you. Let's go get the specials up."

Eric goes over the specials and after we all dig in we head out to our stations. The shift is moving along nicely when my pen runs out of ink. Since I do not have my usual spare in my apron, I zip into the kitchen to get one out of my purse. I reach up and grab my purse out of the middle-divided section of the wood shelf where we all keep our purses. As I grab the strap, I put my other hand out to catch the bottom of my purse as it drops down. When I catch it, the bottom of my purse is wet.

"Why is my purse wet?" I said aloud not expecting an answer and not giving any thought that there is no water anywhere near the shelf. I open my purse, pull out a pen, dry off the bottom and toss it up into a different hole. As I look up, I see Paula is watching me and without saying a word she quickly turns her head back to the line. Obviously, she is still upset about me training earlier and is giving me the cold shoulder.

I do not know what else to do to convince her I am not after her job. I guess she will see that in time, I think to myself. I walk out of the kitchen wondering how long that will be, as I am just as upset about the situation as she is.

By the time Saturday rolls around I am too nervous about bartender training to worry about Paula. John gives me a boost of confidence when he assures me that I can do this in his pep talk before he leaves for work.

It is going to be a long day, so I relax and watch TV until it is time for work. The bartenders wear a tuxedo shirt, black vest, and bow tie with black pants which I have all ironed. As I dress, I decide to put a little lipstick on, and I grab my server shirt to change into later.

I arrive at work on time, punch in and head to the bar. Eric arranged for me to train with Audrey, an attractive woman in her mid-thirties with short dark hair and brown eyes. I am happy to be training with her, I know from when I have talked to her at shift change that she is patient and kind.

"Hi, Audrey, how are you?"

"I'm good and you? Are you ready for bartender training?"

"Yes, I'm ready."

"Ok great. Since we are open, I already have the bar set up, but I will go over that with you."

"Ok great."

"Starting from the ice bin here are all the well liquors, mixers, garnish, and soda gun. Next is the call brands, glass ware, shaker, strainer, and glass washer. The reach in cooler here has all the beer; this shelf has all the top shelf liquors and cordials, the fridge down here has the champagne and white wines, and the reds are above it on the counter. The beer cooler is at that end and the backup liquor is in this locked cabinet. You must sign and date what you take on this list," she said pointing to the cooler, cabinet, and list.

"The sink set up is soap, rinse and sanitizer. Here are the tablets. Put a new tablet in the water each time you change it. The micros are the same as those that you use for the food orders, and the bank is two hundred dollars. The tap beer is here. If the keg kicks let Eric or Tony in the kitchen know and they will change it for you. If you are ok with all of that I want to concentrate on drink recipes."

"I'm ok with all of that."

"Ok good. You know what kind of glasses the different drinks go in so that is good. I made you index cards of the basic drinks: Martini, Manhattan, whiskey Sour, old fashioned, margarita and daiquiri. Those you should get to know by heart. If you cannot remember or get a request for a drink you do not know here is the Mr. Boston Bartender's Guide," she said while holding up the red and black book.

"Ok," I said thinking I know we have that book at home.

"I also made index cards for drinks indicative of New Orleans: a hurricane, Pimm's cup, brandy milk punch, Ramos gin fizz, mint julep, Sazerac and an Absinthe frappe. Tourists like to try these drinks."

"Thank you very much," I said as she hands me the detailed cards.

"Oh, I forgot to show you the regular and spicy bloody Mary mix are kept in here and are both marked," she said as she opens the reach in near the well.

The micros shot out a drink order, and Audrey shows me how to make a frozen daiquiri. As I am pouring it into a tall glass, I see Julia the daytime hostess approaching the bar.

"I'll take care of her," Audrey whispers to me.

"Ok," I said as I move out of her way.

"Hey, how are you doing?" Julia said to Audrey.

"Good, about time you came back here to say hello. Do you want a Coke?" Audrey said with a smile.

"Yes please, sorry but the wicked witch of the south is on the war path upfront," she said referring to Maria the day manager with a laugh and a wink.

"Ok, I forgive you," Audrey said as she puts a couple of cherries on top of her Coke.

"Thank you," Julia said as she takes a sip.

"You're very welcome."

"Hey Chelsea, how's it going?" Julia said, turning her attention to me.

"So far, so good."

"Good luck," she said as she walks away.

"Oh God, look at those eyes, those lips not to mention her breasts, I could get lost in those breasts," Audrey whispers to me as Julia walks away.

"If you like her so much, why don't you ask her out?"

"Well, first of all she's straight and she just broke up with her boyfriend."

"So, people go both ways, and she was definitely flirting with you."

"No, she was not; she was only being friendly. Look at her blonde hair, blue eyes, big, beautiful breasts. Why would she be interested in me? Not to mention I am about ten years older than her."

"Well, to begin with you are an attractive woman yourself, and ten years is not that big of a deal. I am telling you she was flirting with you. She does not talk to the rest of us girls like that."

"You really think she's interested?"

"Yes, I do, and I think you should ask her out. What's the worst that can happen?"

"You're right; what have I got to lose?"

"Exactly, I think it's going to work out better than you think."

We spend the rest of the shift making drinks, restocking the bar, and browsing through the bartender's guide. Eric comes in and has me take a break and get something to eat before the dinner shift.

"Thanks for everything, Audrey," I said at the end of the shift.

"You're welcome; you did good. You will get more confident as you make more drinks. I'll see you tomorrow," she said with a smile.

"See you same time tomorrow," I said as I head to the rest room to change my shirt.

The dinner shift is busy which makes it go by fast; I am glad because it has been a long day. Eric lets me go home a little early. I am happy to get home, have a glass of wine, shower and put my feet up while I study the cards that Audrey made for me.

Sunday's bar shift goes great. I get to make a bunch of different drinks since people like to have cocktails with Sunday brunch. Audrey is a great trainer and I feel confident by the end of the shift. She is happy because she took my advice and asked Julia out and she said yes; they have a date on Monday.

On Monday I get up early to go shopping with Gina. We had made plans over the weekend, and I am meeting her at the shops at Canal Place. As I leave the house, I smell the sweet fragrance of the magnolias that are in bloom this time of year. I admire the lovely pink flowers of the one in our yard. I head out to Canal Place and find Gina already there when I arrive. We greet each other with a kiss.

"Hi, how are you?" she said with a big smile.

"Great. How are you?"

"Ready to shop!" she said with a laugh.

We walk a bit and window shop when Gina sees a sweater on a mannequin in a window and stops to admire it.

"Oh, that's beautiful. Let's go in here."

"Ok," I said as I follow her inside.

The sweater she likes is on a rack right in front of the doors. It is a long-sleeved V-neck sweater with four assorted colors in patches on the front.

"Oh, I love it," Gina said as she takes the sweater off the rack and holds it up to herself.

"It's beautiful," I said.

"I'm going to try it on," she said as she looks at the price.

I see the price is $150 and think to myself that is an expensive sweater. I follow her to the dressing room, and she quickly comes out of the room with the sweater on to show me.

"I love it. What do you think?" she said as she admires herself in the mirror outside of the dressing rooms.

"It's beautiful and it looks great on you."

"I can wear it with several different pants. I must have it."

"Should I tell Eric about it tonight so he can get it for you for an upcoming occasion?"

"I'm not waiting for an occasion," she said. "I will tell him I want it tonight and I will have this sweater by tomorrow."

"You are so spoiled; I hope you know how lucky you are."

"Yes, I know. I cannot wait to wear it out. Oh, I can wear it to work next Monday!" she exclaims with a smile.

Just as she said that it hit me; in all the time we have known each other I have not seen her in the same outfit twice. That is when I realize she is a clothes horse. Well, nothing wrong with that. Although $150 is still too much money for a sweater, especially when you live in the south. But I have no doubt she will have that sweater by tomorrow.

We look around in a couple of other shops and I buy a blouse. We decide to skip lunch and stop to have coffee. As I pay for the coffees, I see a bowl of chocolate mints on the counter with a sign that says "Lagniappe."

"What does that mean?" I ask the girl behind the counter as I point to the sign.

"Lagniappe means something extra, something free."

"Oh, how nice, thank you," I said as I take a mint for Gina and myself while thinking here is another unique New Orleans saying.

"You're welcome," she said, and I join Gina to enjoy our coffee before heading to work.

"Hello. Did you two enjoy your shopping excursion?" Eric said as he gives Gina a kiss.

"Oh yes. I found the most beautiful sweater," Gina said with a smile.

"Oh boy, how much is that going to cost me?"

"It's $150 but I can wear it with so many things," Gina said as she rubs her hands on his chest and smiles at him.

"Ok, we will get it tomorrow."

"Oh, thank you, thank you," she said as she kisses him all over his face.

I can see how he loves to make her happy as his whole face lights up when she smiles at him.

"What did you get, Chelsea?" Eric asks.

"I got a blouse that did not cost $150," I said with a chuckle and they both laugh.

"We had coffee but skipped lunch and I am starving," Gina said.

"Well, I can make you dinner right away if you like."

"That would be great. Thank you," Gina said.

"Coming right up," Eric said as he heads to the kitchen.

"Let's punch in," I said to Gina as we head to the kitchen and punch in.

"Hello, everyone," I call out to the girls.

"Hello, Chelsea. Hello, Gina," the girls call out.

When we get back up-front Gina cashes out the drawer as I check the specials board and menus. I am just finishing when Preston walks in.

Preston is from England and is in the United States on a month-long vacation. He came into the bar one night and hit it off with Eric and has been hanging out with Eric and his friends ever since. He joins them when they come in for dinner and playfully flirts with me when I see him. He is at least six-foot eight, incredibly built with a broad chest, shoulders, muscular arms, and thighs. He has short brown hair, big brown eyes, and a nice smile. He is a friendly, lovable character and has fit right in with our group.

He playfully moves back and forth in front of me until he reaches me then he put his hands, on each side of my waist and picks me up and extends his arms above his head.

"Arg," Preston jokes as he easily lifts me up.

"Put me down," I said laughing as he sets me down and plants a big kiss on my cheek.

"Hello, sexy."

"Hello, Preston. Would you like a table?"

"No, not yet. Thank you, I am going to have a drink at the bar first."

"Ok enjoy."

"See you later," he said as he heads to the bar.

"Here's your dinner, ladies; honey garlic grilled salmon with sautéed zucchini and squash," Eric said as he put our plates on the table.

"Oh, my, that looks wonderful," Gina said.

"Yes, it does. Thank you, Eric," I said as I look at my plate.

"You're welcome. Enjoy."

"Preston is here; he's in the bar," I said.

"I heard him come in. I will go and say hello when you are done eating."

Eric works the front while we eat our dinner, then heads to the bar to see Preston when we finish eating. I can hear Preston laughing as he greets Eric as I head to the bar to get a coke.

"Hey, Chelsea. Eric and I are going out for a drink after work. Do you want to join us?" Preston said with a smile.

"No, I can't. Thank you anyway. I am meeting John after work," I said seeing the disappointment on his face.

I head to Igor's after work to meet John. A great local bar on St. Charles Avenue, it is open twenty-four hours and has a laundromat in the back.

I am glad he is already at the bar when I arrive, and I walk over to him as he pulls out a stool for me.

"Hey, have you been here long?" I said as I give him a kiss.

"No, I just got here. What would you like to drink?"

"Umm, I think I will have a white wine."

"Ok, let me get the bartender's attention."

"How was work?"

"Ok busy. How was shopping today?" he said as he orders a glass of wine for me from the bartender.

"It was fun. I got a blouse."

"That's nice. I am glad you and Gina got to go out together. I like her and Eric."

"Yes, so do I."

"What do you think of their friend Mr. Anal retentive?" John said with a chuckle.

"What, who is that?" I ask.

"Their friend, Adam."

"Oh, why did you call him that?"

"He seems a bit obsessive about his attention to detail."

"That's actually not a terrible thing."

"No, it's not. I just noticed that about him and that name came to mind."

"Oh well, I think he's nice and he's very polite."

"Yes, he is. He just strikes me as odd, that's all."

"Maybe he thinks we're odd," I said with a laugh.

"Hell, I am odd," John said with a laugh.

I wake up Wednesday morning not feeling well at all. I have a sore throat, stuffy nose, body aches and I feel like I have a fever. Damn it, I was fine all day yesterday. Where is this coming from? Maybe if I take something and have a cup of tea I will feel better in a little while. I look through the medicine cabinet for Tylenol and head to the kitchen to make some tea.

"Good morning," I said to John as I enter the kitchen.

"Good morning. You don't sound too good."

"I don't feel too good."

"Let me make you some tea. You feel warm I think you have a fever," John said as he put his hand to my forehead.

"I feel like I have a fever; I just took Tylenol. I am going to have a cup of tea and go back to bed."

"Why don't you go lie on the couch while I make you a cup of tea."

"Ok thank you," I said as I get on the couch and pull the afghan over me as John makes me a cup of tea.

"Here's your tea. Would you like toast or something to eat?"

"No thank you. The tea is all I need right now," I said as I take a sip.

"You seemed fine all day yesterday."

"I was I didn't feel sick until this morning."

"Well, good thing you are off and have nothing to do and you can go back to bed."

"Yeah, good thing."

"I am going to make myself breakfast and get ready for work. Are you ok?"

"Yes, I am going to drink this and lie down; wake me before you leave, ok?"

"Ok."

"I'm going to work. Can I get you anything before I go?" John said as I open my eyes.

"No thank you. Have a good day."

"You, too. I hope you feel better."

"Thank you. See you tonight, I love you."

"I love you too," he said as he walks out of the bedroom.

I decide to take a shower hoping that will make me feel better. After which I realize, I am not going to feel well enough by this afternoon to see Adam, so I call him to cancel.

"Hello."

"Hi, it's Chelsea."

"Hello, Chelsea. You do not sound good."

"I do not feel good. I have a stuffy nose, sore throat, and a fever. Unfortunately, I am going to have to cancel today."

"Oh, I am sorry to hear that. Did John go to work?"

"Yes."

"Let me pick you up and bring you here so I can take care of you today."

"Oh, that would be nice."

"I will be there in a half an hour. You take care."

"Ok, see you then," I said as we both hang up the phone.

I change into a pair of sweats pants, a comfortable oversized T-shirt, socks, and sneakers. I comb my hair but do not bother with any make up. I am at the door in exactly half an hour just as Adam pulls up. As I walk slowly down the steps Adam gets out of the car and comes around to the passenger side and opens the door for me.

"Oh, I am so sorry you are sick. Are you cold? I brought you a blanket," he said as I get into the car.

"Thank you."

"Would you like me to put the seat back?" he said as he covers me with the blanket.

"No that's ok," I said as I close my eyes.

"Well, we will be at my house soon and I will make you nice and comfortable."

"That sounds great."

When we arrive at his house, he helps me get out of the car and wraps the blanket around me.

"You definitely have a fever," he said as he feels my forehead with the back of his hand.

I am pleased to see when we get into the living room that he has the sofa bed out and all kinds of medicine and a thermometer on the coffee table.

"Ok, let's get you into bed and take your temperature," he said while helping me into bed.

"Open your mouth and let me put this under your tongue," he said as I open my mouth and lift my tongue. He glances at his watch as he puts the thermometer under my tongue. He tucks the covers around me as he waits to check my temperature.

"Ok, that's three minutes; let's see what we got," he said as he takes the thermometer out of my mouth and looks at it.

"101.8, no wonder you do not feel good. Let me get you the NyQuil and a cool washcloth for your head," he said as he pours the NyQuil onto a spoon and brings it to my mouth.

"Thank you," I said as I take the medicine.

He goes to the kitchen and is back in a moment with a glass of water and a cool washcloth.

"Would you like a sip of water?"

"Yes please," I said as I take a sip of the water as he holds the cup to my lips.

"Thank you," I said as I lie back down, as he puts the cool cloth on my forehead.

"Let me put some Vick's on your chest," he said as he sits next to me on the bed and pulls the covers back and pushes my shirt up. I close my eyes as he rubs the ointment on my chest, pulls my shirt down and covers me up again.

"Can I get you anything else? Are you hungry?"

"No, I'm not hungry, but do you have any Visine? My eyes are burning?"

"Yes, I will be right back," he said. He returns in a moment, as I start to sit up to take the bottle from him.

"Lie down and close your eyes."

I lie back down; close my eyes and he gently pulls my eyelid open and squeezes the drops in one eye and then the other.

"Thank you," I said feeling the effect of the NyQuil as I drift off to sleep.

"Chelsea, wake up. It's time for lunch," I hear Adam say and as I open my eyes, I see he has a tray of food.

He sets the tray on the coffee table as I sit up. He props a pillow behind me, and I notice there is a movie on the TV.

"I made you some chicken noodle soup, dry toast and some tea," he said as he put the tray over my lap.

"Thank you," I said as he put a linen napkin over my chest.

"You're welcome. Try to eat as much as you can."

"Ok, aren't you having lunch?"

"I had lunch before I woke you up."

"Oh," I said as I sip the tea.

I eat half of my lunch and Adam takes the tray as I lie back down and drift off to sleep again. At five O'clock Adam wakes me up to give me more NyQuil and I go back to sleep.

"Wake up, Chelsea; I want you to eat some dinner before I have to take you home," he said as I sit up and Adam props a pillow behind me.

"How do you feel?"

"A little better."

"Good. Let me take your temperature before you eat; hopefully it has come down," he said as I open my mouth as he put the thermometer under my tongue and checks his watch for the time.

"Ok, that's three minutes," he said as he takes the thermometer out of my mouth and holds it up to his eyes.

"Oh good, it's 99.2; that's much better. Now let me get your dinner tray," he said as he goes to the kitchen and returns with a tray.

"Soup, tea and toast," he said as he set the tray over my lap and put the napkin across my chest.

"Thank you. It looks good; I'm a little hungry."

"That's a good sign."

"Did you eat dinner?"

"Yes, I ate earlier."

"What time is it?"

"It is eight o'clock, I will take you home after you eat. You will be home by nine."

"Ok great, thank you," I said as I start to eat.

I eat all my dinner and Adam clears the tray as I get up to put my sneakers on and go to the bathroom. Adam stands as I enter the room.

"Are you ready to go?" he said as he reaches for the blanket.

"Yes," I said as we head to the door.

Adam opens the car door, helps me in and covers me up.

"Thank you."

"You're welcome."

"Well, I hope you are all better when you wake up tomorrow."

"I hope so too. I already feel much better than I did this morning. Thank you for everything today."

"You're welcome. I am glad I got to take care of you," he said as we head to my house.

When we arrive at my house, Adam helps me out of the car and walks me to the door.

"Thanks again for everything," I said as I unlock the door.

"You're welcome. Call me tomorrow and let me know how you are feeling," he said as he kisses the top of my head once we are in the house.

"Go to bed and get some rest," he said as he shut the door behind him. I head to the bedroom, kick off my shoes, climb into bed and drift off to sleep.

Chapter 10

"**L**et's go, Chelsea, I want to be there before the gates open at eleven o'clock," John calls out to me as I finish dressing for Jazz Fest.

"Ok, I'm hurrying," I said as I put my sneakers on, and grab a hat and a pair of sunglasses.

"I am so happy we both got the day off so we could go together," John said.

"So am I. I have been looking forward to this since Eric told me about it a couple of weeks ago when we were at French Quarter Fest."

"I think today is going to be the best day of the festival."

"It's probably going to be the busiest since it's the last day," I said as I pick up my purse as we go out the door and head to the fairgrounds.

"Let's go right over and listen to Dr. John before we get some lunch," John said as soon as we go through the gate.

"Ok with me," I said as we hustle to get to the tent where he is playing.

We get there just as he comes on and the crowd cheers as he starts to play "Right Place Wrong Time" and people sing along as they dance.

"He is great," I said as I dance to the music.

"Yes, he is," John said.

It is a beautiful day to be outside and everyone is enjoying the music. People are laying in the sun on blankets and families are picnicking as they listen to the music.

Dr. John is only on his third song when John lets me know he wants to eat lunch. We pass craft booths on our way to the food stands, where local artists have beautiful clothing, jewelry, paintings, and pottery for sale. I look forward to checking these booths out later I think to myself.

We get to the food area. I cannot believe the choices of food. If you are looking for a hot dog or a hamburger you are in the wrong place. True to New Orleans culture the menu consists of crawfish beignets, alligator sausage or soft-shell crab po-boy, oysters, crawfish, red beans and rice, jambalaya and muffulettas. This is a perfect place to try something different, and I decide on an alligator po-boy and John gets the jambalaya.

"Well, do you like it?" John asks after I take a bite.

"Yes, it tastes just like sausage. It's just not as tender."

"I knew you would like it."

"Who's on next?" I ask.

"I'm not sure. Let's walk around after lunch and find out."

We finish lunch and walk back to the music stages and come upon Marcia Ball playing piano and singing the blues. I get into the groove of her music and am dancing and feeling good.

"I'm ready to go. It's crowded, hot and I have seen enough," John said.

"We haven't even been here that long," I cry.

"It is just going to be the same thing, a crowd of people dancing around to the music. I would rather be at home on the couch drinking a beer."

I don't bother to try to get him to stay because he will just be unhappy, and I will not enjoy myself. So, sadly, we go home.

The next morning after John leaves for work I decide to go to Victoria Secret, to get something special to wear for Adam on Wednesday. Since it is Monday and I am the hostess today, I dress for work so I can go there directly from the mall.

I stop outside the store to look at a red teddy the mannequin is wearing in the window. The backless red lace G-string teddy has a plunging V-neck. A thin G-string goes up between the butt cheeks that connects to a band at the lower back that connects to the straps from the side. That looks perfect I think to myself; I am going to try that on. I am about to walk in when I hear someone call out my name and I turn to see who it is.

"Chelsea, Chelsea."

"Oh, hi Rich. How are you?"

"Good, how are you?"

"Good, just doing a little shopping."

"I'm glad I ran into you. Are you going in here?" he said, pointing to the door.

"Yes I am."

"Can I come with you?"

"What?"

"Sorry, what I meant to say is can you help me pick something out in here for Emma?"

"Oh, sure," I said with a chuckle.

"Great, thank you," he said as he follows me into the store.

"Ok, what do you have in mind?"

"I don't know. What do you think?" he said obviously feeling uncomfortable in these surroundings.

"Well, how about this one?" I said as I show him the same teddy, I was looking at it in the window outside the store but in black.

"That's nice. I like that," he said touching the material.

"Would you like to get her something else?"

"Yes," he said as he looked around.

"Ok, how about this?" I said holding up a sexy bra and pantie garter belt outfit that comes in a variety of colors.

"Oh, you think I should get her two risqué items?"

"Um yeah; what do you have in mind?"

"Well, I don't want to seem so, um, you know."

"Rich, you are giving her lingerie. What do you think that means? If you want to get her a pretty silk night gown for everyday wear, there are a selection hanging over here," I said pointing to the short night gowns.

"Which I promise you she already has; this relationship is still new. I think you should get her special occasion lingerie that no one else has seen her in." The look on his face lets me know that line was all he needed to hear.

"If you want, get the bra and pantie set in white with the pink garters and flowers. I promise you she will love both choices and after you get her out of them, they will look great on the floor," I said laughing.

"Ok, you're right. I will get these two."

"Good, I promise you're making the right decision," I said as I check that they are in Emma's size.

"Thank you, I'm glad I ran into you," he said as he carries the items to the register.

"You're welcome. Enjoy," I said with a smile.

I go back up front, get the red teddy and look for the dressing room. I hope Adam likes it I think to myself as I admire myself in the mirror. I start to get excited as I think about him. I better get out of here I think to myself as I dress and go up to the register to pay. I also buy a couple of pairs of silk panties that are on sale. I leave the store happy with my purchases and looking forward to Wednesday.

"Hi, Gina, nice sweater," I said as I walk into the restaurant.

"Hello, thank you it's a light sweater so I can still wear it. Doesn't it go perfect with these teal pants?"

"Yes, they match the teal in the sweater perfectly," I said with a smile.

"What are you up to?" she said laughing.

"Nothing, just lingerie shopping for Wednesday," I said.

"Good for you. Adam will like that."

"Well, if it isn't Wednesday's Girl," Eric said as he approaches the hostess station.

"Hi, Eric, how are you?"

"Good, did you enjoy Jazz Fest?"

"Yes, I wish we had stayed longer. John wanted to leave shortly after we got there."

"Oh, sorry to hear that. Next year you can come with us."

"Sounds good to me."

I punch in, say hello to the girls, check the specials and organize the menus. Henry walks in just as Gina and I finish our dinner.

"I'm done, Eric," I said as I get up from the table, grab a menu and seat Henry. As I return to the hostess station Preston and a young pretty woman are walking into the restaurant and Eric seats them in the station near the register.

"Tell Ashley I am cooking for them, and I will let her know what to charge for their meal," Eric said as he heads towards the kitchen.

"Ok, I will."

"Hey, Ashley, Eric is cooking for Preston and his date. He will let you know what to charge for the meal. Just get a drink order for now," I said when Ashley came back from the bar.

"Ok, thanks," she said.

"Hey, Chelsea," Preston calls out as I walk by his table.

"Is everything ok?" I said noting his date had just gone to the restroom.

"Yes, did you see my date?"

"Yes, she's lovely. Is she alright?"

"Yes, I just want you to know that young lady came on my tongue several times last night."

"Well, good for her," I said blushing as I walked away.

I turn to the hostess station and see Adam standing there staring at Preston and he does not look happy.

"Hi, I am so happy to see you. I was thinking about you today," I said with a big smile.

"I was thinking of you as well," Adam said, his face softening as he turned to me.

"Did you enjoy Jazz Fest?" he asks.

"Yes, it was nice."

"I came to see Eric for a minute."

"He's in the kitchen."

"Ok thank you. If I do not see you before I leave, enjoy your day off tomorrow and I will see you Wednesday."

"Yes, I will see you Wednesday," I said with a big smile on my face, as I think about the red teddy as I watch him walk away.

"What did he just say to you?" Gina said.

"See you Wednesday; why?"

"Because you are blushing," she said with a smile.

"Good thing you can't read my mind," I said as visions of a red teddy dance in my head.

"I hope you enjoy yourself."

"I'm sure I will," I said smiling.

I see that John is already out of bed when I wake up. I hear a noise coming from the kitchen, and I head to the kitchen to join him.

"Good morning."

"Good morning, sweetie," he said as he leans in and kisses my lips.

"Have you been up long?"

"No, not long. Would you like a coffee?"

"Yes please. What do you want to do today?" I ask as he fixes me a cup of coffee.

"I was thinking we could go to the Audubon Zoo; would you like to do that?"

"Are we going to be there longer than a half an hour?"

"Very funny. I am sorry; it was boring just standing there. I promise to stay at the zoo for as long as you want today."

"Ok, then yes I would love to go to the zoo."

"Great; we'll eat breakfast and get ready to go."

"Sounds great. It looks like a lovely day. Let's take the streetcar."

"Ok with me," he said as he starts to make our eggs.

We walk the few blocks to St. Charles Avenue and board the

streetcar. It is almost full; luckily, we get a seat. We enjoy the scenery as we hear the clang of the trolley and the driver ringing the bell as cars approach. Stopping as people pull the cable making it buzz to alert the driver, they want to get off. The streetcar is standing room only when a little old lady comes aboard. She is not on long enough to reach for a strap to hold onto when everyone in the front of the streetcar gets up and offers her their seats. I smile as I think, chivalry is alive and well in the south.

New Orleans may be famous for its history, culture, music, art, and cuisine but its real treasure is its people. Young or old, rich, or poor, black, or white, they greet you on the street, respect their elders and welcome you in with southern hospitality that makes you feel at home. I laugh when I think how nervous I was when I first moved here. Now I am in love with the people, culture and everything that makes New Orleans the unique and charming city that it is.

"Audubon Park," the driver calls out.

"Thank you," we both say as we exit the trolley.

"Have a wonderful day," the friendly driver says as we step off.

Audubon Park is 350 acres and is full of graceful old oaks adorned with moss, a golf course, picnic areas and a bike path that leads to the zoo. We enjoy the beauty of the park as we take the path that leads to the zoo.

"Hey, Chelsea, if we get a yearly membership it would pay for itself in two visits," John said when we arrive at the gate.

"Oh, that sounds like a good deal."

"We can come in the morning before work and walk when it is cooler. We wouldn't have to spend the entire day to get our money's worth. We can visit one section each time we come and, on our day off, if we want to spend the entire day we can. Do you want to do that?"

"Yes, that's a great idea," I said thinking I will end up going alone.

We get our membership cards and enter the zoo. There is a pond with a fountain and sculptures of an elephant and lion at the entrance with lily pads that are in bloom. Artists are sketching the statues as balloonists make animal shaped balloons for children going by. It is a lovely 78 degrees, and I am eager to see the animals, especially the white tiger and the white alligators that are a new attraction to the zoo.

As we begin to explore the zoo, we come upon a beautiful statue of a women that touches me. She is nude except for a towel draped from her arm that wraps around her waist just covering her private parts. Her other arm extends in the air holding a bow exposing her small breasts. Her head is looking upwards, her eyes are looking at the bow, her lips are slightly parted, and curls hang around her head above her neck.

Her arm with the towel draped over it bends at her elbow, and her hand is open just beside her shoulder. Her back arches as she extends her arm, and you can just see the top of the crack of her buttocks from above the towel. One foot is on a ball as the other is in the air behind her. There is a dog at her feet; it is on its hind paws, and its front paws are in the air. Its head is looking up towards the bow as its tongue hangs out.

She is beautiful, graceful, and poised and I am immediately taken by her. My eyes travel to the base she is standing on. "Diana," I whisper reading the name engraved on the plaque.

"Are you ready to go?" John said, breaking my concentration.

"Isn't she beautiful?"

"She's all right. Good thing we are members now so you can see her anytime you want. Come on, time to see the animals."

"Ok," I said as I tear myself away from her.

We walk towards the area where the rare white tiger is. He is lying in the center of his habitat; he gets up and walks to the edge of the grassy area that touches the water as we are looking at him.

"Oh, look honey. He came to greet us."

"More like he's thinking of lunch," John said with a laugh.

"Hello, Suri. I've never seen a white tiger before, and you are gorgeous," I said to the tiger after I read his name off the plaque in front of his exhibit.

"Yeah, he is something," John said as we both stood there and admire him.

We enjoy the bear, elephants, and other animals in this area before heading over to see the primates. We enter the primate section and walk into a small, enclosed area between two trees.

There is a small glass enclosed area full of small plants, flowers, and branches. I look at the sign and photo to see what is in this enclosure, a golden lion tamarin. It only takes me a moment before I spot the little monkey; its bright orange mane and face looks just like a lion.

"He is fabulous. I've never seen anything like him before," I said giggling as the monkey hops around and stops in front of me and tilts its head as if it is looking at me.

"Well, I am so glad you are enjoying the zoo," John said.

"Yeah, this was a great idea."

"Ok, let's go see the gorillas next."

"Ok, lead the way."

We see the gorillas and then the sealion exhibit, before going to see the zebras, rhino, and giraffes in their natural habitats. I am in awe of the beauty of the zoo and its natural animal habitats.

As we head to the Louisiana swamp exhibit, we come upon Monkey Hill. Monkey Hill is the highest point of New Orleans, being about thirty feet above sea level. A plaque on top of the hill reads, "Dedicated to the children of New Orleans."

"Well, see that we learned some more New Orleans history," I said.

"Yeah, that's cool."

"Ok, next up is the swamp," I said leading the way.

The swamp is an actual Louisiana swamp with alligators, blue herons, turtles, and frogs. It is full of cypress trees and cypress knees. There is a shack and rowboat on display on the side of the swamp.

The highlight of the exhibit is the white alligators. The seventeen hatchlings were discovered in a nearby swamp and brought to the zoo.

"Look how cute these little alligators are, John," I said as I point my finger at the alligators in the exhibit as they climb on top of each other in front of the glass.

"Just think how cool it's going to be to come here on a regular basis and watch them grow," John said while smiling at me.

"That's going to be fun to watch," I said as we step away from the glass giving the next group of people a chance to see them up close.

Just outside of the swamp exhibit is a stand selling lemonade. The young girl who is working at the stand is singing along to a song on the radio. "They All Ask'd for You" a song about the Audubon Zoo.

"That's a cute song you are singing," I said as she put the lemonades on the counter.

"Oh, I didn't realize I was singing aloud," she said blushing.

"Well, you have a lovely voice," John said as he paid for the drinks.

"Thank you."

"Well, next I would like to see the flamingos and the macaw."

"Ok, let's go," John said as we head over to the flamingo exhibit and then on to the macaw.

"I love this bird. It reminds me of Dr Doolittle," I said referring to the big red, yellow, and blue bird.

"Polly wants a cracker?" John said in a funny voice to the bird.

"Oh look, there is a blue one also," I said pointing to the other macaw in the exhibit.

"Wow, that one is beautiful."

"Yes, it is," I exclaim as I kiss him on the lips.

We walk around a while longer looking at the animals, statues, and oak trees. We come upon two magnificent old oak trees with large branches hanging down and stretching across the ground.

"These trees are incredible, thank you for a lovely day. I love you," I said as we walked out of the park.

"Thank you for a lovely day. I love you too," he said taking my hand.

The next day I am at the door at exactly one o'clock when Adam pulls up. I skip down the steps and hop into his car.

"Hello, how are you?" Adams asks as I get into the car.

"I'm great. How are you?"

"Feeling good. How was your day off?"

"Great. We went to the zoo and had a wonderful time. I am happy that we got a membership and can go any time. What did you do this week?"

"Well, the other day Joel invited Eric and me to his house.

Do you remember him; he was at Eric and Gina's house when we first met?"

"Yes, I know who you're talking about. He comes in the restaurant when Eric's friends come in for dinner occasionally."

"Well, he has been seeing a young girl named Monica; she is about eighteen or nineteen years old. He convinced her that if she loves him, she will sleep with his friends."

"Wait a minute, don't get any ideas of me doing that," I said in a stern tone.

"Trust me I have no such idea; that is not the purpose of this story. So, he invited five of us over there the other day to sleep with her."

"She agreed to do that, and you and Eric slept with her?"

"I assume she agreed since we were all there, and, no, Eric and I did not sleep with her; we left. But Preston was there and two of Joel's other friends stayed and I heard later they all got drunk and each of them had sex with her."

"That's terrible. Why would he ask her to do that?"

"Well, he did not want to see her anymore. So, he figured he would get her to sleep with his friends before he dumped her. She did not know that part of course."

"That poor girl. That's awful."

"You met her actually."

"Oh, I don't recall him bringing any girl to dinner."

"She was the young girl having dinner with Preston the other night. I guess since Joel dumped her, Preston plans to sleep with her while he is still here."

"Oh," I said, realizing the purpose of the story.

When we get to his house, I see the sofa bed is open and there is a movie case on the coffee table. I sit on the end of the bed as Adam fixes us a drink.

"Here you go," he said as he hands me a drink.

"Thank you," I said as I reach for the drink and take a sip.

"I thought we could relax and watch a movie," he said as he lights up a joint and passes it to me.

"Sounds good," I said as I see the movie title on the case, *9 1/2 Weeks*. I remember Emma telling me about it and I laugh as I take a hit of the joint and pass it back to him.

"I thought we might enjoy this movie," he said with a smile.

"Let us get comfortable and lie on the bed. Take off all your clothes and jewelry."

"Ok," I said excited for him to see my new red teddy. I take off my jewelry and place it on the table and I take off my clothes and hang them over the chair. I stand still and wait for him to notice me.

"Oh, I like that," he said as he looks up and sees me.

"Oh good, I'm glad. I wanted to surprise you," I said as I turn around so he could see the back.

"Oh, I like that very much."

"I went shopping on Monday. I could hardly contain myself when I saw you at the restaurant."

"What a pleasant surprise."

As we watch the movie, the erotic relationship starts out sensual and fun. But as the male character's desires becomes more demanding, the relationship begins to take a toll on the woman.

"He does too much all the time. He doesn't give enough time in between," Adam said of the male character and his timing of his sexual actions. I look at him concerned by his comment but do not say a word. When clearly the relationship had gotten out of hand.

I leave the teddy on, and I see Adam looking at me during the movie. When the movie ends, he turns to me and runs his hand from my shoulder down my back to my bare bottom. He gently rolls me over and leans over and kisses me. He stops for a moment and moves himself above me spreading my legs apart with his.

"Put your arms over your head with your hands together."

I follow the instructions as he begins to kiss my neck. His mustache tickles me, and I quiver. He looks into my eyes as his knee rubs between my legs. He kisses me and as his tongue enters my mouth, I hungrily swirl my tongue with his as we kiss. He gently pulls away and he slowly kisses down my neck. His lips move down the center of my chest; he moves the teddy aside and exposes my breast. He kisses all around my breast as I arch my back pushing my breast towards his mouth. I want to grab him and pull him to me, but I do not dare move my arms.

His tongue moves slowly around my nipple making me moan as he pushes the G-string between my legs aside and slips his finger inside my wet vagina. The movie's erotic sex scenes have me all hot and bothered and I know it will not take me long to come.

"Oh yes," I moan as I move my pelvis forward as he fingers me. His tongue flicks my already hardened nipple and I moan breathlessly wanting him to take me into his mouth.

"Oh yes, please don't stop," I beg as his mouth devours my nipple; he sucks it with his lips as his tongue swirls around its tip.

His mouth glides to my other breast, and he bites the fabric of the teddy and moves it over my breast. He takes my nipple into his mouth as he fingers my clitoris as my pelvis arches to meet his finger wanting more.

"Don't stop, please don't stop!" I cry out as he moves his mouth from my breast and slips his finger out of me.

He kisses me through the fabric as he moves down my chest

and stomach and over my mound. His face is between my legs, and he slips his tongue into my vagina.

"Oh yes, yes, just like that," I moan aloud as he lightly licks my throbbing clitoris. I push myself up to him and he pushes his tongue deep inside me swirling it around my clitoris. His tongue slowly licks me as I move my bottom up and down to meet him.

"Oh yes, don't stop!" I cry louder and louder as my hands above me bang on the bed and my head shakes from side to side. He holds my hips down with his hands as his tongue franticly licks my swollen clitoris. I cannot move as his tongue thrashes against me.

"Ah, ah, ah, ah, ahhhh." I hear my screams getting louder and louder as I get closer to coming. My orgasm is intensified by the constant force of his tongue on my clitoris as he holds my hips down. I am screaming with pleasure as I explode, and my screams turn to laughter.

He lays next to me for a moment before he moves above me holding himself in place as he looks in my eyes. I lick my lips and take a breath in and slowly exhale as he lowers himself between my legs stopping just outside of me. He pushes his cock against my mound arousing me and I push my pelvis towards him. He makes me wait before he plunges his hard cock deep inside of me.

"Ah," I moan as he enters me. He smiles as he moves in and out of me pushing himself deeper inside me as my hips meet his thrusts. I want to pull him closer to me with my hands, but I do not dare move them from above my head. I throw my head back with pleasure as I moan aloud. Our bodies move together as our pace quickens and I am moaning louder and louder. I spread my legs further apart and push my hips up one last time as we collapse together. I hear him moan as he comes, and I giggle with pleasure.

We lay quietly for a while then he moves next to me and wipes the hair from my forehead. Then he gently squeezes my skin as his hand moves up my arm as he leans on his side and faces me.

"I want you to do something this week."

"Ok."

"I want you to masturbate three times this week, maybe while you are lying in bed, in the shower or watching TV."

"Ok, I can definitely do that," I said giggling.

"BUT DO NOT HAVE AN ORGASM! Bring yourself just to an orgasm each time and then stop. Do you understand?"

"Yes."

"Good, time to take a shower," he said as he kissed my head.

We get into the shower and Adam begins to wash my hair. We move in sync as he washes my face and body. He takes the shower head out of the holder and begins to rinse the soap from my body. I turn around so he can rinse my back and behind, then he puts his arm around me and pulls my body against his and begins to rinse my front. Moving the sprayer from the top of my chest to between my legs. "Oh," I moan when the warm water sprays between my legs.

"You can masturbate with the shower massage this week," he said.

"I don't have a shower massage," I stated.

"You never masturbated with a shower massage before?"

"No, I've never had one and I didn't realize that I could."

"Spread your legs," he said and as I do, he changes the setting of the sprayer, and it pulsates inside me.

"Oh, that feels good."

He pushes the sprayer up and down as the water jets into me. I spread my legs open a little more as he brings the showerhead just outside my vagina changing the speed again, so the water shoots out in one steady jet directly on my clitoris as I push myself down onto the jet moving in rhythm with the water.

"Oh, that feels so good. Please don't stop," I said as I put my head back and rest it on his shoulder as he circles my nipple with his finger squeezing it a little once it is hard.

"Oh, Oh." I begin to moan louder and louder as I move my pelvis back and forth over the shower head. My legs are shaking as the water pulsates inside me. I spread my legs wider as Adam puts the shower head up against my clitoris.

I reach my hands behind me and hold onto him to steady myself and he holds me tighter with his arm as the jets pulsates me to orgasm.

"AH, AH, AH, AH, AH," I moan louder and louder as I shake my head from side to side. I practically collapse when I come and he holds me tighter, so I do not fall as he moves the sprayer from between my legs.

"Are you ok?"

"Yes, my legs are weak," I said with a laugh.

"Are you ok to get out of the shower by yourself?"

"Yes, I think so," I said as he holds his hand out for me to hold as I step out of the shower. As I grab a towel, I start to feel dizzy. I barely make it out the door and onto the bed.

"Are you ok?" Adam said as he comes out of the bathroom and sees me on the bed.

"Yes, I just need a moment. My legs are like Jell-O. I am so getting a shower massage," I said as I start to get up.

"I can't believe you didn't know about that."

"Well, I do now. I may never leave the bathroom," I said laughing.

"I'm glad you enjoyed that," he said with a devilish laugh as we get ready for dinner.

As we are leaving the restaurant after dinner, I see one of the waiters that John works with that I met at the Christmas party. I stop dead in my tracks for a moment. I start walking again not sure if he saw me or not.

"What's wrong?" Adam asks when we are in the car.

"I saw a waiter that John works with walking towards the door to the restaurant. I am not sure if he saw us or not."

"Relax, you are not doing anything wrong. You are just leaving a restaurant; doesn't John think you usually go out on Wednesday night?"

"Yes, but why would I be out with you?" I said nervously.

"First of all, you don't know if he saw us and if John asks you later you can say you were with Gina and Eric, and I tagged along."

"I guess that would make sense."

"Sure, it would and it's not like we were holding hands or anything."

"You're right."

"Chelsea, unless he sees your naked ass going up and down in the pale moonlight, he can't prove a thing and don't you ever confess to anything."

"You're right. It just made me nervous."

"Relax, I bet it never gets mentioned."

I relax and listen to the radio on the way home deciding not to worry about it. I will deal with it just as Adam said if it comes up. When we arrive at my house, I give him a quick peck on the cheek.

"Have a wonderful week," I said.

"You too, I will talk to you soon," he said as I get out of the car. I zip up the steps, unlock the door, turn, and wave as he smiles, waves, then pulls away.

Chapter 11

"Good morning. Did you sleep well?" I said to John as I pour him a cup of coffee.

"Yes, I did. Have you been up long?"

"No, not too long. I was just about to make breakfast."

"I'll make breakfast; I have been craving a Spanish omelet with salsa."

"Oh, that sounds delicious. I'll set the table."

I sit at the table and watch him chop the vegetables for the omelet. As he cooks the omelet, he holds the handle of the pan, jerks the pan, and flips the omelet on to its other side to brown. He puts the omelet on a plate with some fruit, and a side of salsa in a monkey dish.

"Oh, thank you. That looks wonderful."

"You're welcome; hope you enjoy it."

"Yum, it's so good," I said as I took a bite.

"Do you want to ask Gina and Eric to go out to dinner with us this Tuesday to celebrate our anniversary?"

"Yes, that sounds like a great idea. I'll call Gina later and ask her if they want to go."

"I was thinking of going to The Grill Room at the Windsor Court Hotel. I hear it is an excellent restaurant. How does that sound to you?"

"I have never heard of it, but wherever you choose is fine with me."

"Ok, let me know if they're going to join us so I can make a reservation."

"I will," I said as we finish eating breakfast.

John gets ready for work while I clean up. After he leaves, I jump into the shower. My mind drifts off to yesterday as I put soap all over my body. I run my soapy hands over my breasts as I think of Adam. This would be a perfect time to start masturbating I think as my fingers circle my nipples until they are hard. I squeeze them a little then I slide my hands down my stomach, as I rub the lather over my stomach and the top of my thighs.

I rub my soapy hands over my inner thighs and move them up to my vagina as I take the bar of soap and rub it over my mound. I put the soap on the shelf and work the lather into my bush. I back myself up against the wall, spread my legs as I slip a finger into my vagina. I bring my other hand to my breast and circle my nipple with my finger as I put my finger on my clitoris and begin to move my finger in a circular motion as I rock my hips.

"Oh, that feels good," I think as the warm water shoots down onto my body. My finger and thumb squeeze my breast as I finger my clitoris.

"Oh yeah," I moan aloud as my hips move back and forth. My finger moves faster inside me making quick circles as it pushes down harder on my clitoris. My hips are bucking back and forth, and I am moaning aloud; it feels so good. I am so wet I need to stop because I am about to come. Oh, I can't, it feels so good, one more second.

"Oh, Oh, Oh, Oh," I moan as I quiver into orgasm. I giggle as I think well that did not go as planned. Good thing it is early in the week. I will consider that a trial run as I step under the water to rinse the soap from my body.

I dry off and wrap a towel around me, dry my hair, and apply a little make up. I have time before I must dress for work, so I throw on a romper. I go out to the living room and pick up the phone and call Gina.

"Hello."

"Hi, Gina; it's Chelsea. How are you?"

"I'm ok. How are you? I heard you had fun yesterday."

"Does he tell you guys everything?" I said shaking my head.

"Actually, he tells Eric and Eric tells me," She said laughing.

"Well, that makes it so much better."

"I can't believe you didn't know about the shower massage."

"I can't believe it either. First chance I get I am getting one."

"I guess that means you don't know about the tub faucet either."

"No, what about the tub faucet?"

"Well, you put the water on, lie down in the tub and scoot your butt up to the front of the tub, put your legs up against the wall on each side of the faucet and spread your legs so the water runs on your clitoris until you come."

"No, I never heard of that, but I will definitely try it."

"Trust me you will love it. It's almost as good as getting head," Gina said as we both giggled.

"Well, I called to see if you and Eric wanted to join us for our third anniversary dinner on Tuesday night at The Grill Room at the Windsor Court?"

"Oh, that sounds great. Hold on while I check with Eric. I do not know if he has something else planned. Yes, we would love to join you," she said when she got back on the phone.

"Ok great; I will let John know so he can make the reservation."

"Ok, let us know what time. I am going to take a bath, good-bye," she said laughing.

"Goodbye," I said with a laugh, thinking I will have to try that out another time.

I spend the rest of the day catching up on laundry and cleaning until it's time to get ready for work. I walk into work, stop at the podium to check my station, head to the kitchen, punch in and toss my purse up on to the shelf.

"Hey, everyone," I call out.

"Hi, Chelsea," the girls reply. As I walked out of the kitchen, I see Eric.

"Hey, Chelsea. Dinner on Tuesday sounds great; we are looking forward to it. I brought those tapes and books we talked about; get them from me before you leave."

"Ok great, thanks."

"Hello, ladies," I said as I entered the server station.

"Hello," Emma said.

"Hi," Anna said as she waves her hand.

"What's happening?" I ask as I reach for the sugar basket.

"Well, I would like to say thank you for helping Rich shop for my surprise," Emma said with a smile.

"What are you talking about?" Anna said.

"Chelsea helped Rich pick out some lingerie for me at Victoria Secret."

"You're welcome. I'm glad you liked it."

"Oh, I definitely liked it," she said with a big grin.

"Let's go, ladies. The specials are coming up," Sharon said on her way to the kitchen.

We head to the kitchen and Eric goes over the specials. We all grab forks and enjoy a bite of steak au poivre, Cajun catfish and shrimp meuniere.

"I love meuniere sauce," I said taking a bite of the shrimp.

"Me too. It is good!" Emma exclaims.

"Ok, ladies. Get to your stations," Paula said.

We all head out to our stations as the dinner rush starts. The night is going smoothly, and I am thinking about asking the girls if they want to go out for a drink after work. I am on my way to the bar to pick up drinks when I hear a commotion coming from the kitchen as I walk by. I am waiting for my drinks when Eric enters the bar, and he looks pissed.

"What's going on?" I ask.

"Someone stole $235.00 from Sharon's purse tonight," Eric said.

"What? How? Our purses are out in the open."

"I don't know, but I am going to find out," he said sternly.

"I don't know if this has anything to do with it or not, but when I took my purse off the shelf last week it was wet."

"When was that?"

"The day I expedited. Why?"

"Did you say anything to anyone about that?"

"No, I just said aloud why is my purse wet. Not really giving it any thought. Do you think that has something to do with this?" I said as the look on his face made me think he figured it out.

"Was anything missing?"

"No, but if I bring any money to work, I keep it in my apron."

"Who was there when that happened?"

"Actually, just Paula and me. She didn't say anything because she was still mad at me about the expediter thing."

"Don't tell anyone about that, or that you told me."

"Ok, I won't," I said wondering what he is thinking.

"Nothing I hate more than a thief; people shouldn't have to worry about getting robbed at work," he said as he quickly left the bar.

I pick up my drinks and head back out to my station. Everyone is consoling Sharon, and the mood is somber as we all cannot believe this happened.

"I was supposed to deposit that money into the bank today to cover bills. I didn't make it, that's the only reason I had that kind of cash on me," Sharon said crying.

"I don't understand how anyone can do that when our purses are in the kitchen right where everyone can see," Ashley said.

"Are you sure it was in your purse? Maybe, you left it in the car," Emma said.

"Yes, I am sure I saw it in there when I got my pen out," she said sobbing.

I do not say anything as I listen to the conversation as I try to figure out what Eric thinks happened. I give up and go back to work, deciding not to ask the girls to go out for drinks tonight. I get the tapes and book from Eric when I cash out at the end of the night and head home.

I shower and am in the living room watching TV when John gets home. I explain everything that happened at work tonight and he cannot figure it out either.

"No one could go through our purses without someone seeing them do it," I stated.

"It does not make sense given where they are in the kitchen and people coming in and out of there all night. Hopefully, she misplaced the money, and it will turn up."

"I hope so. I don't see any of the girls that work there stealing, but I know Eric thought of something when I was talking to him tonight."

"I guess we will find out eventually."

"I guess we will, by the way, Eric and Gina will be joining us for dinner on Tuesday."

"Ok great, I'll make the reservation tomorrow."

"I'm going to bed; I am drained," I said as I kiss his lips.

"Good night, sweetie, sleep well."

The next morning after John goes off to work, I am about to get into the shower when I hear the phone ring. I grab my robe and run out to the living room to get the phone.

"Hello," I said as I grab the phone while I tie my robe. No one is on the other end, so I hang up. I start to go back to the bathroom when the V.C. Andrews novel *Seeds of Yesterday* that I just started to read catches my eye. I decide to lie on the couch and read a while instead of getting into the shower.

I grab the book, curl up on the couch and start to read. My mind turns to Adam as my hand caresses my breast and I decide Adam is a great fantasy to masturbate to. Although I am facing the window, I am not worried since the window is on the alley side of the house and all I can see is the side of the house next door.

I lay the book on the coffee table and open the belt to my robe. I bring my knees up and spread my legs. I cup my breasts with my hands and circle both nipples with my fingers. They harden from my touch; I slowly move my hands over my stomach and caress my thighs as my legs fall open. I bring my hand to my mound, and I slip a finger inside my vagina and begin to circle my clitoris. I squeeze my nipple with my other hand and moan aloud as I move my hips up and down as my finger moves slowly over my clitoris.

"Oh," I moan as my finger circles faster inside me. I move

my hand to my other nipple, and it hardens from my touch. My finger moves inside my wet vagina as I moan aloud with pleasure.

"Oh, oh, oh," I moan as my head moves from side to side and I moan louder and louder as my legs spread wide open and I buck my hips up and down faster.

"Yes, yes, yes," I moan as I thrust my hips forward one last time as I explode with pleasure.

"Ha, ha, ha." I giggle as I collapse back on the couch and catch my breath.

"Shit, I forgot to stop again."

"Hey, Chelsea, I need to talk to you for a minute," Eric said as I walked in the door for work on Saturday.

"Ok, let me punch in."

"Just wait a minute."

"Ok, what's up?" I said sensing a problem.

"Well, I caught the thieves last night."

"Thieves? Oh, who was it?"

"It was two of the dishwashers. They were grabbing your purses off the shelf on the way into the kitchen, putting them into the bus pan with the dirty dishes and going through them by the dishwasher. Then they would toss them back on the shelf on their way out of the kitchen. That's why your purse was wet that day. I caught them last night and fired them."

"Oh, I am so glad you figured it out. I knew it wasn't any of the girls. Everyone will be relieved to know that."

"That's not all. They could not have pulled it off without Paula seeing them. Whether she was in on it or just looked the other way I do not know. Of course, she denied it and pitched a hissy fit when I fired her today. She blamed you in our conversation, that I was using this as an opportunity to make my friend the expediter."

"That's ridiculous," I said I do not want that job.

"Of course. It is she was just trying to save face and exonerate herself. I just wanted to let you know what she said."

"Well, I don't like being blamed for other people's mistakes," I said as I head to the kitchen to punch in.

Miss Jane is in the kitchen covering the evening and everyone is in good spirits now that the mystery's solved. While I am happy the mystery's solved, I am upset about what Paula said to Eric. After work, the girls all head over to Madigan's for drinks. Since I am still upset about the situation, I skip going out and head home.

I woke up the next morning and see that John is still asleep, so I slip out of bed and head out to the kitchen to make coffee. While it is brewing, I decide what to make for breakfast. I am pulling the eggs, ham, and cheese out of the fridge when John walks in the kitchen.

"Good morning, sweetie. Did you sleep well?"

"Good morning, honey, no I didn't," I said as I lean in to give him a kiss.

"Oh, I'm sorry," he said as he kisses my lips.

"I am going to make ham and cheese omelets. How does that sound to you?"

"I got this; you set the table and fix the coffee," he said as he starts on the omelets.

"Ok sounds good, thank you," I said as I pour two cups of coffee.

We enjoy our breakfast and I clean the kitchen as John showers and dresses for work. After he leaves for work, I go into the bedroom to masturbate knowing I don't have a lot of time before Wednesday when John is not at home. I am determined not to have an orgasm.

I take off all my clothes and lie on top of the bed. I cup my breasts as my fingers circle my nipples until they are hard. I move my hands across my stomach, as I pull my knees up, and I caress my thighs. I slide my right hand between my legs as my left hand moves back up to my breast. I spread my legs as I slide a finger into my vagina as my other hand circles my nipple, and I squeeze it between my fingers.

My finger moves inside me, and I circle my clitoris slowly as my hips move up and down. I am having a tough time getting into it as I try different fantasies in my head. Well, I will not get to orgasm at this rate I think to myself. I move my finger faster inside me to try to make myself more excited. I slide a second finger in and jerk my hand up and down faster over my clitoris as I move my hips up and down.

I realize this is not working and am about to change positions when I have a small uneventful orgasm. "Wow, I did not even feel that coming on," I said out loud. I realize I did not stop again but think it's ok. I am always so excited to see Adam, it will not matter. As I lay in bed I think about Adam, how attentive he is and how great the sex is. At this point I could not give up Adam even if John and I had sex every day. I push my thoughts aside and get ready for work.

I am happy when I get to work and see a new expediter has started and everyone is in a good mood.

"Well now that everything's back to normal around here, how about we go across the street and have a beer afterwork?" Anna said.

"Sounds good to me," Emma calls out.

"I'm in," Ashley said.

"Me too," I said thinking that is just what I need, a night out with the girls.

"Ok ladies, specials are up," Eric calls out as he passes the server station and we all head to the kitchen.

"First of all, this is our new expediter, Denise. Please make her feel welcome and help her as she trains."

"Hi everyone," Denise said with a smile.

"Hi Denise," we all said in unison.

"Now, tonight's specials are creole shrimp over rice with broccoli, barbecue ribs served with coleslaw and sweet and spicy cornbread, and southern fried chicken served with macaroni and cheese and hush puppies. Whoever sells the most specials will get a free drink or appetizer; your choice."

"Oh, this is so good," Ashley said as she tastes the cornbread.

"Yes, it is. Do you plan to win the specials contest?" I ask.

"As a matter of fact, I do. Anyone care to challenge me?" Ashley states.

"You're on," Emma said with a smile.

As I finish dressing for The Grill Room, John calls me into the living room. I am wearing a clingy blue skirt and white V-neck top. I slip on dark blue heels and grab my dark blue evening bag as I head to the living room to join John.

"You look lovely."

"Thank you, so do you," I said admiring his blue suit, white shirt, and blue tie.

"Let's have a toast," he said as he hands me a glass of champagne.

"Thank you," I said as I take the glass.

"To our anniversary and another wonderful year. I love you, Chelsea."

"Happy anniversary, John. I love you too," I said as we ring our glasses.

"For you, my love," he said as he hands me a small box.

"Oh, it's so beautiful, thank you," I said as I open the box and reveal the opal pendant inside.

"You're welcome. Do you like it?"

"Oh yes, I love it," I said as I kiss him on the lips.

"Ok, let me get yours," I said as I walk across the room, retrieve his gift, and hand it to him.

"Thank you, I love them!" he said as he opens the box and sees the pewter beer mugs inside.

"To us," he said as he raises his glass of champagne.

"To us," I said as we ring our glasses.

"Let me help you put this on," John said as he takes the necklace out of the box.

"Thank you. How does it look?" I said after he put it on me.

"Beautiful, just like you," he said as we kiss.

"I love it," I said as I admire it in the mirror on the wall.

We head to the CBD (Central Business District) to the Windsor Court Hotel. Gina and Eric are waiting for us in the lobby just outside The Grill Room. The restaurant lobby has beautiful paintings of subjects who look like royalty and large ornate gold mirrors adorn the walls. The leather Queen Anne chairs, rich wood tables and mauve couches bring out the pattern of the burgundy carpet.

"Hello, happy anniversary," Gina and Eric say in unison when we arrive, as they stand and greet us with kisses and handshakes.

The maître d' escorts us to our table and is about to hold out our chairs when John and Eric hold out the fabric covered armchairs for each of us.

"True gentlemen. Carl will be your server this evening. Enjoy your meal," he said as he places menus in front of us.

Eric reaches for the wine list, and we all look at the menu as the busser fills our water glasses. When Carl comes to greet us, Eric orders a bottle of champagne.

"Happy anniversary," Eric and Gina said as they raise their glasses.

"Cheers," we said as we ring our glasses with theirs.

"Let's all sign the cork and date it so you will remember tonight," Eric said as he picks up the cork.

"This is a fun idea," I said as I sign the cork.

The food and service are five-star dining at its finest. We enjoy redfish, seared scallops, duck, and lamb chops all cooked to perfection. We order a round of after dinner drinks, and we all enjoy a couple of bites of crème brulee and chocolate mousse. Eric pulls out a small camera and has the waiter take a picture of the four of us.

"This is delicious," Gina said as she tastes the crème brulee.

"Well, shall we have a drink at the Hotel Monteleone after this?" Eric said.

"That sounds like a great idea. Is that ok with you ladies?" John asks.

"Sure," Gina and I reply.

The Hotel Monteleone is located on Royal Street in the French Quarter. When we arrive, I look up at the beautiful architecture of the building as we step off the street through the glass doors and into the opulent lobby.

The lobby with its rich dark wood furniture, beautiful couches, chairs, paintings, and grandfather clock is one of the most beautiful lobbies I have ever seen. We step into the bar off the lobby. An elegant bar with couches, tables and chairs grouped in living room like settings throughout the room with two bars in between. A server approaches our table and takes our drink order. He serves our drinks on napkins pictured with a crown and lions with The Monteleone New Orleans, USA printed on it. While I have become accustomed to fine dining, I still appreciate the elegant touches.

"Cheers to friends," John said as he raises his glass.

"To friends," we all said as we raised our glasses.

I look around at all the beautifully dressed people and the gorgeous jewelry the women have on. Certainly, a significant difference from where I grew up.

"I love coming to this bar on special occasions when we are dressed up," Eric said.

"Oh, I love it. I am so glad we came here," I said.

"I know. It's so elegant," Gina said as she sips her juice.

We enjoy another round of drinks before parting ways with kisses and head home.

"That was a wonderful evening. Thank you very much," I said as we get into bed.

"I am so happy you enjoyed it. Happy anniversary, my love," John said as he kisses me on the head.

"Happy anniversary. I love you, John."

"I love you too; goodnight," he said as he turns off the light, rolls over, and goes to sleep.

I am waiting at the door at exactly one o'clock when Adam pulls up. I close the door, skip down the steps and get into his car.

"Hello, how are you?" I said as I put my seatbelt on.

"Very well, and you?" Adam said as he turns to me and smiles.

"Did you enjoy your evening last night?" he asks.

"Yes, I did."

"I like The Grill Room; it is a very nice restaurant," he said as we drive towards his house.

"Yes, it is, and I love the Hotel Monteleone lobby and bar."

"I am glad you enjoyed yourself."

We arrive at his house, and I settle in the living room while he fixes us a drink. The sofa bed is open and made up. He appears from the kitchen with two glasses in his hands and he gives me one.

"Happy Wednesday," he said.

"Happy Wednesday," I said as we ring our glasses.

He watches me as we sip our drinks and when we finish, he sets his glass on the table.

"Take off all your jewelry and clothes and lie in the center of the bed with your legs together, your hands at your sides and your eyes closed."

"Ok," I said, and I do as he instructs.

When I am in position on the bed, I hear him as he approaches me from the side of the bed and his finger lightly touches my nipple. He quickly removes his hand and places his hands under my back and legs and rolls me over with force.

"WHEN I TELL YOU TO DO SOMETHING YOU DO IT!" he said as his hand comes down and strikes my buttocks with a hard slap that stings.

I realize he knew the minute he touched me when I did not react how I should have if I had not had an orgasm. That instead I had over satisfied myself this week. I did not think of that before now and I certainly never expected this anger. I lie there stunned as I hear him walk out of the room. I just lie there on my stomach afraid to move, not knowing what to do when I hear him re-enter the room.

He grabs my hands in his and I feel the cool steel around my wrists. I hear the click of the cuffs as they lock around my wrists. As he rolls me over, my body lies on my hands. I am afraid to open my eyes, but I can hear him taking off his clothes. He gets on the bed, spreads my legs apart and moves himself between them.

His head is between my legs, his finger's part my vagina as his tongue enters me. My body betrays me as his tongue pleases me and I move in sync with his tongue as it slowly circles my clitoris. The force of his tongue moving inside me and my hips moving to meet him pushes on my hands and the cuffs behind my back. The pain of the cuffs pushing into my back competes with the pleasure his tongue gives me. I give in to the pleasure as his tongue moves in and out of me faster and harder.

"Oh, oh, oh, oh," I moan aloud as my hips move up and down. My head shakes from side to side, and I moan louder and louder. He holds me down with both hands as his tongue licks directly on my clitoris with a thrashing until I am screaming, and my body stiffens as I explode.

He quickly moves on top of me and rams his hard cock deep inside of me. The weight of his body pushes the cuffs into my back. My body jerks and I stop breathing for a moment as the pain shoots through me. I open my eyes and see his face is close to mine and he is staring into my eyes as he holds himself above me. He does not move as he looks intently into my eyes for a moment before moving himself slowly in and out of me. When he moves his weight is not so heavy. I move to meet his thrusts and our pace starts to quicken. As he pushes himself inside me, I push my hips up to meet him.

He thrusts himself in and out of me faster and harder and his weight is on top of me again. I feel the cuffs in my back for a moment, then the pleasure of his cock makes me forget as we move together until I am moaning again.

He pushes himself deep inside me one last time as he comes. His weight crushes the cuffs against my back. "Ahhh!" I cry out from the pain, as he moves himself off me. We both lay in silence for a moment, then he gets up to retrieves the key to the cuffs.

"I am going to roll you over and uncuff you," he said as he places his hands under me and gently rolls me over. My arms are stiff from the weight on them and when he moves my hands to uncuff them I feel a sting.

"The cuffs cut into your back; don't move," he said as he takes them off.

I stay on my stomach as I hear him leave the room. I move my arms above my head and stretch them for a moment as he re-enters the room.

"I am going to put some Neosporin on your back. Don't move."

"Ok," I said wincing a little as he applies the ointment.

"This will stop it from stinging in the shower as well. You will need to put this on for the next few days," he said matter-of-factly.

"Ok," I said as I think he does not seem terribly upset about the cuts, whether he realized this would happen or not.

We head to the shower, and I am quiet as he washes my hair and my body. The ointment helps to keep the water and soap from stinging and Adam avoids the area as he washes me. I try to see the cut on my back in the mirror when I get out of the shower. Since the mirrors fogged up, I cannot see so I dry off and dress thinking I will check it out when I get home.

Adam finishes showering, dresses, and joins me in the living room as I am putting my jewelry back on.

"I am going to make us burgers and potatoes. Is that ok?"

"Sure," I said curtly.

He quickly makes dinner, and we eat in silence. I am at a loss for his lack of remorse. I am glad we finish eating quickly and we immediately leave for my house. We are both silent as we drive, and I am glad when we finally reach my house. I have my purse in hand, quickly unlock my seat belt, open the door, and get out of the car.

"Goodnight," I said as I get out of the car without my usual peck on the cheek.

"Goodnight," he replies.

I head up the stairs, unlock the door and go into the house without turning around. Although I know he is still there, I hear him pull away as I shut the door.

I rush to the bathroom, take off my clothes and look in the mirror. There are three cuts on my back, one is about an inch long, the other two are smaller. The longest cut is the deepest. The other two are not as deep but still bad. I hope none of them will leave a scar.

I feel like this is my fault as well, I should have stopped him after he yelled at me and smacked me. He shocked me since he has never behaved that way. I was not thinking that the cuffs would leave a mark. As the pleasure diminished the pain I got, caught up in the moment. The fact that he yelled at me and smacked me was upsetting enough but his indifference to the cuts on my back upset me even more. As I think of him punishing me, I realize this has gotten out of hand and it is time to end this.

I change into my pajamas, pour myself a glass of wine and curl up on the couch. I flip through the channels trying to find something to watch but I am too preoccupied to concentrate on anything. I am happy when John comes through the door.

"Hi, how was your day?" I said as he kisses me.

"Good, how was yours?"

"Ok."

He heads to the kitchen, gets a beer, pours it in his new mug, and joins me on the couch before taking a shower. He comes back to the living room after his shower, and we watch TV for a while before heading to bed. I am happy the day is over as I drift off to sleep.

The weekend goes by quickly and work happily distracts me. We all go out after work on Saturday night and have drinks, which is just what I need. I decide to call Adam on Monday after John leaves and before I go to work to break it off. I take a deep breath and am ready with what I am going to say. I do not plan to have an argument; I plan to end it nicely on a friendly note. I pick up the phone and dial his number. Ring, ring, ring, the machine picks up and I hang up the phone not wanting to leave this on the answering machine. I decide to try to call him tonight and if I do not get ahold of him, I will call him Wednesday morning.

I walk into work and see Gina behind the register and Eric standing at the hostess station next to her. He does not look happy, nor does he say hello. He walks away before I get to the desk.

"Wow, what's wrong with him?" I said to Gina.

"He is mad because when Josh and I had sex yesterday we ended up on the floor and now I have an open mark on my back from the carpet. He is furious that I did not realize and stop."

"Oh, I see," I said, thinking how interesting the same thing happened to both of us the same week. I also realize that Adam, who tells Eric everything about our encounters, had not told him what happened on Wednesday. I had not thought about it until now but realize I would have heard about it from Eric if he knew. Interesting that he did not tell him that and I decide not to say anything about what happened on Wednesday.

"You know how it is when you get caught up in the moment."

"Yeah, but you have to realize that it is upsetting for Eric to hear that and see marks on you from another man caused during the throws of hot wild sex."

"Well, I wasn't going to lie about it."

"I know you and Eric do not lie to one another and you tell each other everything, but sometimes the truth is hard to handle especially given the situation. Knowing what is going on and hearing and seeing that is a different story. I can see why he is upset."

"I know, but there is nothing I can do about it now."

I punch in and get to work checking the specials and organizing the menus. Eric brings our dinner just as Henry comes in the door and I try to make small talk to lighten the mood.

"I wonder why Henry does not have dessert after his dinner. Why does he go home and then comes back out?"

"He doesn't go home. He goes to the grocery store up the street. He organizes the shelves with the staff there to pass the time and not be home all alone. After a couple of hours, he comes back here for his coffee and dessert before going home," Eric said.

"Oh, no wonder he's always so happy to see all of us," I said as I finish my dinner. Eric heads to the bar the minute I finish eating, just as Preston and Monica come in for dinner. I seat them and when I get back to the register Adam is sitting at the table right behind Gina.

"Hello, Chelsea."

"Hello, Adam, would you like a menu?"

"No thank you," he said, and I turned back to him and face the door. He speaks to Gina in a faint voice, but I can hear what he is saying. "Gina, you have to think about it like this, when you borrow something from someone you should return it the way you got it."

I realize he is referring to the marks on her back. I am furious to hear him say that to her given his reaction on Wednesday. I turn around and am about to excuse myself and go to the restroom to get away from him for a moment. Then I see his face, he is looking at me as he speaks, and I see the sadness on his face.

"Obviously, you both did not realize that would happen as you both got caught up in the moment, but you should be more careful. When you have something special you should be careful to take care of it," he said as he stares at me.

"I am sure you were both caught off guard by what happened, but that is not acceptable, and this is a serious matter. If you were mine, I would be beside myself and make sure something like that never happens again," he said as I stood there looking at him and listening knowing he is talking to me.

"I know, you're right," Gina said.

I see the sincerity on his face as he looks at me. Customers entering the restaurant divert my attention. I seat them and when I get back to the register Adam is standing. He walks towards me and takes my hands in his.

"I meant every word I said. I hope I will see you on Wednesday," he said while looking intently into my eyes.

"Yes, I will see you on Wednesday." I said after a moment.

"Good, I will be there at one," he said with a smile.

"See you then," I said as he turns and walks toward the bar.

"So, I better be more careful in the future. I certainly never wanted to upset Eric," Gina said.

"Tell him all the things that Adam just said. It won't change what happened, but I think it will make a difference."

"I will."

I go to the server station to find Anna to see if she wants to have a drink after work. Since I finish before her, I wait in the bar while she finishes her side work. I am sipping a glass of wine when Preston walks in the bar door and sits on the stool next to me.

"Well, hello. I'm happy to see you here."

"Oh, where's Monica?"

"I took her home; can I get a glass of champagne, please?" he said to the bartender. The bartender pours him a glass of champagne and returns to stocking the beer.

Before I realize what, he is doing, Preston jumps off the stool, bends down, slips off my high heel, pours the champagne in it and holds it up to make a toast.

"What are you doing? Are you crazy. Don't drink out of my shoe," I said.

"I think you are a very sexy woman and I have wanted you since the moment I laid eyes on you. Come home with me and your every wish will be my command," he said, and he drinks the entire glass of champagne from my shoe. He dries it with a couple of beverage napkins and puts it back on my foot while his hand caresses my calf. I move my leg from his hand. As he stands up, he looks at me waiting for an answer.

"I'm flattered, but I can't."

"I'm disappointed."

Before I can say another word, Anna comes into the bar and calls out to me.

"Let's go, Chelsea."

"I got to go, goodnight," I said to Preston.

"I guess this is goodbye as I am leaving in two days."

"Goodbye, it was nice to have met you."

"It was nice to have met you too," he said as he gives me a hug and holds me for a moment. I gently pull away, smile, and walk over to Anna.

"Did I interrupt something?" Anna said as we walk out of the bar.

"No, your timing was perfect."

Chapter 12

$\mathcal{I}$ wake up the next morning and find John in the kitchen bending over as he looks in the fridge.

"Good morning."

"Good morning, I was fixin to make breakfast, but we are out of eggs," he said as he stands up and kisses me.

"Oh, I didn't realize that." I said as I get a cup of coffee.

"I'm going to run to the store and get some; I'll be right back."

"Ok, see you in a bit."

He heads out the door and I sit at the desk looking over a couple of bills that I need to write checks for. I forgot to check the mail yesterday, so I put some clothes and sandals on, and I step outside to check the mail. A breeze blows the door shut behind me as I reach for the mailbox.

"Oh shit," I said aloud as I turn the doorknob and realize I locked myself out. I sit on the steps and start to go through the mail while I wait for John to get home. I jump up as it starts to pour, and I stand in the doorway to get cover from the small awning over the door. I am getting soaked when one of the guys from next door pulls up and offers to let me wait inside their apartment until John gets home.

"Oh, thank you very much," I said as we head up the stairs.

"No problem. Let me get you a towel."

"Thank you," I said as I reach for the towel and start to dry my hair and face. As I stand in their living room and look out the window, I look down and see everything in our living room. From our apartment I see the outside wall but since their apartment is above ours, they can see everything. Something I did not realize until now.

"Wow, you can see our whole apartment from here."

"Only the living room and kitchen," he said with a smile.

"Well, I certainly did not realize that." I said as visions of me masturbating on the couch make me blush.

"I think your husband just pulled up."

"Great, thank you," I said as I hand him the towel.

"You're welcome," he said as he walks me to the door. I run out the door into the rain and into our apartment.

"Hey, where were you, are you ok?" John said as I enter our apartment soaked and wet.

"Yes, I went to get the mail and locked myself out. It started to rain just as the neighbor came home, so he let me wait in their place."

"Oh, sweetie, I'm sorry that happened to you," he said as he put a towel around me.

"While I was in their place, I found out they can see in our apartment. We will need to get blinds for the kitchen and living room. Lowering them part way will stop them from seeing in unless they bend down to look. Good thing we keep the bedroom curtains closed and the bathroom has textured glass on the windows."

"Ok, we'll get blinds and put them up today," John said as he starts to prepare breakfast.

"Thank you," I said with a smile.

I spend the afternoon ironing clothes for the wine and food event we are going to tonight. John has been looking forward to this for a month. The restaurant he works for has a booth at the tasting, along with some of the finest restaurants in New Orleans. At six o'clock we dress for the event and head to the convention center in the warehouse district.

I chose a long black skirt with a slit up in the center, and a long-sleeved purple blouse with shoulder pads. The blouse hangs over the skirt, and I accent it with a black leather belt at my waist. Black heels and a small black evening purse complete the outfit. John looks handsome in his black trousers, white shirt, and black sports coat. As we walk up the steps to the convention center, I see people walking up the steps in shorts and jeans.

"Oh, John, I think we're overdressed. I thought you said this was a dressy event."

"Trust me it is either they're not dressed properly or maybe they are going to another event."

As we enter the room for the event, I am happy to see everyone dressed up. The room looks great, the booths, tables and bars are all elaborately decorated with ice carvings and beautiful flower arrangements. The delicious aroma of the food fills the room, and we are eager to sample the gourmet food that is available.

The event's hosted by local restaurants, for their employees as an evening of food and drink with peers to reward their demanding work. We get a glass of wine and walk from booth to booth sampling the incredible food. There is gumbo, barbeque shrimp, trout almandine, softshell crab, crawfish, fried oysters, lamb chops, veal with crab meat, steak au poivre, and all kinds of sides and salads. Everything tastes exquisite and the wine offered with the different dishes is superb.

There is a band playing jazz music as people dance. John

introduces me to more of his coworkers and it is nice to put a face with the names he has mentioned. A group of us settle at a table together where we enjoy food, drinks, and laughter with his coworkers for the rest of the evening.

I am waiting at the door when Adam pulls up at precisely one o'clock. I see he is smiling as I get into the car.

"Hello, how are you?"

"I'm fine, how are you?" I said as I put my seatbelt on.

"Good, how was your day off yesterday?"

"Very nice, we went to a food and wine tasting."

"That sounds nice. I have a special day planned for you today."

"Oh, what do you have planned?" I said, thinking it could be anything.

"I am taking you across Lake Pontchartrain to go target shooting. Have you ever shot a gun. Do you and John own a gun?"

"No, we don't own a gun and I have only ever shot a BB gun."

"Well, that will change today. Everyone should know how to shoot a gun."

"Ok."

"We will be going across The Lake Pontchartrain Causeway; it is over twenty-three miles long. It is the longest bridge over water in the world. It is a beautiful bridge to cross."

"Sounds nice. I have never been on that bridge."

It is a lovely sunny day, and the sky is clear blue. I look out at the water as we get on the bridge. The radio is on low, and I am relaxing as I take in the beauty of the lake.

"Put your seat all the way back and close your eyes."

"Ok," I said as I put the seat back and close my eyes.

His hand caresses my cheek for a moment before it moves down my neck to the top of my chest. He slides his hand inside the V-neck of my shirt, inside my bra and cups my breast. His finger circles my nipple and I moan as it hardens.

"Oh, that feels nice," I whisper.

He gently squeezes it between his finger and thumb, and I lick my lips as I take a breath.

I move my head slowly back and forth as his hand moves to my other breast. It quickly hardens from his touch, and I put my head back and arch my chest forward as his finger slowly circles my nipple.

"Oh yes," I said aloud as his finger circles the tip of my nipple for a moment.

He removes his hand from my breast, and he slowly moves it outside my clothes and down my stomach. He unhooks the belt to my shorts, unbuttons and unzips them. He pushes my shirt up and slides his hand into my panties. His finger slides into my wet vagina as I spread my legs open.

"Oh yes, don't stop," I cry aloud as his finger moves slowly in a circle inside me.

I move my hips up and down as he pushes his finger deep into my vagina, first one then two. He pushes them in and out of me as I rock my hips to meet his hand as his fingers move faster and deeper inside me. My hands grab the sides of the seat and I spread my legs wider and thrust my pelvis up and down to meet his fingers.

"Oh, yes, yes, yes, yes," I cry aloud.

He gently pulls his fingers out of me and begins to slowly circle my wet throbbing clitoris, making me cry out in pleasure.

"Oh God, please don't stop," I beg as his finger moves faster and faster over my clitoris as my hips buck franticly up and down as I grip the sides of my seat as my head shakes from side to side and I moan louder and louder.

"Ah, Ah, Ah, Ah," I moan louder and louder until I am screaming. I growl like an animal as I have an explosive orgasm. My body thrusts forward and stiffens as I come before collapsing as my growl turns to a fit of laughter.

"Ha, ha, ha, ha, ha," I laugh as he gently pulls his hand out of my shorts.

I lay quiet for a moment while I catch my breath before I zip and button my pants and put my seat up.

"Oh, I enjoyed that," I said breathily.

"I enjoy satisfying you," Adam said with a devilish laugh. "I know a guy who does crazy things so he does not come, so he can last longer to please his wife. When he could easily do that by satisfying her first. He thinks about spinach and brussels sprouts while having sex with her, so he does not come too quick."

"I certainly don't want anyone thinking of spinach and brussels sprouts while their having sex with me."

"I agree. That does not seem very enjoyable," he said with a laugh.

We arrive at the shooting range and Adam carries a locked box of weapons and ammo into the range. We register and go over the gun and range safety and put on our goggles and earplugs. We settle into a lane and Adam loads a Glock 9mm. Taking care to show me how the slide kicks back. Adam hands me the gun and I feel the weight in my hand as he puts a paper target of an outline of a person in the clips and sends it all the way back with the lever on the side of our lane.

"I will go first," he said as he aims and shoots seven times. He pulls the lever on the wall to bring the target back in. I see as the target approaches us that Adam's shots are divided between the head and chest. Three shots in the center of the forehead and four shots in the center of the chest.

"Wow, that's good," I said as he holds the target and admires his shots.

"This is what you want to aim for if someone is coming at you with a gun. You would unload your weapon into their chest," he said pointing to the chest of the target. He put a fresh target on the clip and sends it halfway back.

"Now, stand up straight and look through the site. Cup your hand and aim for the dot in the center of the chest and squeeze the trigger."

I get into position aim and shoot; the power of the weapon startles me. I stop for a moment before I shoot again.

"Good you hit the target, now aim a little higher and to the left."

"Ok," I said as I shoot again.

He pulls the target back in and I am happy that I hit the target five times, but my shots are not together.

"Pretty good, you hit the target most of the times that's good for your first time. Now we need to work on your grouping."

"The gun is heavy, but I am getting used to it," I said as he sends the target back again.

He shoots again with the same results, and I improve when I shoot the next time, getting two shots in the right side of the chest. We take turns shooting for about an hour and he is happy with my progress.

"You did great. You will get better with practice," he said with a smile.

"Thank you," I said happy that I did well.

"Would you like to keep the targets."

"Sure," I said as I reach for the paper targets and roll them up.

Adam locks up the weapon and ammo and we head to the car for the hour ride back across the bridge. I settle into my seat as we head towards New Orleans.

"Have you ever heard the story "The Monkey's Paw," Adam asks.

"No."

"It is a story by W.W Jacobs. In the story the owner of the monkey's paw gets three wishes. An older couple makes a wish for two hundred pounds, just enough to pay off their mortgage. They get their wish. The next day the old couple find out that their grown son died in a machinery accident at work and the settlement is two hundred pounds. His parents are horrified and that night his mother wishes for her son's return. During the night they hear a knock on the door, and they think it is their son. The father realizes he will be returning the way he died, all mangled from the machinery. So, while his mother is trying to open the door the father looks for the paw and wishes for the knocking to stop and for the person to go away."

"The moral of the story is you get everything you ask for just the way you ask for it," he said as I wonder how this story pertains to me and why he told it to me as we drive across the bridge towards his house.

"Make yourself comfortable in the living room while I fix us a drink," he said as we walk through the door.

I head to the living room and sit on the couch. Adam enters the room with two glasses and hands me one and sets the other on the coffee table.

"I will be right back," he said as he goes back into the kitchen and returns with two shot glasses and joins me on the couch.

"Happy Wednesday," he said as he raises his glass.

"Happy Wednesday," I said as we ring our glasses.

I make a face after I drink the shot and quickly take a sip of the rum and Coke. Adam joins me on the couch and smiles as he looks at me as we sip our drinks.

"Take off all your jewelry and come with me," he said as he stands and holds his hand out for me. I take off my jewelry, lay it on the table, stand and place my hand in his. I wonder what he has planned as he leads me towards his bedroom.

"Take off all your clothes and lie on the bed," he said in a soft tone. I take off my clothes as he takes off his and we get on the bed together.

As I lie on the bed, he takes me in his arms and kisses me gently. His mouth slowly moves over my neck, and he sensually kisses my neck. His mustache feels good as it brushes my neck. His slowly kisses his way down to my breast and his tongue circles my nipple as his hands cup my breasts.

My nipples harden and I moan with pleasure as his tongue teases me. He kisses his way to my other breast and his tongue lightly dances over my nipple.

"Oh yes, that feels so good," I said as he sucks my hardened nipple.

He gently kisses my stomach making me quiver. He continues to my mound as his hands spread my legs open and he moves himself in between them. He slips a finger inside me followed by his tongue.

"Oh, oh, don't stop," I moan as I push my hips up.

As his tongue circles my clitoris darting in and out of me, I move my hips to meet his tongue as he fingers my wet vagina. His finger moves in and out of me faster and faster as his tongue licks my throbbing clitoris.

"Oh, yes, yes, yes," I moan aloud. As I move my hips up and down, my legs quiver and my hands grasp the bedspread under me. He pushes my legs up, so my knees are pointing up and my feet are near my bottom. He spreads my legs, so my knees drop to the side.

"Oh my God!" I scream as his tongue licks me faster and faster as he pushes another finger in and out of me.

"Ah, Ah, Ah, Ah, Ahhhh," I scream as my body shakes to orgasm.

He quickly moves on top of me and moans as he plunges his cock deep inside me in one thrust. He holds himself above me, his arms are on each side of me on the bed. He looks into my eyes with a piercing stare. Our eyes lock as he slowly moves himself in and out of me.

"Ooh," I moan as he enters me.

I move my hips slowly to meet him without breaking from his gaze as I moan aloud with pleasure. He moves himself in and out of me faster and faster as I keep his pace as he thrusts himself deep inside me.

"Oh," he moans aloud as he thrusts himself deep inside me one last time as he comes inside me, keeping his gaze until he gently collapses on top of me.

We lay in silence for a moment, then he moves next to me and caresses my forehead. His hand moves down to my shoulder and caresses my arm as I close my eyes and begin to drift off to sleep.

"Time to take a shower," he whispers in my ear.

"Ok," I said as I opened my eyes.

We walk to the bathroom and get into the shower. He washes my hair and body with barely an instruction. I am about to move to get out of the shower when he hands me the shampoo bottle.

"Will you wash my hair?"

"Ok," I said as I am shocked by this request. I take the bottle and I pour the shampoo into my hand. He is standing under the water and steps forward, as I reach up and put my hands on his head and work the shampoo into his hair. I take my time and enjoy touching him as I wonder why I am getting this reward. He moves his head back under the water as I run my hands through his hair with the water to get the shampoo out.

"Thank you," he said as he moved his head from the water.

"You're welcome," I said with a smile.

"Start to dry yourself off. I will be out in a minute then we can have dinner."

"Ok," I said as I take his hand and step out of the shower.

I grab a towel and go into the bedroom, dry myself off and start to dress. Adam enters the room with a towel wrapped around his waist. I watch him as he walks over to the chair where his clothes are. He lets the towel drop to the floor as he reaches for his clothes.

I enjoy the view of his tight, toned bottom and his deep tan line. A view I rarely get to see, and I find myself staring at him as he puts his underwear on. I go back to dressing when he grabs his pants and turns around.

"This is for you," he said as he hands me a T-shirt.

"Thank you," I said laughing as I open the folded shirt, hold it up, and see a Jägermeister bottle on the front of the shirt.

"You're welcome, I thought you would get a kick out of that."

"I'm going to grill our steaks. Would you like something to drink?"

"A Coke would be great."

"What are your plans for the rest of the week?" he said as he pours us each a Coke.

"I have to work, probably not much else. What do you have planned?"

"I have things to do around the house and I have a business meeting this week."

"Sounds like fun," I said as he prepares dinner.

"Did you enjoy shooting today?"

"Yes, I did. It was a wonderful day."

"Good, I am glad. Dinner is served," he said as he put the plates on each end of the table.

"How is your steak?" he said as I take a bite.

"Perfect, thank you. How is yours?"

"Very good. Would you like butter for your potato?"

"Yes please," I said as he passes the butter.

I enjoy the rest of my dinner and relax as he quickly cleans up before we head out to the car.

"I hope you enjoy the rest of the week," I said as I lean over and give him a quick peck when we pull up to my house.

"Thank you. I hope you have a wonderful week as well," he said as I got out of the car.

I walk up the steps, open the door, turn, and wave. He waves as he pulls away. Since it has been a long day and it is later than I usually get home, I put my pajamas on. I just bought *The First Deadly Sin* by Lawrence Sanders and decide to read it in bed. My mind drifts back to "The Monkey's Paw;" you get everything you ask for just the way you ask for it.

The rest of the week flies by and Sunday night after work the girls and I have plans to go to Ms. Mae's bar on Magazine Street. As

Anna calls it, a great late night local 24/7 bar. I do not care where we go, I need a night out.

"Ok, let's get our side work done and get out of here," I said to the girls.

"Yeah, let's get this party started," Emma said.

"I am ready to party," Anna said.

"I asked the other girls if any of them want to join us, but I don't think anyone wants to come," Ashley said.

"Oh well, their loss," Anna said.

We finish our side work, set our stations, cash out and head to Ms. Mae's. On Anna's advice I mentioned to John I may be out late, and he is welcome to join us. He said he was going to go home and told me to enjoy myself.

Located on Magazine Street, Ms. Mae's has all the makings for a great girl's night out. A juke box, pool table, drink specials and shots.

"Ok, let's start with a pitcher of beer and shots of Jägermeister," Anna said as we walk in and head to the bar.

"I'm having my cranberry and club soda," Ashley said.

"You got it."

We all throw money in a pile on the bar as the bartender pours our shots and pitcher of beer.

"Here's to great friends and the end of the summer," Anna said as we all raise our glasses.

"Cheers to friends," we all said in unison, and I grimace as I drink the shot.

"I'm going to play the juke box," Ashley said as she slides off the bar stool.

"Play some Billy Joel, please," I call out to her.

"Ok, I will."

"Let's order some food," I said.

"Good idea. Order a couple of things for all of us to share," Emma said.

"Ok."

"Let's grab that table near the pool table," Emma said.

"Sounds like a plan," I said as I grab the pitcher and we move to the table.

"Who wants to play?" Anna said as she put quarters in the pool table and the balls drop down.

"I do," Ashley said.

"I got winners," Emma said.

"I'll go after that," I call out as Anna lines the quarters up on the table.

"It's Still Rock and Roll to Me" comes over the juke box and I move to the beat as they begin to play pool. The bartender brings our food, and everyone digs in. The music keeps us upbeat, as the beers go down.

"Who's ready for another Jager?" Emma calls out.

"Get three," Anna said.

"Ok," Emma calls out as she heads to the bar.

"Here we go," Emma said as she set the shots down on the table.

"Cheers," we all said.

"Ok, it's finally my turn to get beat by Ashley on the pool table," I said as everyone laughs.

"Be glad I'm not playing any of you for money," she said with a smile.

"I am," I said with a laugh.

"I'll go easy on you," she said with a wink.

"Gee thanks," I said as I picked up a pool stick.

The next few months fly by as Halloween, Thanksgiving, and Christmas come and go. Thank goodness for Wednesdays, it gives me something to look forward to. Eric's birthday is coming up and Gina has planned a dinner party at a restaurant with a limo for the evening. She invited a group of his friends so of course Adam, John and I are all invited. We all meet at Don and Cindy's house, friends of Eric and Gina, for cocktails and hors d'oeuvres before dinner. Don's a successful advertising executive, and his girlfriend, Cindy, is a model.

I feel uncomfortable being with John and Adam and try to keep my distance which is easy since there are other people to mingle with. John, however, heads right over to Adam and strikes up a conversation. Feeling nervous and curious I follow.

"Hi, Adam, nice to see you again," John said as he held out his hand.

"Nice to see you too," Adam said as they shake hands.

I have all I can do not to cringe as I stand and watch, always worried that something will give us away. Although I know Adam can manage any situation it still makes me uneasy. Thankfully, Eric comes over to intercede.

"Hello, everyone, thanks for coming," Eric said while shaking the guy's hands and kissing me on the cheek.

"Happy birthday, Eric!" we all said in unison.

Gina joins us, and I relax a little but not completely. I am overcome with guilt, and I am glad these occasions are rare. "We better get going. We have reservations," Gina said as we all set down our glasses and head out to the limo.

"Ok, let's get this party started," Don said as he opens a bottle of champagne.

"Happy birthday to my wonderful husband, I love you," Gina said.

"Happy birthday, Eric," we all said as we raised our glasses. Someone lights a joint and we pass it around. We enjoy the luxury of the limo ride as we head across the river to The Steam Room on the West Bank.

Deirdre and Jeremy, who own a shop in the Quarter, and Ken, who is another friend of Eric and Gina's, gave us a party of ten.

The Steam Room is a casual restaurant whose specialty is buckets of steamed shrimp, lobster, clams, and crab legs. Eric orders appetizers and wine for the table to start the dinner off. We all pass the champagne cork from the limo ride around and sign it. Sensing my nervousness Adam sits at the other end of the table from us so I can relax.

"Let's split a bucket. That should be enough food with all the appetizers Eric ordered," I said to John.

"That sounds like a great idea," John said as he reaches for his wine glass.

I look towards the end of the table at Adam who at that exact moment turns to me and smiles. I quickly smile and turn my attention to Gina who is sitting across from me.

"This is a wonderful place. I have never been here before," I said to Gina.

"I picked it because Eric loves it and there is a fun bar up the street that we're going to after dinner for a drink."

"Oh, that sounds like fun especially since we have a limo."

"Yes, we are friendly with the owner, and I told him we're coming there after dinner."

We all delight Eric with gag gifts and bottles of wine and champagne as we enjoy the appetizers. The server brings the entrées. Adam and Ken's steaks look delicious as does the steamed buckets.

"Oh, this is so good," Gina said as she dips a piece of her lobster tail in the butter warmer cup next to her plate and seductively licks her fingers.

"Oh, can I have a taste of that?" Eric said.

"That's for later." Gina said to him with a smile.

As the waiter clears our plates Gina lets everyone know we are having after dinner drinks and dessert at a bar close by. The waiter brings the check, and everyone chips in.

We barely settle in the limo before we get to the bar. As the driver pulls up to the bar door to let us out, the owner Rick greets our party as we walk in. Rick takes us to a large table he has reserved for us. As one waiter takes our drink order another pours champagne for the table and Rick comes out of the kitchen with a big birthday cake. The people in the bar join us as we begin to sing happy birthday.

"Happy birthday, dear Eric, happy birthday to you."

"Thank you very much everyone. This has been a great birthday and thank you to my beautiful wife, I love you," he said as he kissed Gina on the lips.

Since it is a Tuesday night the bar is not that busy and the owner joins us for drinks as Don goes to play the juke box.

"Take your shoes off ladies and get ready to dance," Gina said.

"Why are we taking our shoes off?" I said thinking I am not the only one wondering why.

"Because we are dancing on the pool table," Gina said as kicks off her shoes and leads us to the pool table.

The guys help us climb on top of the pool table. Someone turns the juke box up and we begin to dance. All the girls have fun dancing as the guys enjoy their drinks. As I raise my hands over my head and sway to the music I look down and see Adam watching me and he smiles. I smile back and return my attention to the other girls as we dance together.

"Ok, that's enough dancing. Time for you girls to rejoin us," Eric said as he helps us off the pool table.

"That was fun," I said as I stepped onto the floor.

"Let's have one more drink before we go home," Gina said.

We all enjoy one more drink before the limo takes us back to New Orleans.

Chapter 13

New Year's Day 1987. I wake up a little hung over, and much to my surprise, John is up and in the kitchen. I am happy that we met in the Quarter after he got off from work and celebrated last night.

"Happy New Year, sleepy head," he said as he kissed me.

"Happy New Year. What are you making?"

"Black-eyed peas, cornbread, and collard greens, a New Year's Day southern tradition," he said as he pulls the warm cornbread from the oven.

"That looks good," I said as I poured myself a cup of coffee.

"You are supposed to make a dollar this year for every black-eyed pea you eat, so try to eat a million. Last year we didn't eat enough," he said laughing.

"Right now, I think I will just eat some of this cornbread. I will make a plate of the rest later."

"Ok, I'm going to eat some before I go to work. I made enough to have some later tonight as well."

"Did you have fun last night?"

"Yes, I probably should have only had one Hurricane," I said as I look at the two new Hurricane glasses on the shelf.

"Well, I am glad you met me at work last night and that we rang in the New Year together in the Quarter."

"Me too," I said as I took a bite of the cornbread.

"This is so good. You don't know what you're missing," John said as he takes a bite of black-eyed peas.

"I'll have some later."

"Ok well, I better get ready for work."

"I'll clean the kitchen and put everything away," I said.

"Thank you," he said as he leans in and kisses my cheek.

After I clean up, I settle on the couch while John showers.

"Ok, I am off to work. Are you going out with the girls tonight?" he said as he leans over and kisses me.

"Probably not. Hope you have a good day. I love you."

"Ok, I'll see you at home tonight. I love you too."

I watch him walk out the door as I pull the afghan off the back of the couch and cover myself. I have time to lie on the couch for a while until it is time to get ready for work.

My mind drifts off to being with Adam yesterday. He gave me a body massage while we watched the movie *Blue Velvet*. A bizarre movie about a man who kidnaps a woman's husband and son and forces her into a S and M relationship with him. We had a late dinner and toasted together before we headed to the French Quarter. He went over to Eric and Gina's, and I joined John to ring in the New Year. I fall asleep for a while and wake up to a ringing phone.

"Hi, this is Gina. Happy New Year!"

"Happy New Year to you. Did you all have fun last night?"

"Yes, we did; did you?"

"Yes, probably shouldn't have had that second Hurricane but I'll live."

"Adam told us you both had a wonderful day and that you finished your resume. Eric wants you to bring it to work so he can see it."

"Ok, and I will bring back the tapes as well."

"Ok great, see you next week. Enjoy your weekend."

"See you," I said as we both hang up the phone.

"Happy New Year," I said to Eric as I walked in the door.

"Happy New Year. Did you have fun last night?"

"Yes, we went to Pat O's. It was crazy busy, and I had a little too much to drink, but I had fun. How about you?"

"We had a wonderful time; we went out for a drink right after Adam got there but we were back at our house by mid-night toasting with champagne."

"Here are the tapes you loaned me and the wine book. Thank you very much," I said as I handed him the tapes and book.

"You did watch all the tapes, because you can't put it on your resume if you didn't."

"Yes, I suffered through every one of them." I said with a sarcastic look on my face.

"Good, the wine book is yours to keep, to use as a reference in the future," he said as he hands me back the book.

"Oh thanks. I like this book," I said as I took the book back.

"Let's see your resume."

"Here it is," I said as I handed him the folder holding my resume.

"Thanks, I will look at it during the shift and give it back to you later. Knowing Adam I am sure it is perfect."

"Ok, let me get to work," I said as I went to the kitchen to punch myself in. I call out hello to everyone as I punch in and go to the bar to get a Coke, my hangover cure.

"Happy New Year, Chelsea." Julia said to me from a seat at the bar.

"Happy New Year. Did you have a fun night?"

"Yes, Audrey and I celebrated together; we have been spending a lot of time together. I am so happy."

"That's great," I said just as Audrey comes up behind me and kisses my cheek.

"Happy New Year," she said with a kiss.

"Happy New Year, Audrey," I said as she joins Julia at the bar for an after-work drink.

"I better get to work. Enjoy your evening, ladies."

"See you later," they said together.

"Happy New Year ladies," I said as I entered the server station.

"Happy New Year," Anna said as she hands me a peach flavored daiquiri.

"Thank you; maybe this will work better than the Coke."

"I set all of our stations," Ashley said.

"Oh, thank you!" Emma said to her.

"You're welcome," Ashley said as she sips her daiquiri.

"Let's go check the specials," Anna said.

"Yes, I need food," Emma said as we all headed to the kitchen.

"Ok, for today's specials we have black-eyed peas, served with cornbread and collard greens, blackened drum fish served with rice and glazed beef tournedos served with a twice baked potato. They all come with a salad and the prices are on the eighty-six board. Whoever sells the most specials, gets a free dessert tonight," Eric said as we all grab forks and taste the specials.

"So, are we having a drink after work tonight, ladies? We got to celebrate the New Year together. Besides, I have news," Anna said.

"I wasn't planning on going out. What's your news?" I said as Anna holds up her left hand.

"Oh, that's beautiful," Ashley said as we all gather around her to admire her ring.

"Well, I guess we have to celebrate now," Emma said.

"All right, I'm in," I said.

"Ok, ladies, let's get out to your stations." Eric said as we all go out to the dining room.

Being New Year's Day, we are not busy, and the night drags on. Finally, we are cleaning up and cashing out.

"Hey, Chelsea, here is your resume. It looks great, very professional," Eric said as he hands me the folder.

"Thank you, I am very happy how it turned out thanks to you and Adam."

"You're welcome; I would be impressed if someone handed me that resume."

"Thank you, I really appreciate all you have done for me," I said thinking what a great boss he is.

"You're welcome. Go enjoy the night with the girls," he said, as I walked out the door and headed across the street.

"So, how did Mike propose?" Ashley said as we sip our drinks.

"Nothing exciting. I already knew he had the ring we talked about it. You know me, I'm not mushy."

"So, when is the big day, what are you planning?" I ask.

"Well glad that you asked, Chelsea. I was hoping you would help me with that since you have time and are into that stuff."

"That stuff, sure I'll help you," I said with a laugh.

"Great, I was hoping you would come with me to my parents' house and meet my mother and help her plan."

"Ok, I'll do whatever you want."

"Great thank you. My mother and you will get along great."

"Ok, here's to a Happy New Year and congratulations to Anna and Mike," Emma said as we all ring our glasses.

I have one more quick drink with the girls and rush home. Since I am feeling better, I hope to have a dish of black-eyed peas with John.

"Hey, you are just in time," John said as he is finishing heating up our dinner.

"Great, thanks. Sorry I'm late. I had a quick drink with the girls for New Year's and Anna got engaged," I said as I gave him a kiss.

"I figured y'all went out for a drink. How was work?"

"Slow since everyone went out last night. How about you?"

"Same."

"John, I heard about this great night club that's downtown called the Rainforest and I was wondering if you would like to have a date with me on Saturday night and go dancing?"

"I heard of that place; sure, we can do that," he said.

"Oh, great," I said.

"Here, eat this while it's hot before you take a shower," John said as he set our plates and beer on the table.

"Ok thank you," I said as I joined him at the table.

"This is even better than it was earlier today."

"It's very good, better than what we served at work tonight," I said as I took another bite.

"So, Anna and Mike are engaged. Well, we knew that was coming."

"Yes, but I didn't know she was going to ask me to help her mother plan her wedding."

"Wow that's interesting; you'll enjoy doing that."

"Actually, I am glad she asked me. I will enjoy doing that." I said as I finished my plate.

"Well, I guess we're not going to make a million dollars this year," John said with a smile.

"We will if you eat a whole lot more," I said with a laugh as I leaned over and give him a kiss.

On Saturday morning after John leaves for work I decide to try out Gina's tub faucet masturbation technique. I go into the bathroom, take off all my clothes and get in the tub. I turn the water on, and I check the temperature with my hand. Knowing it will feel hotter between my legs I turn it down a little.

I lie on my back in the tub and slide my bottom towards the faucet. I scoot my butt up against the tub wall as I put my legs up against the wall on each side of the faucet and spread them allowing the warm water to run between my legs.

"Oh yeah, I like this," I said aloud as the warm water flows between my legs. I spread my vagina open with my fingers as the water gushes down on my clitoris. "Oh, Gina was right; this is just like getting head." I think to myself as I move my pelvis up and down as the warm water flows on me.

"Oh, oh, oh," I moan aloud as I move my hips up and down faster as the water thrashes down on me. The water is rising around me, and I push my hips up closer to the faucet and let the water come down full force directly on my clitoris.

"Ah, ah, ah, ah, ah," I moan louder and louder until I come, thrashing my head from side-to-side, splashing in the water as I giggle with delight and my bottom splashes down into the water.

"Wow, I liked that. Best masturbation trick ever!" I said aloud as I brought my legs down and pushed myself away from the tub wall. I sit up in the tub while the water keeps filling around me. I turn the water off and relax in the tub enjoying the warm water for a while thinking I should take baths more often.

Then I rub the soap in my hands and rub the lather over my arms breasts and stomach. I grab the washcloth, rub the soap over it, and place it between my legs and then glide it over my thighs, calves, and feet. I push the lever and stand up as the water starts to drain from the tub. I finish washing and turn the shower head on to rinse the soap from my body. I wash my face, turn the water off, and grab a towel as I step out of the shower. I cannot wait to tell Gina I finally tried it; this is absolutely my new favorite way to masturbate.

I am changing in the bathroom after work for my date with John. Happy to be going out for a night of dancing. I slip my black dress off the hanger and put it over my head. I reach my arms through the cap sleeves and pull the body-hugging dress down over my black stockings. I reach my hand in the boat neck and adjust the shoulder pads as I put on my heels. The dress goes to my mid-thigh and on the right side there is a drawstring that pulls it up a little. I adjust the string as I look in the mirror, fix my make up and put on a little lipstick.

I am waiting in the bar when John walks in looking as handsome as ever. He is sporting black leather pants, a tight black mesh shirt with his hair spiked and a smile on his face.

"Oh wow, you look great," I said as he walked over to me and gives me a kiss.

"You look hot yourself," he said as he looked me up and down.

"Do you want a drink?" the bartender said.

"No thanks, we're going to head out."

"Hope you have a wonderful time tonight," Eric said as he walked into the bar.

"Thanks, see you tomorrow."

"Have fun, Chelsea," Ashley calls out as we walk out the bar door.

"Do you know where this place is?" I ask as we head downtown.

"Yes, it's located at the top of the Hilton hotel on Poydras Street."

"Oh, I'm so excited!"

"From what I hear from the girls at work you are going to love this place," John said as we drive.

"I hope you are ready to dance."

"I'm ready," he said as he smiled at me.

The Rainforest looks like the bayou, and in the center, there is a dance floor with rain sprinkling off to the sides. You can hear thunder and see lightning. Fog comes over the dance floor as people are dancing and between songs you can hear crickets chirping.

"Oh, this is fabulous," I said with delight.

"I knew you would love it. Let's get a drink," John said as we made our way to the bar.

"What can I get you?" the bartender said.

"I would like a glass of champagne, please."

"I will have a Corona, please," John said as we look at the dance floor as the bartender makes our drinks.

He is back in a moment with our drinks and John puts a twenty on the bar as he reaches for his beer.

"To us," he said as he raised his glass.

"To us," I said as I ring my glass with his.

"Let's grab a table and enjoy this drink before we hit the floor," John said as we made our way to one of the small tables that are around the dance floor.

We settle at a table and sip our drinks while watching the people on the dance floor when the song "Kiss" by Prince begins to play.

"Ok, let's dance," I said to John as I stood up.

"Walk like an Egyptian" by the Bangles follows "Kiss" and the club is hopping. I am happy to be out dancing and glad that John is enjoying himself. After a couple of songs, we take a break and get another drink.

"Are you having a good time, sweetie?"

"I'm having a wonderful time," I said smiling just as "Venus" by Bananarama starts to play.

"Let's get back on the floor," I said as I stand and dance my way to the dance floor as John follows my lead. We enjoy the night dancing, drinking, and laughing together.

"Good morning," I said as John walked into the kitchen.

"Good morning, sweetie. Did you have fun last night?"

"Yes, thank you. I had a wonderful time," I said as I gave him a kiss.

"I'll make us some breakfast while you get ready. I know you are going to see Anna's mother today."

"Ok, great, thanks. I already showered; I'll go get dressed," I said as I headed to the bedroom.

"Breakfast is ready." I hear John call out just as I finish dressing and I join him in the kitchen for breakfast.

"That is great. Thanks." I said as I tasted my omelet.

"You're welcome. You better hurry. Anna will be here any minute."

"I know," I said as I quickly finished eating and grab my uniform just as I hear a horn beep out front.

"Have fun. See you tonight. Love you," John said as he walked across the room to give me a kiss.

"Love you too. See you tonight," I said as I headed out the door.

I open the back door of Anna's car and hang my uniform on the hook. As I get in the front seat, I notice how nicely dressed Anna is.

"Hey, did you have fun last night?" she asks.

"Oh yeah, you know I love to dance."

"Thanks for coming today. There isn't that much to plan but my mother really wanted to meet you."

"No problem, I'm looking forward to meeting her as well. What type of wedding are you thinking about having?"

"Very simple in fact. A small church service because my mother insisted; we would have gone to a justice of the peace. Followed by dinner at a restaurant, thirty people max."

"You're kidding right, that's it?"

"No, I'm not kidding, that's it."

"No music or dancing?"

"No, just dinner."

"What about a cake?"

"I guess a small cake will be ok. That can be dessert."

"Wow, what are we planning then?"

"Well, the restaurant, menu, cake, and I will need a small bouquet. You know me, no fuss."

"That's not much to plan."

"I know but it will be fun for my mom to start thinking about it and to have someone to plan it with."

"Aren't you going to plan it with us?"

"No," Anna said laughing as we pulled up to her parents' house. I am shocked when I see a huge house on a beautiful piece of well-groomed property.

"Wow, this is beautiful. Is this where you grew up?"

"Yeah," Anna said with a smile as she parks the car.

We start up the walk as the large front door opens and a small woman with dark blond hair pulled up in a bun greets us with a smile as she waves.

"Hi, Anna. Oh, you look so nice."

"Hi Mom, this is Chelsea. Chelsea this is my mother," Anna said as we got to the door, and she gave her mother a hug and kiss.

"Hello, Chelsea, so nice to finally meet you. Just call me Vicky," she said as she gives me a hug.

"So nice to meet you, Vicky."

"Come in, come in," she said as we walked through the doorway.

"Oh, thank you," I said as we follow her into the house.

We enter the foyer and I see a large round table in the center. There is a huge fresh flower center piece on it and a winding staircase to the right. We follow her into a large living room that is about the size of my apartment. The room looks like it came right out of *Southern Living Magazine*.

"Please sit down. Would you like a glass of iced tea?"

"Yes please," I said as I sat on the couch.

"Anna tells me you are married; your husband is a beverage manager and that you are from New York," she said as she hands me a glass of tea from a pitcher she has set on a tray on the table.

"Thank you. Yes upstate New York."

"A beverage manager is a good profession to be in when you live in New Orleans. Have you given any thought about taking classes at the university?"

"Actually, I have been thinking of taking some classes lately."

"I think you should, even if it's only one or two, to start to broaden your horizons."

"That's what I was thinking to start."

"Yes, see what interests you. You can never go wrong when you are learning something new."

"So, Anna, I was thinking of what you told me you want for your wedding. Although I wish you wanted something a little more traditional, I guess we should start by picking a restaurant," Vicky said.

"Whatever restaurant you want is fine with Mike and me."

"Chelsea, although there is not much to do I appreciate your help. It will be nice to have someone to make plans with; let us exchange numbers before you leave."

"I'm happy to help. I think it will be fun," I said thinking Anna's mother is wonderful.

"Good, we can meet to decide on the cake and flowers," she said with a smile. "Now, let's go into the dining room and discuss some ideas over lunch before you girls have to go to work." She spoke.

"So, how did the wedding plans go?" John said as we finished breakfast the next morning.

"Good, there really is not much to plan. Anna wants everything simple; it was nice to meet her mother, she is fabulous. I am looking forward to seeing her again."

"What does she have in mind?"

"A small church service followed by dinner for about 30 people at a restaurant with a cake."

"That is simple."

"You know, Anna, no frills. You should see the house she grew up in. It's beautiful," I said as I clear our plates and start to clean the kitchen as John heads to the shower to get ready for work.

"Well, I'm off to work," John said as he walked into the living room dressed for work.

"Ok, have a wonderful day. I love you."

"Love you too," he said as he leans in and gives me a kiss.

The phone rings shortly after John leaves and I cross the room to answer it.

"Hello."

"Hello, Chelsea," I hear Adam sing my name.

"Hello, Adam. How are you?" I said as a smile comes across my face.

"I'm good, how are you?" Adam said with a devilish tone.

"I'm good. Are you having a nice week?"

"Yes, I am. I just wanted you to know that I am thinking of you, and I am looking forward to Wednesday."

"That's nice, I'm also looking forward to Wednesday."

"I'll see you Wednesday. You take care," he said as he hangs up the phone. I sit there thinking he sounds extremely excited, and I get aroused as I wonder what he has planned.

I am waiting at the door at exactly one o'clock when Adam pulls up. I see a smile come across his face as I walk down the steps and get into his car.

"How are you?" I said as I put my seatbelt on.

"Very well, and you?" he said as he looked at me and grins.

"Good, thank you," I said wondering what he is up to.

"How was the rest of your New Year's Eve?"

"Good, how was yours?"

"Good."

"Did Eric mention that I showed him my resume. He loved it."

"Yes, he did. He was happy with the way it came out."

"I am too. Thank you again."

"It was my pleasure," he said as we drive towards his house.

"Make yourself comfortable in the living room while I fix us a drink," he said as we walked into the house.

"Ok."

"Here you go," he said as he hands me a drink, sets his on a coaster and goes back to the kitchen.

"Happy Wednesday," he said as he hands me a shot of Jägermeister.

"Thank you, happy Wednesday," I said as we ring our glasses and drink the shot.

He laughs as I quickly take a sip of the rum and Coke. He joins me on the couch as we sip our drinks, smiling at me.

"Why are you smiling like that? What are you planning?"

"I am going to hypnotize you!" he states.

"What for?" I said as I begin to get nervous.

"Relax, I am going to hypnotize you, so you have the most powerful orgasm of your life."

"Oh, how do you plan on doing that?" I said as I relax as I think to myself this is not going to work.

"I will show you. Take off all your jewelry and clothes and follow me."

I take off my jewelry and place it on the coffee table, I take off my clothes and drape them over the chair. He watches me as I do this and holds his hand out for me when I am naked. I place my hand in his as he leads me out of the living room. When we reach the doorway, we do not turn right towards his bedroom. We turn left, and he opens the door to his office.

I do not know why he calls this his office when he works out of a smaller room across the hall that has a desk, computer, copier, and phone. That is where we worked on my resume. This is a small room that faces the side of the house. There is a window covered by drapes and a leather couch in front of the window. On the wall to the right are two tall wooden filing cabinets, one has a globe on a brass stand on top of it.

The back of the room has a double closet with accordion doors. To the left of the closet is an ornate wooden desk and leather chair with a desk calendar, lamp, and pencil holder on it. Beside it is a small bookshelf.

Between the couch and desk in the center of the room is an Oriental rug that sits on the polished hardwood floor. The beautiful plush beige, green and black rug runs the length of the couch and looks about three feet wide.

"I want you to lie down on the rug with your legs together and your arms at your sides," he said pointing to the rug.

"Ok," I said thinking it is strange that he wants me to lie on the rug instead of the couch, but I do as he says.

"Are you comfortable?" he asks when I am on the rug.

"Yes," I said feeling the soft plush rug under me as he sits cross-legged on the floor next to me.

"Good. Close your eyes, relax and listen to my voice," he said in a soft tone.

"Ok," I said as I take a deep breath and exhale.

"You are getting very sleepy; I am going to touch your shoulder and when I touch your shoulder you will fall into a trance." He repeated this several times before he put his hand on my shoulder.

I open my eyes, look up at him and see him staring down at me. The last thing I remember was him touching my shoulder. He stands, holds out his hands, helps me up and leads me out of the room. He holds my hand as we walk the short distance into his bedroom. The room is dark, and I can barely see but I notice the walk-in closet door is open and he stops in front of it.

"Turn around and stand in the doorway," he said in a soft tone.

I stand in the doorway, and he takes my arm in his hands and stretches it up towards the doorframe.

"Hold your arm here," he said as he wraps a band around my wrist. The band is somehow connected to the door frame. He pulls the band and hooks it like you would a watch band. Then he slides the band in the keeper.

He checks the band to make sure it is not too tight, then he stretches my other arm up and I hold it in place as he locks the band around my wrist. Checking it to make sure it is not too tight. I see his figure in front of me as he stops for a moment. He caresses my cheek with his hand, and I tilt my head towards his hand. My heart races as my excitement heightens as he straps me to the doorframe.

He drops down to his knees, picks my foot up and stretches it towards the door frame, I hold it there as he locks the band around my ankle. He stretches my other foot to the frame, and

I hold it there while he wraps and locks the band around it. He checks both ankle bands to make sure the bands are not too tight. His hand runs from my ankle to the top of my inner thigh, and I cry out with pleasure.

"Ah."

As Adam stands back and admires his work, I take a deep breath and lick my lips as I cock my head to the side a little.

He takes off all his clothes, stands in front of me and kisses my lips. I open my mouth as my tongue hungrily meets his. As our tongues swirl together my tongue tingles. He slowly kisses his way to my neck and his mustache makes my neck tingle as it brushes over it.

"Oh," I moan as I put my head back as he slowly, sensually kisses me down my neck. He opens his mouth slightly and I feel his tongue on my neck as he kisses me.

I try to move my arms as I turn my head to the side offering him my neck as his soft mustache caresses my skin. He slowly kisses his way to the other side of my neck, and I cry aloud as his mouth touches me, the hairs stand up on the back of my neck. I am so excited and my whole body is tingling.

"Oh yes!" I exclaim.

He gently pulls away from me and I see his outline before me staring at me as I arch my back pushing my breasts forward. He carefully leans down but does not touch me, then his tongue lightly licks the tip of my nipple.

"Ohhh yes," I moan aloud as his tongue teases my hardened nipple. He slowly, lightly flicks his tongue all around my nipple as I whimper and beg for more.

"Oh yes, don't stop!" I cry as he takes my nipple into his mouth.

"Oh God, that feels so good," I moan as he sucks on my

nipple. My excitement is heightened by his every touch, and I cannot get enough of him. I want to rip my arms out of the restraints and grab him.

"Ahhh!" I moan as I breathe a deep breath in as his mouth moves to my other breast. Teasing me again as I beg for him to take me in his mouth. His hands are on my sides as his mouth moves down my stomach. His mustache tickles me and my body jerks as his hands move up and he squeezes a nipple with each hand.

"Oh, yes, yes," I moan as I push my pelvis forward. I am wet, throbbing, and my heart is beating so fast. I pull on the restraints and try to move my arms and legs as I arch my whole body forward.

He drops to his knees as he slowly kisses me down to my mound. He kisses all around the top of my mound as I moan with pleasure. His hands caress me slowly from my ankles to the top of my inner thighs.

"Oh, oh," I moan as he kisses the top of my mound as I push myself forward. He spreads my vagina open with his fingers and I moan aloud as his tongue follows and lightly licks me. I push myself forward again wanting more. He holds back as I do, teasing me. His tongue lightly dances on my clitoris as I move my pelvis slowly back and forth.

"Oh yes," I cry as my clitoris tingles with pleasure. I have never felt these intense feelings before.

He gently holds my backside in his hands as I move slowly back and forth in sync with his tongue. He pushes his tongue deep inside me and slowly circles my clitoris with its tip.

"Oh yes, don't stop," I beg as his tongue circles my clitoris faster and faster. I try to move my arms and my legs but cannot. I stand on my toes and move myself up and down on his tongue.

"Oh yes, yes, yes," I yell as he holds my bottom as his tongue licks directly on my clitoris in a fast steady pace.

My heart is beating faster as I struggle to move my pelvis into his tongue as he holds me and lashes his tongue against my clitoris. I am moaning louder and louder as my body shakes and quivers. My head thrashes from side to side as my hands bang against the doorframe.

"Oh, oh, oh, oh," I moan louder and louder as I stand on top of my toes as he holds me firmly in his hands as my body jerks and I am screaming louder than ever.

"AH, AH, AH, AH, AH, AHHHHH," I scream as I throw my head back and I have the most explosive orgasm of my life. My screams turn into an animal growling as I pick my head up and look forward as I growl. As I bare my teeth like an animal, I see a flash of light like lightning before me.

"ARG, ARG, ARG, ARG," I growl as I throw my head back and let out the most devilishly wicked laugh.

My head falls forward, my hands hang down as my feet fall to the floor and my body slumps. The bands around my hands and ankles are the only thing holding me up.

As Adam unhooks the bands around my ankles my legs give out. He holds me up with his body as he unhooks my left hand, my body collapses on his as soon as my hand is free. He holds me while he unhooks my other hand and puts an arm under my legs as he wraps his other arm around me. He picks me up and gently lays me on the bed as I whimper with pleasure. I hear him leave the room as my body continues to tingle as I lie there.

"Would you like a sip of water?" I hear him say as he enters the room.

"Yes please," I whisper as I hear him set something down on the nightstand. As I struggle to lift my head, he put his hand behind my head. He holds it up while he brings the water glass to my lips as I take a small sip. He moves the glass, keeps hold of my head and waits a moment as I swallow the water.

"Would you like more?"

"Yes please," I whisper as he brings the glass back to my lips and I take another sip.

"That's enough, thank you," I whisper, and I hear him set the glass on the nightstand.

I lay quietly as I hear water wring from a washcloth. I feel the cool cloth on my face as he moves my damp hair that clings to my forehead and wipes my forehead with the cloth. He wipes my face and neck; then he dips the cloth into the water again.

I let out a small sigh as he wipes the cloth over and under my arms and glistening chest, moving slowly around my nipples. He wets the cloth again and wipes my stomach and I squirm as it tickles me. He gently spreads my legs with his hands as he places the cloth between my legs. He gently pushes the cloth inside of me with his fingers moving his fingers inside me as he does.

"Oh," I whisper as his fingers move inside of me.

He gently moves his hand and I hear him dip the cloth in the water again. He wipes the cloth over each of my legs and feet tickling me when it touches the bottom of my feet. I hear him place the cloth in the bowl and he gets on the bed putting his legs between mine and a hand on each side of me as he holds himself above me.

He lowers himself to me and pushes his cock against my mound as he kisses me. I spread my legs a little as I push my hips forward wanting him. He stops kissing me and stares intently into my eyes making me wait as his cock slightly enters me.

"Ah," escapes my lips as I push myself forward wanting to pull him into me, but I keep my hands at my side as our eyes lock in a gaze. He holds back for a moment before plunging his hard cock deep inside me. I take a quick breath in as he does, and I slowly exhale as I moan.

"Ahhh!" I cry out as I move my bottom up and down to meet his thrusts.

He slowly moves in and out of me; his skin feels so good against mine. He pushes himself deep inside me and holds himself there for a moment. A whimper comes out of my mouth; then he pulls himself out of me and slowly plunges deep inside me again.

"Oh, please don't stop," I cry as he stops for a moment before moving himself in and out of me at a steady pace as I meet his thrusts. We move faster and faster together as I push my hips forward and moan with pleasure. I buck my bottom up and down faster and faster as he pushes himself in and out of me.

"Ooh, oh, oh, oh, ooh..." I moan louder as he brings his face close to mine, cups my chin and stares into my eyes, as he plunges his cock deep inside me one last time and I hear him moan as we come together. I giggle with delight as he gently lowers himself on top of me. As we lie in silence, I enjoy the feeling of his skin against mine.

He gently pulls himself out of me, moves next to me and wipes my damp hair from my forehead moving his hand to the top of my shoulder.

"WOW! I did not think that was going to work!" I exclaim.

"Oh, I knew it would," he said as he turns on his side and looks at me as his finger and thumb gently squeezes my skin as they move down my arm.

"Time to take a shower," he said as he turns and gets off the bed. He turns on the lamp next to the bed and holds his hand out for me.

"Ok," I said as my eyes adjust to the light, and I place my hand in his as he helps me off the bed.

I follow as he heads towards the bathroom, stopping in front of the closet. I see there are four little pink kitty collars with small silver buttons on them nailed to the closet frame. I reach up and touch one of them. I imagine him buying them at the store, bringing them home and hammering them into the frame on Monday before he called me. I turn and realize he is looking at me and smiling. I smile as I drop my hand and follow him into the bathroom.

He turns the water on, checks it with his hand and helps me into the shower. My legs are weak and ache as I step over the tub. He gets in after me as I stand with the water on my back. He reaches his hands up as I put my head back under the water as he rubs the water through my hair.

"Do you have a passport?" he asks as he washes my hair.

"Yes, why?"

"I was hoping we could get away for a long weekend after Mardi Gras, maybe in early March and get out of the cold," he said as I tilt my head back and he rinses the shampoo from my hair.

"I don't know how I would get away with that," I said as I think only a true southerner would call 60 degrees cold as he lathers the washcloth with soap.

"Well, can't you say you are visiting one of your sisters. Wouldn't one of them cover for you?"

"Yes, I guess I can say that. Where do you want to go?"

"I was thinking Cancun Mexico would be nice and warm, and you would have time to plan so it wouldn't be a last-minute trip and look suspicious," he said as I hold my arms up as he washes me.

"Ok, let me see what I can work out and I will let you know," I said as he drops down and I put my foot on his knee, and he washes it.

"Ok great," he said as he washes my other leg.

I turn around as he stands so he can wash my back and bottom. Wrapping his arm around me as he pulls me against him as he washes between my legs. He reaches for the showerhead and rinses the soap from my body holding it between my legs for a moment before he releases me. I turn when he finishes rinsing my back so he can rinse the soap from my front.

"Ok, all done. You can dry off; I will be out shortly," he said as he helps me step out of the shower.

I pick up a big plush white towel and begin to dry myself off as I go out to the living room to dress. I towel dry my hair and am putting on my jewelry when Adam enters the room all dressed, with a bag in his hand.

"I got this for you," he said as he hands me the bag.

"Thank you," I said as I took the bag and opened it. Inside is a knife in a black sheath with buckles on it. I look at him with an inquisitive look as I hold it in my hand.

"It is a diver's knife, and the sheath buckles to your calf. I got it as I was thinking about our trip."

"Will we be going shark hunting or something?" I said laughing.

"No, I was just thinking about the trip and saw this, so I bought it."

"Well, that's good," I said as I placed it back into the bag.

"I stopped at a travel agency and got some brochures of different resorts and of the Mayan ruins that I want to show you," he said as he handed me the brochures.

"You have been thinking about this," I said as I look at the brochures as he pours us each a glass of wine.

"Yes, I have. Look at this one; it's a five-star resort," he said as he points to one of the brochures.

"That's beautiful," I said as I looked at the pictures.

"Wouldn't it be nice to lay at that pool?" he said as he prepares our dinner.

"Yes, that would be lovely."

"It has a spa, restaurant, bar, nightclub, pool, and it is on the beach where there are water sports. We can go swimming, diving, parasailing or just bask in the sun."

"Oh, that sounds nice."

"Here's another brochure of the Mayan Ruins. We can take a day trip there."

"I would definitely like to see that."

"See what you can arrange and let me know so I can make the resort and plane reservations."

"Ok, I will start working on it right away."

"Great," Adam said as he put our dinner plates on each end of the table.

"Oh, this looks delicious," I said as I look at the barbeque chicken, baked potato and green beans that are on my plate.

"Enjoy," he said as he watches me as I take a bite.

"It's very good, thank you."

"Good, I was thinking we could leave early on a Wednesday and come back on a Monday. That would give us four full days there. How does that sound?"

"That sounds like a nice getaway."

We finish dinner and Adam cleans up while I look at the brochures some more. When he finishes cleaning, I gather my purse and gift bag and we get in his car and head to my house.

The next morning after John goes to work, I shower and dress, and head to Canal Street to go shopping. I decided last night to send Adam a dozen roses and I want to get a vase to put them in. I remember when I looked at the crystal in his china cabinet. I noticed that he did not have a vase. I think it will be nice to get him one and have the flowers delivered in it.

I go to D.H. Holmes's department store and find the china department. I see beautiful silver, china and crystal and begin to look around. I see a stunning Waterford vase that matches his crystal and would be the perfect size for a dozen roses and although it is expensive, I decided to get it. The clerk wraps it and puts it in its box. I pay for it and carefully carry it out of the store. I head to the florist down the street. Since I know exactly what I want I go straight to the counter.

"May I help you?" the lady behind the counter asks.

"Yes please. I would like to send a dozen long stemmed red roses to this address, and I would like them arranged in this vase," I said as I handed her a piece of paper with Adam's address on it, and I take the vase out of the box.

"Oh, what a beautiful vase. Would you like to fill out a card to send with the flowers?" she said as she writes up the bill for the flowers and delivery.

"Yes," I said as I select a card and envelope and quickly write my message, thinking Adam will get a kick out of this as I look down at the card and read it to myself.

"Oh God, I truly am your slave." I sign my name as I laugh to myself, and I put it in the envelope. I hand it to the clerk, pay the bill and leave the store smiling as visions of yesterday fill my head.

Chapter 14

The following day after John goes to work, I call my sister Ann who lives in Florida to get my plan started. This will be tricky to plan as countless things can go wrong with this plan. I feel bad about lying like this to John, but I also don't want to disappoint Adam. Of course, my sister will cover for me. Any one of them would, that is not a problem. I ask Ann because she lives in south Florida so it would make sense when I come home with a little color. I just hung up the phone from my sister when it rings again.

"Hello."

"Hello, Chelsea," Adam sings my name.

"Hello, how are you?"

"I am looking at the most beautiful flowers in a stunning Waterford vase. Thank you very much. You shouldn't have done that."

"I wanted to."

"I love the card," he said with a laugh.

"I thought you would get a kick out of that."

"Eric thought it was perfect."

"Well of course he did," I said shaking my head.

"Hope you have a lovely day. You take care."

"You too, see you soon," I said as I hang up the phone.

I decide to go to the zoo and see the primates, stopping first to look at my Diana statue. As I sit and gaze at her my mind wonders to Wednesday and Adam and how intense that was. It certainly was the most powerful orgasm of my life.

The weeks fly by, and I plan my trip to see my sister as Adam and I plan our trip to Cancun. It is carnival season, and I am enjoying my second year of parades. I get the *Gambit* for the locations of the parades leading up to Fat Tuesday.

I like the small local parades that start in January and run through February on weekends and during the week. There are parades uptown, downtown in the Quarter on the Westbank, in Metairie and other towns surrounding New Orleans. Families come out and watch the parades together. It is nice that it is just the locals and not crowded, since the tourists come for the last weekend leading into Fat Tuesday.

I also learn more about the parades, krewes and the time it takes to make the floats and costumes. How they go to work on the next year's floats and themes right after Mardi Gras and that each krewe has a masquerade ball. There is a good amount of time, planning and money that goes into Mardi Gras. I bet it would be fun to be a member of a krewe and be on a float.

I am happy we catch a couple of smaller parades during the week, since we will miss Bacchus and all the other big parades on the last weekend because of work. We do catch Thoth on Sunday before Mardi Gras Day before going to work.

"I'm glad I am able to go in late today; this is a nice parade," John said as we watch the parade come down Tchoupitoulas Street.

"Yes, and the weather is nice also, oh, here comes another float," I said as a float follows the marching band.

"Ok, get ready," John said as we both put our hands in the air.

"Throw me something mister," I call out as I wave my hands in the air and catch a strand of beads as the sound of doubloons hitting the street makes everyone look down.

"I got one," John said as he stomps his foot on a doubloon.

"Oh, look at this," John said as he picks the doubloon up from under his foot.

"Krewe of Thoth 1987 40th Anniversary" I read as I hold the doubloon.

It is Mardi Gras Day; John and I are spending the day together going to parades. We miss Zulu again this year, but we catch Rex and Comus staying uptown this year instead of walking and fighting the crowd on Canal and Bourbon Street. We walk uptown starting on Magazine Street. Then we walk down Napoleon Avenue to St. Charles Avenue making our way to Que Sera. Home of the three for one on Wednesdays where the place is always overflowing with people to the street every Wednesday like it is for Mardi Gras. I have seen the drunken crowds here when Adam brings me home.

"Wow, this is quite the crowd," John said as we make our way to the bar to get a drink.

"Yes, the bar on Magazine Street wasn't as packed. Of course it was earlier," I said laughing.

"Happy Mardi Gras, sweetie," John said as he raises his beer.

"Happy Mardi Gras," I said as I ring my can with his.

"Maybe one of these years we will catch Zulu," I said.

"That would be great if we can get up early enough," he said with a laugh.

"Ok, breaks over. Let's get back out there."

"Ok, since clearly you don't have enough throws yet," he said pointing to the full bag of throws we collected on Magazine Street and Napoleon Avenue as we walked here.

"No, I don't, we need more cups," I said laughing as we head outside. "Throw me something, mister," I call out as another float approaches and I catch a pair of gold panties with Happy Mardi Gras written in purple with pictures of green colored beads, doubloons, and a crown.

"I'd like to see you in those later," John said with a laugh, as I winked at him.

I enjoy watching the efficiency of the clean up after the parades are over as we have a drink on the porch of Que Sera. I like this tradition. The crowd parties long after the parades are over, and we hit a few bars on our walk home.

A couple of weeks later I decided to have a drink after work while I was on my way home. I stop at a bar on Magazine Street close to my house. It is not busy. I see an empty stool at the bar. I sit down and order a beer. There is a young woman sitting alone to the right of me.

"Hello," she said to me.

"Hello. How are you?"

"Ok, how are you?"

"Great thanks. I'm Chelsea nice to meet you," I said as I extend my hand to the pretty petite woman next to me with long blonde hair and big brown eyes.

"I'm Diana. Nice to meet you too," she said shaking my hand.

"I just got off of work and am happy to be having a beer close to home."

"Oh, do you live around here?"

"Yes, just up the street."

"Oh, me too I just moved here from New York."

"That's funny. I moved here from upstate New York a couple of years ago."

"What brought you to New Orleans?" she asks.

"My husband got a job here. What about you?"

"I have a friend who lives here. She is always telling me how great it is so I thought I would check it out."

"Oh, you are going to love it here."

"So far, I do, I will be happy when I get a job. Right now, I am going to bartender school."

"Well, there are plenty of bars in New Orleans that's for sure."

"Did you enjoy your first Mardi Gras?" I ask.

"Actually, I moved here just after Mardi Gras so I will have to wait until next year."

"Oh well, don't worry. There will be parades on St Patrick's Day."

"Sounds like fun."

"Then there's jazz fest and French Quarter fest. One thing about New Orleans, there is always a party."

"So, I heard."

"How do you like the food?"

"The food is so good. I especially love the red beans and rice," she said with a smile.

"It is hot and humid in the summer here, but most of the year is lovely."

"I know; we would be buried in snow if we were up north at the end of February."

"Oh yeah. I don't miss winter, but I do miss fall and the color of the leaves."

"Well, maybe you should go home to visit during that time."

"That's an excellent idea," I said as I ordered another beer.

"I am wondering where to look for a job once I finish bartending school. Any suggestions?"

"The French Quarter, but it is hard to get a job there if you have not lived here long. But I think any bar on Magazine, St. Charles Avenue or Canal Street would be good."

"Yes, my friend told me that about the French Quarter. I have time to look around while I finish the class," she said as she ordered another drink.

We have another round and talk some more. She is extremely sweet, and I feel like I have known her forever. We exchanged phone numbers and plan to get together when I get back from my trip. I give her a hug before we both head home.

I am excited that it is two days before I go to Cancun and Gina, and I are going shopping. Adam and I finalized all our plans when I saw him last Wednesday. I am smiling as I head to the Riverwalk to meet Gina to go shopping before work.

"Hey, I bet you're in a good mood. Lucky you are going to Cancun in two days," Gina said as I greeted her outside of the shops at The Riverwalk.

"Yes, I am. I can't wait."

"So, are you shopping for anything in particular?"

"I am looking for a couple of pairs of shorts and tops. Other than that, I am all packed."

"Well, let's go and see what we can find."

"Let's go in here," I said as we approached the Banana Republic.

"Good idea. They'll have shorts in there."

I quickly find a couple of pairs of shorts and cute tops to go with them and Gina finds a shirt she likes. We leave the Riverwalk with just enough time to get to work.

"Well, hello, ladies. Did you have fun shopping?" Eric said as we got to work.

"Yes, I got a new top," Gina said as she kissed his lips.

"Yes, I am all set for my trip."

"That's good. I better make you ladies some dinner before we get busy."

Eric makes us a nice dinner and the shift goes by fast. I pop into the server station to say goodbye to the girls who also think I am going to see my sister.

"I'll see you next week," I said to Gina and Eric.

"Have a wonderful time," they both said together.

"Thanks, I will," I said with a smile as I walked out the door.

I wake up early Wednesday morning extremely excited. I quietly get out of bed, so I do not wake John and head to the kitchen to make coffee and to start breakfast. The coffee is just finishing brewing when I hear John coming down the hall.

"Good morning, sweetie," he said as he gives me a kiss.

"Good morning, would you like a cup of coffee?"

"Sure. Are you all set for your trip?"

"Yes, I am all packed and ready. I was about to make breakfast. What would you like?"

"Whatever you like."

"How about scrambled eggs and toast?" I ask.

"Sounds great, I'll help."

"This looks pretty good," I said as I plated up the eggs, toast, and orange slices.

"Yes, it does," John said as he tops off our coffee cups.

"I hope you have a wonderful time on your trip. Please be careful."

"Thank you, I will," I said feeling terribly guilty.

"Very good breakfast, thank you very much," John said as he brings his plate into the kitchen.

"I'll clean the kitchen; go get ready for work."

"Ok thanks," he said as he swoops down and kisses me.

I clean the kitchen and get a couple of last-minute things together. I am about to go lay my clothes out when John comes into the living room all dressed for work.

"Ok, I am ready for work. Have a wonderful time and be careful. I will miss you and I love you very much," he said as he put his arms around me.

"I promise to be careful; I love you too and will miss you very much," I said as I give him a big hug and kiss and walk him to the door and wave as he drives off.

I am waiting at the door for Adam when he pulls up at exactly eleven o'clock. He parks and gets out of the car to help me with my bag.

"Do you have your passport?" he said as he put my bag in the trunk next to his.

"Yes."

"Great," he said as he opens the door for me.

"I am so excited I woke up so early this morning," I said.

"So did I, I was thinking our vacation is finally here."

Of course, Adam planned for us to get to the airport early. Once we check our bags the time goes by quickly. In no time at all we are in the air looking at a magazine from the seat pocket of the beautiful blue ocean.

"That's you," Adam said as he points to a picture of a woman swimming in the ocean.

"That water looks so beautiful," I said remarking about the clear blue water in the picture.

"We are on our way," Adam said as the beverage cart comes by, and we each get a Coke.

We land in Mexico, get our bags and head to customs. We have our passports ready for them to check and that's when it hits me. They are going to stamp my passport, I did not think about that until now, not that there is anything I can do about it. I relax a little as I think; it is not like John looks at my passport. I will just have to worry about that later.

"Next." I hear someone call and I step forward and hand the man my passport.

He quickly looks at my photo, looks at me and picks up his stamper. Fortunately, he flips to the back of the passport and stamps it leaving blank pages in between.

"Ok, you're all set," he said to me as he hands me back my passport.

"Thank you," I said as I took my passport back.

We take a taxi to the resort, check in and meet with the Concierge. He tells us briefly about the resort, the beach activities and tours including the Mayan Ruins. We have been traveling all day and since Mexico is an hour ahead of us it is past dinner time, and we are both starving.

"Let's unpack and then get some dinner," Adam said.

"Ok great, I'm starving," I said as I unpack my clothes.

"Look what I brought to play with," Adam said as he holds up four white cable ties.

"Oh, I look forward to playing with them," I said with a smile.

"Let's have some dinner and drinks. Then we can walk around and check out the resort."

"Sounds good to me."

The dining room is a lovely room with large windows, big potted plants, and colorful artwork on the walls. The tables are occupied by couples with a few parties of four and six.

"Someone will be right with you. Enjoy your meal," the host said as he shows us to our table and gives us menus.

"Oh, I want to have a Mexican specialty," I said as I pick up the menu.

"Sounds good, just be careful and don't drink any water. It will make you sick," Adam said as he looked at his menu.

The waiter comes by, and Adam orders two rum and Cokes while we look at the menu.

"Happy Wednesday," Adam said as he lifted his glass.

"Happy Wednesday," I said smiling as I ring my glass with his.

I order salbutes, a lightly fried tortilla topped with lettuce, tomatoes, shredded cheese, and chicken. I am surprised that Adam orders a grilled white fish. We are happy that the food comes out quickly since we are both starving.

"This is delicious," I said after my first bite.

"Mine is tasty as well," he said as he pushes the rose garnish made from a tomato off his fish.

We skip dessert and wander around the resort. We find the spa, nightclub, giftshop and bar, leaving the rest for morning when it is light out.

"Let's have a drink at the bar and then head up to the room for a good night's sleep so we can get an early start tomorrow," Adam said as we walked into the bar.

"Ok, I am a little tired."

We enjoy another rum and Coke before heading up to the room. We both put on our pajamas and brush our teeth. We get in bed and fall asleep as soon as our heads hit the pillow.

I wake up the next morning feeling completely refreshed, as I roll over, I see Adam is not in bed.

"Good morning. How are you?" he said from a chair in the corner of the room.

"Good morning. I feel good, how are you?" I said as I stretched my arms above my head.

"Not good. I have a terrible stomachache. I did not have any water, but something did not agree with me."

"Oh no, I'm sorry. What can I do for you?"

"After we shower, I will get something for my stomach at the gift shop."

"Maybe some ginger ale and toast will help," I said.

"I hope so."

We shower, dress and head down to the gift shop so Adam can get some Pepto-Bismol before going to the dining room. Adam has dry toast and a ginger ale while I have scrambled eggs, pan dulce and fresh pineapple, papaya, and mango.

"This pineapple is so good; I'm sorry you're not feeling well and are missing it."

"It's ok, I am glad you are enjoying it."

"Do you want to go back up to the room and lie down?" I ask.

"No, let's go up to the room, get into our swimsuits and go out to the pool."

"Ok, if you're sure you are up to it," I said as I finished my breakfast.

"I'm ok."

We get into our swimsuits and head out to the pool. We find a spot right on the side of the pool and settle into two lounge chairs. We both put suntan lotion on ourselves and on each other's backs. Then I lay back with my sunglasses on as Adam relaxes next to me.

As I bask in the sun, I see couples getting in the pool. When they get in the men are all picking up the woman and holding them while they float on top of the water and spinning them around for a moment. A romantic gesture I think as I watch from my chair.

"Let's get in the pool," Adam said.

"Ok," I said as I stood up and we walk to the steps of the pool.

The water feels good, and I walk down the steps and dip down, so it covers my shoulders. Adam is beside me and I am shocked when he picks me up and holds me as I float on top of the water as he spins me around while looking down at me smiling. I smile as this rare romantic gesture touches me and he kisses me before he puts me down. We enjoy the water for a little while before returning to our chairs to enjoy the sun.

"I think I would like to head up to the room for a while. Do you want to stay here?"

"No, I'll come with you," I said as I gather my things.

As we pass the gift shop on the way to our room, Adam stops and looks in the window.

"Let's go in and look around."

"Ok."

"I saw some nice things in here earlier."

As I browse through the store the sterling silver jewelry catches my eye. I look at the different pieces as Adam is browsing at another counter.

A braided silver necklace that is about an inch wide with a matching bracelet stands out to me and I decide to get it. I see Adam is looking at a long strand of colorful beads and I take the jewelry and head over to him.

"I am going to get this for my mother," he said holding up the necklace.

"That's nice."

"I got myself a T-shirt. Did you find something you like?"

"Yes, I found this necklace and bracelet set."

"That's beautiful."

"Are you ready to check out?" the woman at the register asks.

"Did you want anything else?" Adam asks.

"No thank you. This is it."

"Yes, we are ready to check out," he said as we put our items on the counter.

"Thank you."

"I also got you this," Adam said when we got back to the room as he hands me one of the bags.

I open the bag, pull out a white T-shirt and hold it up to read the inscription. "Good Girls Go to Heaven and Bad Girls Go to Cancun."

"That's perfect. Thank you," I said giggling.

"I thought it was perfect also."

"I would like to rest a bit before dinner. I'm not feeling too good."

"Ok, can I get you anything?"

"No thank you."

"I should call John."

"Good idea. Let's call Eric also."

"Ok," I said, deciding to call Eric first as I looked at the dialing instructions on the phone and call Eric. The phone rings and as Eric and Gina's answering machine picks up, I hear,

"This is the Mexican operator. Go ahead with your call."

Wow, good thing I called Eric first I thought as I heard that. I leave them a brief message as I realize now I cannot call John while I am here. We rest for a while before dressing and going down for dinner. I wear a pretty sundress with sandals and my new jewelry.

"You look very nice," Adam said.

"Thank you. How are you feeling?"

"Not too great. I think I just want to get a little something to eat and go back to the room."

"Ok."

At dinner Adam orders plain chicken and a baked potato. He barely eats half of it while I try another Mexican specialty. We head back up to the room right after dinner. I feel so bad that he is sick.

"Do you think you can go to the bar and ask the bartender or one of the servers if they have a joint you can buy? I think that will help me feel better."

"I will do my best."

"Great, thank you," he said as he gets into bed.

"I will be back in a bit."

"Do not leave the hotel."

"I won't," I said as I head out the door.

The bar is empty, I take a seat at the bar and order a glass of wine. I explain my problem to the bartender, and he finds me a joint. I leave him a nice tip and head back to the room. Happy with myself that I accomplished my mission.

"I got a joint from the bartender," I said as soon as I got in the room.

"Great, thank you very much."

"I hope it makes you feel better."

"So do I," he said as he lights the joint and takes a hit.

"Can I get you anything else?"

"No thank you, this is perfect," he said as he takes another hit of the joint. Then we climb into bed and drift off to sleep.

"Good morning. How do you feel?" I ask Adam as soon as he wakes up.

"A little better. That joint helped."

"I'm glad."

"Let's get some breakfast and go to the beach today."

"Ok, are you sure you feel up to that?"

"I'm ok."

We head down to the dining room where Adam does not eat much. I admire him for trying to push on with the day, as we head out to the beach and settle in lounge chairs.

There is an abundance of activities on the beach. People are water skiing, parasailing, snorkeling, and diving. I watch the activity as I lie in the sun. I see people going up in the air parasailing and I watch them floating high above the water as the boat pulls them through the air over the water.

"Let's do that," Adam said pointing to the sky.

"What, parasail?"

"Yes, let's go," he said as he gets up with a burst of energy.

We walk over to the area of the beach where you get on and off and I look at how you get strapped in.

"You get on and I will pay," Adam said as they start to hook me up.

"For an extra fee, once you are up there if you want to go higher flap your arms like this," the man said as he spread his arms out and flaps them up and down.

"Ok," I said while Adam smiles as he watches them hook me up.

"Ready, here you go," the man said as he raises his hand, signaling the boat to move pulling me up into the air.

"Have fun," I hear Adam say as I fly into the air.

"Oh my," I said as I go up in the air as I hold on to the harness. When I get to the intended height, I do not flap my arms. I enjoy the view of the ocean, beach, and coastline. I see buildings but concentrate on the beautiful blue water below me. What I really enjoy is the peacefulness as I am one with my surroundings and cannot hear a sound. This is not an everyday experience. I look up and down, left, and right taking it all in. I feel myself going down as I begin my decent to the beach where the men catch me as I come in.

"How was it?" Adam said as I land.

"That was great, you are going to love it," I said as they take the harness off me and start to hook Adam up.

I watch as he flies into the air and quickly flaps his arms when he gets to the intended height, having them send him up higher. I watch him the whole time he is in the air.

"Wow, I enjoyed that," he said as he lands.

"Definitely a unique experience," I said as they took the harness off him.

"Do you want to take a dip in the ocean?" he said as we walked back to our lounge chairs.

"Ok."

We head into the ocean, not too far in as we cool off in the clear blue water. After a while I decided to get out and start to make my way back, swimming the short distance as Adam stays in the water. As I approach the beach the undercurrent drags me back in. Every time I approach the beach the same thing happens. I begin to get exhausted and scared especially since no one notices, not even the lifeguards, when I am finally able to get out. I turn to look for Adam to make sure he is ok and not having the same problem. When I turn, I see he is just coming out of the water.

"The undercurrent kept pulling me in. I had a terrible time getting out of the ocean. Did you have trouble getting out?" I said as I dried myself off.

"No, not at all. I am sorry you had a tough time getting out. Are you ok?"

"Yes, it was just a little scary. I got so tired fighting the waves."

"I am glad you are ok. I would like to go to the room for a while. I am not feeling very well. Do you want to stay here?"

"No, I will go with you," I said as I collect my things.

We rest for the remainder of the afternoon until dinner time. We head down to the dining room for a quick dinner where Adam hardly eats before returning to the room.

"Can you please go to the bar and see if you can get me another joint?" he said as he climbed into bed.

"Sure, I'll be right back," I said as I head out the door.

I get to the bar, order a drink, and ask the bartender that helped me yesterday for a joint but unfortunately, he strikes out. I do not bother to ask anyone else because he told me he asked everyone there. I feel terrible as I head back to the room.

"I'm sorry, no joint tonight," I said when I returned to the room.

"That is ok. Thanks for trying. I will take some of the stuff I got at the gift shop," he said as he takes some Pepto-Bismol and returns to bed, where we both quickly drift off to sleep.

I wake up early the next morning as Adam is getting out of the shower. He walks in the room naked as he is towel drying his hair.

"Good morning, how are you feeling?"

"Ok, a little better. I was thinking we could have a quick breakfast then go to see the ruins today. Would you like to do that?"

"Sure, if you feel up to it. That would be great."

"Great, hurry and get ready. The bus leaves early."

"Ok, I will," I said as I jumped out of bed.

Once we are in the lobby Adam heads right over to the concierge to sign us up for the trip, while I get us a table for breakfast. We have a quick breakfast and are just in time to get on the bus. The bus is a small luxury bus that seats about ten to twelve people with a bathroom. The ride is two and a half hours each way and in addition to touring the ruins we will be stopping at a restaurant for lunch. I enjoy the scenery of the long drive as the driver points out different points of interest that we pass as he drives to the Yucatan.

"How are you feeling? Are you comfortable?" I ask.

"I feel ok. I am comfortable; are you?"

"Yes, thank you. I am looking forward to this tour," I said looking at the brochure.

"Chichen Itza was once a large pre-Columbian city built by the Mayan people located in the Yucatan." The tour guide tells us about the Mayan people and the city once we get to the ruins.

"This is incredible. I have never seen anything like it." I exclaim to Adam as we stand at the bottom of the Temple of Kukulkan next to stone serpent head carvings.

"Are you ready to go up?" Adam said as he started up the ninety-one steps.

"Let's go," I said as I followed.

"It is a pretty impressive view," Adam said when we reach the top.

"It is beautiful!" I exclaim as I gaze at the view from atop the temple. I notice people descending the steps of the temple slowly, and some people are going down on their bottoms moving down one step at a time.

"Ready to go down?"

"Yes," I said not feeling so confident as I look down.

I begin to walk slowly down the stairs as Adam takes off and briskly goes down the steps. I am in awe as I watch noting few people get down that way. Going down is not as easy as going up as it is very steep. Since the Mayans did not put in a handrail, I stopped and get down on my butt and go down that way.

"Are you ok?" Adam asks.

"Yes, I don't know how you did that so quickly."

Next, we see the main ball court where they played a ball game much like volleyball. Followed by the Temple of the Skulls which displays the heads of sacrificed victims and losers of the ball game.

"That's eerie looking," I said of the Temple of Skulls.

"I think it's interesting," Adam said.

The Sacred Cenote was the most interesting. A large natural well used for sacrificial ceremonies where people, gold, jade, turquoise, cooper, pottery, and other treasures were thrown in the well as a sacrifice to the Gods for rain.

"Jacques Cousteau asked the Mexican government for permission to dive into the well and photograph the contents but was denied," the tour guide tells us as we look at the well.

"It is believed that severe drought brought an end to the city and its people," the tour guide tells us as I think of the people sacrificed here.

"Very interesting tour. Did you like it?" Adam said as we looked down into the well.

"Yes, I did. I'm glad we came."

"Me too," he said as we walked to the bus.

"Good morning," Adam said as I opened my eyes.

"Good morning. How are you feeling?"

"Ok, sorry we just had dinner and went to bed again."

"That's ok. I'm sorry you weren't feeling well again."

"I was thinking today we can check out that secluded beach area the concierge showed us on the map."

"Sounds good to me. I'll start to get ready."

I put my swimsuit on under my clothes since we are going to walk to the beach after breakfast. I pack a bag with two towels, a hat, suntan lotion and two waters.

We go down to the dining room where there is a beautiful Sunday brunch buffet. Adam eats more than he has eaten since he got here. After breakfast we walk to the secluded area we saw on the map.

"I think this is it," Adam states as we get to the end of the road where there is a break in the trees.

We see a path heading down to the beach. We turn towards the path and as we get closer, we see a man standing in front of the pathway.

"Excuse us," Adam said as he tries to go around him.

"I'm sorry, I can't let you go down there," the large man said as he moves in front of Adam blocking his way.

"Why not?" Adam said politely.

"Because the President is down there waterskiing."

"The President of what?" I said as I see a large yacht through a break in the trees.

"The President of Mexico," he said as he gives me a look like who else would it be.

"Ok, no problem," Adam said as we turned to leave.

"Well, that was an interesting finale to our trip," I said with a laugh as we walked back to the road.

We arrived back in New Orleans late Monday afternoon. Adam parks in front of my house, gets my suitcase out of the trunk and carries it up the stairs for me while I unlock the door.

"Thank you, I had a wonderful time," I said with a smile.

"You are very welcome. I had a wonderful time also, even though I was sick."

"I guess we will have to try out the cable ties another time," I said with a smile.

"Yes, we will."

I kiss his cheek, go into the house, and watch him pull away. I unpack, wash my clothes, shower, and wait for John to come home. I am worried since I did not call.

"Hello, is that my beautiful wife?" John calls out as he comes through the door.

"Hello there," I said as I got off the couch, walk over to him and greet him with a big hug and a kiss.

"Did you have fun?"

"Yes, I did. How are you? Is everything ok here?"

"Yes, now that your home," he said with a smile.

I smile back thinking how lucky I am.

Wednesday's Girl

Part Two

Chapter 1

$\mathcal{I}$t is May 1987; Vicky and I have finished making all the plans for Anna's wedding. I enjoyed spending time with Vicky; she really took an interest in me and has convinced me to take a couple of college courses. All I need to do now is to find a dress for the wedding. I decide to go to Canal Street to start looking. I am about to leave the house when the phone rings.

"Hello," I said as I picked up the phone.

"Hello, Chelsea," Adam sings my name.

"Hello, Adam, how are you?" I said with a smile.

"I'm good, I was wondering if you would like to have lunch with me at the Windsor Court today?"

"Well, I'm actually heading near there now, I need to go dress shopping for Anna's wedding."

"How about we do both together?"

"Ok, that sounds great."

"We can have lunch first. I will pick you up in thirty minutes, you take care," he said as he hangs up the phone.

I am at the door when Adam pulls up in exactly thirty minutes.

"Hello, I'm glad you called," I said as I get into the car.

"Hello, so am I. I want you to try this artichoke baked with brie for lunch. Eric ordered it yesterday when he, Gina, and I had lunch at Windsor Court. Eric, let me taste his and it was delicious. I have been thinking about it ever since." Adam said as we pull away from my house.

"That sounds wonderful, but you do realize that's a vegetable."

"Yes, I am aware it is a vegetable," he said with a smirk.

"Well, I can't wait to see this."

"After lunch we can look for a dress. What kind of dress are you thinking about getting; is it a formal wedding?"

"No, it is a simple service followed by an early dinner or actually lunch at a restaurant."

"It should be easy to find an appropriate dress at the shops downtown."

"I think so too."

We arrive at Windsor Court in time for an early lunch, and the artichoke baked in brie does not disappoint.

"This is delicious," I said as I gently pull off a leaf with melted brie, holding the end while I eat the soft part and discard the rest.

"I told you it was delicious," Adam said before he eats another bite.

"Maybe next you can try some broccoli." I said with a laugh.

"I wouldn't count on it."

We finish lunch and drive the short distance to Canal Street. We window shop a bit before going into a shop that has nice dresses in the window.

"May I help you?" A woman asks as we walk in.

"Yes please, I am looking for a dress for an afternoon wedding."

"This would be nice for a day wedding," she said pointing to a bold print dress hanging up in front of us.

"Don't get that dress, the print is too big and there are too many colors it is too busy." Adam said aloud.

"Well, have a glass of wine or champagne, and you will like it better," The woman said as someone approaches us holding a tray with glasses of wine and champagne.

"Oh, no thank you," I said laughing as she turns and offers one to Adam.

"No thank you," Adam said.

"What do you think of this one?" I said as I point to a stylish beige clingy knee length dress with a boat neck, cap sleeves and a belt at the waist that ties to the side.

"That looks nice, why don't you try it on."

I find it in a size four and head to the dressing room to try it on. Once I have it on, I step out of the dressing room to show Adam.

"That looks lovely on you, do you like it?"

"Thank you, yes, I think I will get it."

"I think it is perfect for the occasion."

"So do I, let me get changed," I said as I head back into the dressing room.

"I will take this," I said to the saleswoman as I exit the dressing room and hand her the dress.

"Beautiful choice, let me ring it up," the saleswoman said as she takes the dress from me.

"Since we're so close and we have time before you must go to work, how about we stop where Gina works. We can have a Coke and show her your dress?" Adam said.

"That's a great idea." I said smiling as I pay for my dress and take it from the saleswoman.

We get to the restaurant and take a seat at the bar. I hang my dress over the empty seat next to me, as Adam looks around for Gina. The bartender who is the size of a linebacker has his back to us, but I recognize him instantly. I haven't seen him since the day I told him I could not leave John and ended our brief affair.

"Hello, Chelsea, how are you?" Luke said smiling as he turned around.

"Good, how are you?" I ask.

"Great, I just started working here and I love it. What can I get for the two of you?" he said as he places a beverage napkin in front of each of us as he glances at Adam.

"Luke, this is my friend Adam, Adam this is Luke."

"Hello, nice to meet you," Luke said.

"Hello, we will have two Cokes please."

"Oh, there's Gina," I said as I waved to her.

"Hey, what are you two doing here?" she said as she walks over to us and greets us with kisses.

"We were dress shopping in the area for a dress for Anna's wedding and I wanted to show it to you."

"Oh, let's see," Gina said as I pull the bag up so she could see the dress.

"That's gorgeous, I love the material," she said as she touches the fabric.

"It looks great on her!" Adam exclaims.

"We had lunch at Windsor Court; the artichoke with brie was wonderful," I said as I cover up the dress.

"I know it is so good. Well, I better get back to work."

"See you Monday," I said as I reach for my Coke.

"Thanks for stopping to see me."

"Take care," Adam said as she walked away.

"Excuse me while I go to the restroom," I said as I get off the bar stool, as Adam stands and pulls the stool out for me.

"Thank you." I said, turning to make my way to the restroom.

I am on my way back to the bar when I see Luke coming towards me. He stops in front of me blocking my path.

"You look great, Chelsea," he said smiling.

"Thank you."

"I see you're still married," he said glancing at my ring finger.

"Yes, I am."

"I've missed you and I'd love to see you again, on your terms," he said with a smile.

"I'm sorry, I can't," I said feeling awkward.

"I see, well, you know where I am if you change your mind," he said with a smile.

"I better go, take care of yourself Luke." I said as I walk away.

"Are you ready to go?" Adam said when I get back to the bar.

"Sure," I said as I take a sip of my Coke and pick up my dress.

"How do you know Luke?" Adam asks the minute we leave the restaurant.

"I had a brief affair with him before I met you. He wanted me to leave John, so I ended it," I said figuring there was no reason not to tell him the truth.

"Looks to me, he would like to see you again."

"Well, I let him know I wasn't interested," I said hoping that would put an end to this conversation.

"Let me take that," he said as he takes the dress from me and carries it to the car. Hanging it in the backseat after he opens the door for me.

"I'm glad I found a dress, thank you for helping me pick it out," I said as we head towards uptown.

"It was fun," he said smiling at me.

"Thanks for lunch. I had a nice afternoon," I said when we get to my house, as I lean over and give him a quick kiss.

"You're welcome. So did I, see you Wednesday," he said as he gets out of the car to get my dress from the back seat.

"See you Wednesday," I said as I take my dress. I head up the steps and watch him pull away as I enter the house.

I wake up and see that John is already out of bed. I go to the bathroom, brush my teeth, and wash my face before heading to the kitchen.

"Good morning, did you sleep well?" John said as he kisses my cheek.

"No, I had a nightmare," I said as I poured myself a cup of coffee.

"Oh, I'm sorry sweetie."

"It would wake me up, then I would fall back to sleep and be right back into it."

"What was this one about?"

"Someone was chasing me, and I was running and running as they were getting closer and closer."

"I am sorry sweetie, sit down and relax. I was just fixin to make us breakfast. What would you like?"

"One of your famous omelets would be great."

"Ok, coming right up."

"You remember we're all going to Tipitina's Saturday night, after work to see War, right?"

"Yes, I remember, I am sorry I can't go to Anna's wedding with you on Sunday. I wish we didn't have a big party booked that day at work."

"That's ok, Ashley isn't bringing a date so we can sit together. There's no dancing anyway."

"I guess the party is the night before the wedding."

"Yup, that was the only detail that Anna did plan," I said as I set the table.

"Here is your ham and cheese omelet," John said as he put our plates on the table.

"Thank you, that looks delicious."

"It should be a fun night. I bet War puts on a great show."

"I'm looking forward to it, sorry you have to work the next day."

"Yes, me too," he said as he finished his breakfast.

"Would you like more coffee?" I ask.

"No thank you, I have to start getting ready for work," he said as he put his plate in the sink and headed to the bathroom.

I carry my plate into the kitchen and start to clean up, when I hear someone running through the alley outside our kitchen window. That's strange, I think to myself, I wonder who that is. I cannot see anything since the blinds are down and I continue cleaning the kitchen. I am in the bedroom changing the sheets when John comes into the room to finish dressing.

"I'm leaving, have a good day. I'll see you tonight," he said as he gives me a kiss.

"You too, I love you," I said as we kiss.

"Love you too."

I finished changing the sheets and am heading to the living room when I see John coming towards me.

"Did you forget something?"

"No, the car has a flat tire. I'm going to take the bike," he said grabbing his helmet.

"Ok, be careful," I said as he goes out the back door.

"The bike has a flat too," he said as he comes back into the house.

"You're kidding?" I said with a sarcastic tone.

"I wish I was."

"I guess some kids were out playing pranks," I said.

"Well, it's not very funny, I'll have to take the streetcar to work and deal with this tomorrow."

"Your right it's not, be careful." I said as I gave him a kiss.

As I am getting ready for work, I think about my day with Adam yesterday. We watched the movie *Angel Heart* as he gave me a body massage. It was a good movie, and I liked seeing the scenes shot in New Orleans. I am glad I finally got to see it given all the hype surrounding the movie. The media made a big deal about the nudity and the sex scene. I do not see what all the hype was about. I was glad he did not mention us running into Luke last week. My thoughts are interrupted by the phone ringing, and I walk across the room to answer it.

"Hello."

"Hello, Chelsea," Adam sings my name.

"Hi Adam, how are you?"

"You don't sound very happy, what's wrong?"

"Some kids must have been playing pranks and flattened a tire on the car, and the bike, and John is not happy."

"That wasn't kids, it was Luke," Adam said instantly.

"Luke? he wouldn't do that."

"Yes, he would, he's mad that you turned him down last week."

"He wouldn't do that," I said as I think the person running through the alley did not sound like a linebacker, running through the alley to me.

"Yes, it was," he said persistently.

"All I know is we have two flat tires we have to fix."

"I am sorry to hear that. I just called to say I had a wonderful time yesterday and I hope you enjoy the wedding."

"Thank you," I said.

"See you Wednesday, you take care," he said as he hangs up the phone.

"Bye." I said as I think about the conversation and what Adam said about Luke. I do not for a minute believe it was Luke. No matter how hard Adam tried to convince me he did it. However, I do not believe that it was kids playing pranks anymore either.

"Ok ladies let's get going on our side work so we can get the hell out of here," Anna said as she bursts into the server station at the end of Saturday's shift.

"We are on it, Miss Anna on your last night as a single lady," Ashley said as she marries the ketchup bottles.

"I cannot wait to hear "Low Rider" I was jamming to that in my car the other day thinking about tonight," Emma said.

"I am glad all the guys are meeting us there, this is going to be a fun night," I said as I wipe down the beverage trays.

"We're done, let's get dressed," Anna said as we all follow her to the rest room to change.

"I hope you ladies have fun tonight and tomorrow. Congratulations, Anna," Eric said as we all cash out.

"Thank you," we all said in unison.

"Laissez les bons temps rouler!" Emma said as we all walked out the door together.

Tipitina's is jam-packed when we get there. We make our way to the bar to get a drink; while we wait for War to come on and for the guys to get here.

"What is everyone having to drink?" I said as we get to the bar.

"Shots of Jägermeister!" Anna calls out.

"I'll have a Coke," Ashley said.

"Get us each a beer also please," Emma said as the bartender makes his way over to us.

"Can I get three shots of Jager, three Amstel lights and a Coke please?" I said as I lay money on the bar as he starts to get our drinks.

"Hey, there's the guys," Emma waves as she spots Mike and Rich.

"You're just in time," I said to the guys. "Can I get two more shots, and two more beers please?" I said as the bartender comes back with the beers.

Emma hands everyone a shot and a beer and gives Ashley her coke as everyone throws money on the bar for the drinks.

"Here's to the happy couple and their last single night," Emma said as we all hold up our shots and cheer before we chug them together.

"Good evening, everyone, and thank you for coming, on behalf of Tipitina's I am proud to announce War!" announced a man on the stage. The rest of what he said is drowned out by applause and screams as War comes on the stage.

"Good, evening, New Orleans!" the singer yells out as they break into "Why Can't We Be Friends" and the crowd cheers.

"Let's get on the dance floor," Ashley said as she moves to the beat and starts to sing.

"Hey, Chelsea, glad I found you have they been on long," John said as he gives me a kiss.

"It's the first song," I said in his ear.

"Let me get a beer," he said as he tries to get the bartenders attention and orders a beer.

"Wow, they are great," John said as they start to play "Galaxy."

"Let's Dance," Emma said pulling us to the dance floor and we all move to the beat.

I get into the harmonica, saxophone, and bongo drums that they play during their songs. They have the crowd in the groove as they continue to play.

"Time for another shot," Anna yells out to the group and we all head to the bar.

"To the happy couple," Rich said as we all raised our glasses and drink the shot.

"Time to dance," Anna said as she leads the way to the dance floor.

"Isn't it time for the guys to rest?" Rich said aloud.

"No, it's not," Emma said pulling him along.

We all hit the floor and dance together until Anna decides it's time for another shot.

"I think she's trying to get me drunk and take advantage of me," Mike said laughing.

"What's she trying to do to the rest of us?" John said with a chuckle.

"Here's to the best roommate, and to her lucky fiancé," Emma said as we all chug the shot.

"I know an eligible roommate if you need one," Rich said smiling as Emma smiles back.

More dancing is followed by another shot and a beer, when "Low Rider" begins to play. We all dance our way in a single file through the crowd to the dance floor. Then we get in a circle around Anna, she puts her hands in the air and moves around. Then she pulls us towards her, and we all join in and dance together.

"That was awesome!" Ashley said when the band stops playing.

"Ok, we better get going, see everyone tomorrow," Emma said as she starts to sing "Going to the Chapel" and we all join in as we walk out together.

"Goodnight, everyone, see you in the morning," Rich said.

"It is morning!" Mike exclaims as he looks at his watch.

"Goodnight, everyone, thanks for a great night," Anna said.

"Oh, that was fun," I said to John as we headed home.

"Well, I was definitely out later than I wanted to be."

"I'm sorry, but I am glad that Anna had fun."

"Me too, War was great, it was a perfect evening." John said as we make our way home, get in the door, take off our clothes and get into bed.

"Goodnight, sweetie, I love you." John said as he kisses me.

"Goodnight, honey, I love you too." I said falling asleep as my head hits the pillow.

"Chelsea, Chelsea, wake up," John said as I roll over covering my ears.

"Shush."

"Chelsea it's late, you better get moving," John said as I sit up and look at the clock.

"Holy shit," I said as I jump out of bed.

"We overslept," John said.

"By the time I shower, and the time it takes to get there. No way I will be there on time."

"Get your butt going."

"Well, I could move a lot quicker if I wasn't hung over," I said as I grab my robe and head to the shower.

"I hear you, at least you don't have to work today."

I am in and out of the shower in a flash. I quickly apply my makeup and dry my hair as John brings me a Coke in a Bacchus cup and two Tylenol.

"Thank you, see why we need more cups," I said as I take the pills with a sip of Coke.

"You're welcome, yes definitely the good china," John said as we both dress.

I pull the dress down over my body, then I slide on a pair of stockings. I put on my shoes while I scan the room for my beaded purse. I rummage through my closet until I find it, then I quickly put my jewelry on and a splash of perfume.

"Ok, I'm ready," I said as I look in the mirror pulling a couple of hairs down over my forehead and grabbing a pair of sunglasses to put on.

"You look like Miss Sunglasses." John said to me. Referring to the name we affectionately call the woman, in the Patrick Nagel print in our living room.

"I hope I look that good, since I don't feel too great."

"You look beautiful, have fun. I'll see you tonight, love you," he said as he kisses me.

"Thank you, hope your party goes well. I will see you tonight, love you, too," I said as we both rushed out the door together.

I get to the church and am rushing up the stairs, as the pastor is coming out of the door. He closes it behind him as he puts the key in the door and locks it.

"Oh, I guess no one called you either, the wedding is off," he said as he turned to me.

"What?"

"The wedding is off, no one is here, I waited almost a half an hour."

"Pastor, I assure you, the wedding is not off they are just late."

"Everyone?" he said as he points to the empty parking lot and starts to head down the steps.

"Well, I can't explain it, and it does seem strange. But I promise you the wedding is not cancelled, please don't leave." I said as my head pounds harder, just as a couple of cars enter the parking lot.

"Oh, here comes some people now," I said with a sigh.

"I've never seen anything like it," he said shaking his head as he walks back up the steps and unlocks the door.

I rush down the steps as Ashley gets out of her car; followed by Rich and Emma getting out of Rich's car as more people begin to show up.

"Oh, my goodness, I had to convince the pastor not to leave, that the wedding wasn't cancelled that everyone is just late."

"You mean we didn't miss the wedding?" Emma said as she smoothed her dress.

"No, other than me, you're the first ones here."

"Oh, I thought I missed it, Anna isn't here yet?" Ashley asked.

"No, Miss let's have another Jägermeister Anna is not here yet," I said as we all burst out laughing.

"Here she is now," Emma said as Anna pulls up with her parents.

"Oh, you look so beautiful, absolutely gorgeous, stunning," we all said at the same time as Anna walked toward us.

"Thank you, sorry I'm so late," Anna said as she joined us.

"Well, good thing Chelsea convinced the pastor that the wedding was still on. He was about to leave since no one was here," Ashley said as people pass us to enter the church.

"What, you're kidding?" Anna said.

"I'll tell you about it later, right now let's just get this show on the road."

"Mike is inside, and everyone is here. You girls go in and sit down," Vicky said as we walked up the steps.

"See you inside," I said with a wink.

"Good luck," Emma said as she blows Anna a kiss.

"Let's go in," Ashley said as she loops her arm in mine, and we head into the church.

We watch Anna and her father walk up the aisle. They join Mike at the altar, where they recite the short but traditional vows and are quickly married.

"You may kiss the bride," the pastor said as Mike leans in and kisses Anna.

We all clap as they walk down the aisle and head out the door into the sunshine. Where Anna banned us from throwing traditional rice or birdseed.

"Ok, let's get some pictures," Vicky said.

"Oh Mom!" Anna said.

"We'll take pictures with our parents and meet all of you at the restaurant," Mike said to the group.

"Sounds good to me, let's get out of this sun," I said.

"I am ready for a drink!" Rich said laughing.

"We need something for this hangover," Emma said as we walked to our cars.

As we arrive at the restaurant the hostess escorts us to a small banquet room in the back. The tables are set as six tops with a small flower arrangement on each table. The cake table is set in the front of the room. We sit at a table together as the server begins to take drink orders as more people start to arrive. Anna and Mike enter the room, and everyone stands and claps.

"Thank you," Mike said as he waved to everyone. They take a seat at a table with their parents as Mike's brother Eddie makes a toast to the couple.

"I wish you both all the best and may you both have a long and happy life together," he said as he raises his champagne glass, and we all cheer before drinking.

In the center of each table is a small bowl with muffuletta olive salad on a platter surrounded with crostini. Everyone enjoys that as the servers bring an appetizer plate of shrimp remoulade and raw oysters.

"Oh, my, this is so good," Ashley said as she tastes the olive salad.

"Well, save room, there is more food coming. What her mother could not plan in other areas, she made up for in food," I said.

"You know what they say, the rest of the world eats to live, but in New Orleans we live to eat," Rich said as he pops an oyster in his mouth.

We enjoy shrimp bisque and Caesar salads. Followed by petit filets with jumbo lump crab cakes, served with saffron rice and asparagus.

"I am not going to have room for cake after all this," Emma said.

"Well, there's bananas Foster being done table side as well, so you better save room," I said laughing.

"I guess you noticed my mother enjoyed herself planning the menu," Anna said as she approaches our table.

"Oh yes, everything was wonderful, did y'all enjoy your meal?" Ashley asks.

"Yes, we did, now scoot over we want to eat dessert with y'all," Anna said as she and Mike sit in the other two chairs.

"Are you going to cut the cake and feed each other a bite before we serve it?" the server asks Anna.

"No, you can just cut it and serve it," Anna said as the server begins making the bananas Foster tableside. Lighting the pan as the alcohol is poured in, making the dish flame for a moment as part of the show.

"What are y'all planning to do for the rest of the day? We are spending the rest of the day with our parents." Anna said.

"We are going home and going back to bed," Emma said as Rich smiles.

"Hey, Chelsea, do you want to go see the Neville Brothers they are doing a show in the park this afternoon?" Ashley said.

"That sounds like a great idea!" I spoke.

"This is so good," Anna said as she eats her dessert.

As we all get ready to go, and we are saying our goodbyes. Vicky gives me a gift bag with a Passion perfume collection inside.

"Thank you so much for all your help, I really enjoyed planning this with you. Now don't be a stranger and promise me you are going to take some classes," she said as she gives me a big hug.

"Oh, thank you what a pleasant surprise." I said as I take the bag. "I had a wonderful time planning this with you too, I would love to meet for lunch whenever you want. I promise I am going to take a couple of classes," I said as I give her a hug.

"Oh, glad to hear you're taking some classes," Emma said.

"Yes, definitely happy to hear that," Anna said.

"Have a fun time at the park." Emma said as we walked out.

We can hear the music and see the crowd as we walk towards the stage. We walk a little faster as we get closer. Some people have brought blankets and chairs, but most are standing. Ashley takes my hand and moves us through the crowd. She stops when we are right in front of the stage. Everyone is dancing, and we join right in.

They began to sing "Tell It Like It Is" as I slowly sway to the music my mind drifts off to Adam. As the song ends a man approaches us, bringing me back to reality.

"Hi ladies, I am the manager of the band. How would you two like to dance on stage on top of the speakers?" He said pointing to the two giant speakers on each end of the stage.

"Yes, yes, yes," Ashley said as she jumps up and down clapping.

"Ok, I guess it's a yes," I said as we follow him to the stage.

"Have fun," I said to Ashley as we each walk towards a speaker.

"You too," she said smiling.

I walk up the steps on the side of the stage. Two stagehands are waiting, to lift me up and put me on top of the huge speaker. I look across the stage and see Ashley is already on top of the other speaker dancing away. As I begin to dance, I look out at the crowd, and I feel a little nervous for a second. Then I close my eyes and get into the beat as they begin to play, "Ain't No Sunshine When She's Gone" as I dance.

The perfect weather makes for a wonderful day to be outside. We dance on top of the speakers to "Hey Pocky Way," "Iko Iko" and "Fire on the Bayou" we dance away until the end of the show.

"That was incredible!" Ashley said when we meet in front of the stage at the end of the show.

"Yeah, that was a blast, you don't get to do that every day."

"No, you don't," Ashley said.

"What a great show, I am so glad you suggested it. I love the Neville Brothers." I said as we headed out of the park.